BY A SLENDER THREAD

BY A SLENDER THREAD

Barrie Skelcher

NAVIGATOR BOOKS

Published by Navigator Books
Ringwood, Hampshire

ISBN 0 902830 46 5

Typeset by Moorhouse Typesetters
Printed by The Cromwell Press, Melksham, Wiltshire

To the work of all my fellow health physicists
and their contribution to the safety
of the nuclear industries.

Cover design by Catherine Press

About the Author

Barrie Skelcher has spent all his working life with the nuclear industries. He joined the United Kingdom Atomic Energy Authority in 1956 and was involved in fuel reprocessing, including waste management and fissile material storage at their Dounreay site. Six years later he changed employer to work for the Central Electricity Generating Board on their nuclear power station at Sizewell in Suffolk. As Health Physicist he was part of the Station's management team and had responsibility for radiological safety including environmental monitoring and emergency planning. When application was made to build the first pressurised water reactor at Sizewell, in 1980, he became Head of the Sizewell Information Service.

He is passionate about sailing and small boats, which take up a large part of his time. In younger days he was a successful racing dinghy helmsman, now he has taken to cruising at sea and on inland waters.

By a Slender Thread is his first novel in which he draws heavily upon his technical and sailing experience.

PROLOGUE

Although not common, it has not been unusual during man's progress down the centuries for apparently unrelated events, occurring in widely different parts of the world, to come together as a hinge upon which the fate of nations hang. The story I am about to relate, which has hitherto been kept from public knowledge, is a modern example. For a time, known only to a few, the future of Eastern Europe, the unification of Germany, hopes for democracy in Hungary and other "satellite" states of the USSR, and the policies of Glasnost and Perestroika all hung in the balance.

In Britain, at the end of 1980, the Electricity Supply Authority which generates the power used in England and Wales, made an application to build a new type of nuclear station at Layness on the Suffolk coast. At that time the future of atomic energy was in doubt. The accident at Three Mile Island in the USA was still fresh in people's memory, Sweden had held a referendum which resulted in a long term policy to phase out nuclear and other countries were dithering. North Sea oil and natural gas supplies looked assured for the next two decades while a nuclear programme would mean heavy capital investment. Certain organisations, such as those opposed to nuclear weapons and some environment groups, sought to arouse public opposition and demanded a wide ranging inquiry. The Minister agreed and throughout 1982/83 an eminent barrister examined the evidence presented by all sides in the longest planning inquiry ever held in the United Kingdom.

After due deliberation he came down firmly on the side of further nuclear development. He accepted the Industry's economic case, its assurances on safety, and the need for more power stations. The arguments that had been put forward by the objectors did not withstand his close examination, he found them flawed in all aspects save one, the security of the plutonium bye-product. Hitherto, although it belonged to the ESA, it was held in trust at Sellafield by British Nuclear Fuels, a Government owned company. Under such circumstances there could be no guarantee that, on secret instructions from some future unscrupulous government, it would not find its way into the weapons industry. Indeed the development of laser enrichment meant that this would now be a practical possibility. His report recommended to the Minister that while consent should be granted, all plutonium produced by civil nuclear power stations, past, present and future, should be held in a separate repository under the control of the ESA.

Both Government and Parliament accepted these recommendations and the Electricity Supply Authority constructed its own facility on part of an old wartime airfield in Lincolnshire. Four years after the inquiry had ended the Watersthorpe Plutonium Depository was officially opened and the process began of transferring existing plutonium from Sellafield to its new home.

Even before the British Inquiry had started, on the other side of Europe the centrally planned economics were in trouble. Behind the "iron curtain", established by Stalin and maintained by his successors, the Communist peoples were becoming increasingly dissatisfied with their austere existence. The uprisings in Hungary and Czechoslovakia, which had been so ruthlessly put down more than two decades ago, were now in danger of repeating themselves. The Kremlin realised that long term coexistence with the West was not possible, their policy of "non perception", which had attempted to stop the people of Eastern Europe from knowing what the West was like, had not succeeded. The jamming of radio programmes, the restrictions on travel and the flood of false propaganda against the Free World, the huge sums spent in the construction of the Berlin wall, had all failed to conceal the truth. The facts about the good society of the democracies were leaking through the Iron Curtain like water through a crumbling dyke. The hardliners who held power saw only two alternatives, either the West would have to be subjugated by military force or its prosperity destroyed. The presence of nuclear weapons made the former impossible so they had invested heavily in trying to destabilise these economies. Amongst the many tactics they deployed were the funding given to nuclear agitators and the placing of "sleepers" who, when activated, would create havoc in the energy industries. In those days it was well understood in the corridors of Soviet power that the West had a great weakness, its fuel supplies. If Middle East oil could be disrupted by political moves, coal by industrial action and nuclear by "environmentalists" then the Democracies would sink into massive unemployment and degradation. Just taking out the nuclear power component would be a major advantage, it would force Europe to turn to Russia for natural gas and coal.

But now in the Kremlin things were changing, there were reformers who wanted to come to terms with capitalism and live in harmony. They argued for mutual disarmament, freeing of trade and a market economy. First Secretary Gorbachev took office with liberals in the ascendancy. Glasnost and Perestroika were intended to pave the way for the revitalisation of the Soviet economy and introduce a measure of competitive capitalism within the Communist system. They came too late and instead started a rapid decline in Soviet power. The Old Guard foresaw that this would lead to revolutions in satellite states and possibly the reunification of Germany under Western influence. They reasoned that this could only be prevented if Gorbachev were discredited and/or a last desperate effort succeeded in destroying the affluence of their European neighbours. So it was that in the heart of Moscow a score of solemn men and women sat round a table discussing the situation. They were accommodated in one of those special meeting rooms that exist in the heart of the Kremlin. The high walls were decorated with flags of the Soviet Union and pictures of its past heroes. The windows were shuttered and the heavy oak doors firmly locked and guarded from the outside by hard faced soldiers. The meeting was drawing to its close and the man who wore the uniform of a Marshall of the Soviet Union, and who was clearly the senior rank of all those present, summed up.

'Comrades we are all agreed, the energy supply of the West must be disrupted if our socialist society is to survive. The plan we have devised is beautiful in its simplicity. If it succeeds, and there is no reason why it should not for we already have the personnel in the positions we need, then Europe will be forced to close down all its nuclear power stations. Just think what that will mean. France alone generates eighty percent of its electricity from nuclear reactors and exports to other countries. Belgium, Germany, Sweden more than thirty percent and a number of other countries around twenty percent. The sudden loss of nuclear power would plunge them overnight into years of austerity. Our recent unhappy event at Chernobyl has already prepared the ground, their public are jittery and hyped up, our little escapade is bound to catalyze the necessary outcry. On the other hand, if by some means the public backlash from the 'event' is contained we will ensure that the plot is revealed as coming from Mother Russia. After that no Western politician will trust our revered General Secretary and we will be thrust back into the days of the Cold War. As I see it we win either way.

The other conspirators nodded their assent.

'Very well then let us proceed with Operation Firewater, we do not have time on our side.'

CHAPTER 1

The dark green, mud spattered, single decker bus bearing the letters E.S.A. and the logo of a lightning flash, turned off the public road onto what was once a wide concrete runway used by bombers in World War II. It had not seen an aircraft since 1947, and now on either side were anaemic looking hedges and ploughed fields beyond. The land was flat, the immediate 'scape being broken only by the occasional tree. At 0800hrs on an April morning, when a mist of drizzle persisted, the place was neither hostile nor inviting. The bus trundled on some four hundred yards then came to a halt in front of two substantial iron bar gates which filled a gap in the concrete posted, barbed wire fence. One gate was open and a stream of men and women shuffled through, showing their credentials to a heftily built, six foot tall guard, clad in the dull blue uniform of the E.S.A. Security Branch.

The doors of the bus rattled open and it disgorged its human contents who joined their colleagues. John Grimley was last to leave. He stepped down, or at least hobbled down using his stick for extra support as he eased his injured leg onto the road. Glancing left then right, more out of habit than the need to exercise caution when crossing, he limped over to the tail end of the human line and, like others before him, presented his pass to the man at the gate.

'Abandon hope all ye who enter here,' Grimley muttered to himself. The length of a cricket pitch from this first gate was another security fence, access through which was by means of a turnstile operated by a man inside an armoured and bullet proof gate house. A microphone and loud speaker permitted two way conversation between him and a colleague who was checking the personnel entering the site. Secured to the fence was a large notice in white letters on a dark blue background, it read:

Watersthorpe Plutonium Laboratory
Property of the Electricity Supply Authority
Authorised Personnel Only

Grimley was an average man in every sense of the word, so average that he could blend into any group without them even realising that he was there. Not only in appearance, but also in personality, he was a chameleon, changing to match whatever background he was in.

He had brown hair, pale blue eyes, and wore a sports coat under his khaki anorak. At five foot eleven he would have passed as the British Standard Man. He did not socialise or make conversation for conversations sake, to those who came into contact with him he was a mild mannered, ordinary sort of chap, who kept himself to himself. Little did they know just how unusual John Grimley was. Only twelve months before graduating he had been recruited, by the successors of the Philby school, to serve a foreign power but for years he had not been used.

He was then what was known in the espionage profession as a sleeper. His technical career was exemplary and unexciting, doing all the right things at the right time without distinction. Three years ago he had joined the Electricity Supply Authority and shortly after that had managed to get himself transferred to the Watersthorpe Project as a laboratory leader.

In the last days of April yet another depression had settled across the Irish Sea sending its fronts as far as the Lincolnshire countryside. The farmers grumbled, so did the security guard at the check point, as he inspected John Grimley's Identification Card.

'Another grotty day,' he remarked. 'How's the leg mending?'

It was Joe Kitchen the more talkative and cheerful of the 'keepers and he spoke to everyone who passed.

'Teach you to go off on those dangerous holidays, 'suppose the plaster will be coming off soon?'

John grunted, showed his pass and shuffled through the turnstile. The road from the gate house led directly onto a traffic island, to the left of this lay the Administration Block which included the library and senior staff offices. To the right, some hundred yards or so from this island, was a low level building with a red brick facade. It was the entrance to the plutonium areas. From it ran a long wide corridor which gave access to a series of laboratories and the plutonium storage vaults, in some way it resembled the leaves on the stem of an ash tree twig. Grimley turned right and followed the road to the brick faced building which, on its glass faced door, etched in bold letters, was the simple inscription B301. It housed his laboratory. The single storey building was strong in construction and utilitarian in finish. Inside the walls were painted brick, the windows were opaque and barred, at the entrance a security officer sat behind a waist high counter to check, once again, the credentials of those who wished to pass into the change room which lay beyond. It was no ordinary change room, not the type in cricket pavilions or golf clubs. It could accommodate a hundred employees. A wooden barrier some eighteen inches high divided it in half across its width such that the grey metal lockers, which lined up in rows like soldiers on a parade ground, were on the entrance side of the barrier. This was the non radioactive side. Beyond the barrier, in the radioactive area, there were rows of coat hooks from which hung coveralls and laboratory coats. John again showed his pass and the security man inspected it to make sure that it was endorsed for entry into this particularly sensitive area. Grimley noted that he had not seen this guard before and concluded that he must be a new addition. With the assistance of his stick he limped through the "in" door and across to his locker where he deposited his jacket and took out a small metal pill box which he pinned to his shirt. It contained several small disks of Teflon impregnated with lithium fluoride, each in a different wrapper. Should a criticality accident occur[1] these small white disks, when suitably processed, would indicate the radiation dose that he had received and possibly justify some exotic treatment such as bone marrow transplant. As Grimley pinned the container to his shirt he reflected upon the purpose of these devices but then dismissed the thought as being of only academic value

---

[1]*It is a property of the atoms of a fissile material, such as plutonium, that when they are struck by a sub-atomic particle called a neutron, they may split and liberate heat, radiation, <u>and more neutrons</u>. Thus if too much of this material is contained in any particular geometry, such that the neutrons produced when one atom splits are not lost from the surface but are able to split more atoms, they create a chain reaction, the material is deemed to be "critical" or "super critical". The quantity of material necessary to just produce a self sustaining chain reaction, is known as it's critical mass. It is standard practice, when handling fissile material, to make sure that the critical mass for any particular shape can not be exceeded accidentally. Thus, if (say) plutonium were kept in cubes, it would be necessary to ensure that each cube contained less than the critical mass and they were kept sufficiently far apart to prevent them inter-reacting with each other. When handling plutonium great care has to be taken to make sure that too much of the material does not come together accidentally, this is usually done by controlling the mass in any particular container, or by controlling the shape of the container itself. Should something go wrong with these control systems and criticality were to occur, there would <u>not</u> be an explosion like that of a nuclear weapon, but there would be very high radiation levels in the area. These types of accidents have occasionally happened in the past. For the treatment of anyone involved it is necessary to know the radiation dose that has been suffered, consequently it is general practice to wear special devices which measure very high doses of neutron and gamma radiation.*

since such accidents did not occur in well run establishments like Watersthorpe. He hobbled across to the barrier and, before he sat on it, mused that all the routine safety checks would at least keep the Health Physics Department[2] in business.

George Watkins, the Area Manager of the assay laboratories and John's immediate boss, joined him at the barrier as they each pulled on white polyester cotton overshoes. George liked to think his special attribute was his understanding of people and he made great efforts to get to know his staff. John's reserved attitude had always defeated his approach but he kept on trying.

'Hi John, how much longer in the concrete?' he said pushing a nod towards the plaster cast. 'Reckon we'd better get Health Physics to check it over when it's cracked off just to make sure you've not got it stashed full of plut,' he jested as he swung his legs over the barrier and moved off. John, as ever, made no audible comment to his manager but for a few seconds his heart beat a little faster for the joke had been too close to the truth for comfort.

'Piss off you twit,' Grimley muttered under his breath when his boss was out of earshot and he concentrated on the task of persuading a reluctant overshoe onto his plaster encased foot. Having won the contest he too lifted his legs over the barrier, picked up his walking stick and hobbled over to the hooks where he selected his white laboratory coat. He passed a row of hand wash basins and then pushed through double doors into the main corridor of the radioactive area. The walls were plain brick covered with a light green gloss paint, which not only gave it an austere and utilitarian look, it also indicated that he was in a "green" area. This formed a buffer zone between the outside world and those areas which held the deadly radioactive material called plutonium. To the right, at the head of the corridor, were the Health Physics offices and stores, to his left the corridor extended some hundred and fifty yards with spurs off to the Control Laboratories on the left and the Plutonium Stores on the right. Each had its own security guard and another change room. John turned left and limped down to the second of these laboratories.

---

[2]*Health physics is a science that has grown up in the nuclear industry. It concerns the health effects of radiation exposure and the physics of measuring radiation. All nuclear establishments have Health Physics departments, they are responsible for making radiation measurements and advising on all aspects of radiation safety.*

'Morning Mr. Grimley,' the security guard glanced at John's pass.

'Morning,' he muttered in reply and shuffled through a set of double doors, one of which bore a plaque bearing his name as Laboratory Supervisor. Beyond was the small change room, similar in layout to the first except for its colour scheme. At the shoe barrier the green gave way to a pale yellow which not only indicated an area contaminated with radioactive material, it was also aesthetically more pleasing, but not much. For some reason, probably known only to the design office, John's lab was designated L-05, it measured 35ft by 50ft. The pale yellow walls were windowless and now sported a display of technical drawings, notice boards, and a selection of cuttings from calendars and magazines whose purpose in life it seems is to improve the decor of such drab working places. The light was artificial and so was the atmosphere. Two rows of glove boxes[3] ran parallel down the laboratory. A process worker was seated at each. John's desk, cluttered with papers, was at the far end. As he made towards it he stopped and spoke casually to some of his staff before he sat down to look through the pages of analytical results on his desk. L-05's function was to check the quantity and grade of the incoming plutonium[4] before it was placed in the fissile material stores.

---

[3]*Glove boxes are standard equipment for handling highly toxic materials both in the nuclear industry and elsewhere. They consist of a sealed box with sides usually made from Perspex. Port holes, fitted with long gauntlet type of rubber gloves, enable operators to handle material inside the box and thus prevents any escape to the outside. Slight suction is applied so that any leakage is inwards. The air drawn from the box is passed through highly efficient filters before being discharged to atmosphere outside the building. Material may be taken in and out of the box through special posting ports which have sealed doors at each end and so form an air lock. The operator handles the material inside the box by placing his hands inside the long gauntlet gloves which are, in any case, drawn into the box by the suction.*

[4]*Plutonium produced in a power reactor is a mixture of several isotopes, namely Pu 239, Pu 240, Pu 241. The proportion of Pu 239 to Pu 240 determines whether or not it is suitable for use in weapons. If there is a substantial proportion of Pu 240, as is the case with the material produced in civil nuclear power stations, then it is generally regarded as being unsuitable for weapons although there are processes under development which will enable the removal of the Pu 240. Reactor grade plutonium can be used in specially designed reactors such as the Fast Reactor and is therefore a useful nuclear fuel.*

Normally such plutonium would have come direct from the reprocessing line at Windscale but the present work involved the relocation of plutonium which had been in store there for many years. It arrived in special containers, fifteen inches square and just under three feet high. The outside was made of half inch thick steel plate and had a lid bolted and secured with two padlocks. They were green and had, on two sides, the yellow trefoil radiation signs. Inside each steel canister was a close fitting solid block of specially selected African hardwood. This had been bored with four, evenly spaced, two inch diameter holes. Each of these were lined with a cadmium plated steel cylinder which had a screw top and which held four six inch long plastic bags containing black aspirin sized pellets of plutonium oxide. The top of the box was so designed that when the lid had been removed a steel cover only allowed access to one hole at a time. These containers met the International Atomic Energy Agency's specification for the safe transport of plutonium and as such they would withstand both fire and mechanical accidents.

John sensed someone at his side, he glanced up. The process worker from the nearest glove box fidgeted.

'We're ready for loading K-21,' he muttered.

'Are the air sample checks okay?' queried Grimley as he got up and walked over to the box that the worker had just left. The nod he received was a good enough reply. Using the key he had picked up from his desk he released the padlocks then stepped half a pace backwards while the lid was removed. The container, on its special trolley, was moved to be under the glove box. There it was latched onto a leak tight loading port on the underside of the box. Grimley picked up a paper tissue, wiped it around the inside of the lid, then presented it to the RD5[5]. He had supervised this operation many times before and on every occasion there had not been any trace of contamination.

'Clean,' was all he uttered. He hobbled back to his desk and, carefully easing his injured leg into a comfortable position, sat down to resume his scrutiny of the papers he had been working on before the interruption. Out of the corner of his eye he watched the first of the cylinders being fed through the bottom of the glove box. He saw the

---

[5]*Health physicists usually refer to their instruments by their makers type number. For the purposes of this story the RD5 is a contamination monitor which will measure both alpha, beta and gamma radioactivity.*

Artists impression of a possible design for a Watersthorpe Glove Box, submitted as part of an unsuccessful tender.

process worker, hands in gloves, reach inside, unscrew the cap and take out four bags of plutonium oxide pellets. Supplemented by the occasional glance he noticed the worker slit open each bag in turn and select, at random, twenty of the black tablets. From each of these a small sample was taken using a special tool that looked not unlike a leather punch. These were then placed in a small labelled container ready for analysis. The operator's next task should have been to place each of the opened bags inside a new clean one, seal it, and return it to the cylinder, which would then have been lowered back into the transport container. As John Grimley had anticipated, indeed as was necessary for his scheme, the operator's work was interrupted by the clanging of the tea break bell. The other workers left their boxes and drifted to the door but the man with K-21 hesitated. Laboratory rules said that pellets must not be left unpacked in an unattended glove box. Trying to appear calm and natural, while at the same time experiencing a tingle of excitement, Grimley picked up his walking stick and limped over to the reluctant worker.

'Okay George, go and grab your coffee,' he half commanded. 'I'll package these up while you take your break.' The man didn't look surprised for John Grimley had made this gesture before. 'Not worth lugging this lump of rock all the way up the corridor just for a cuppa,' the Laboratory Supervisor added with the best excuse for a smile that he could muster. The process worker muttered his thanks and left the laboratory a little astern of his work mates.

Grimley worked fast, he had just ten minutes to himself but now he could move without the pretence of a broken ankle. He unscrewed the lower third of his walking stick and from it extracted two aluminium containers, each about five inches long and half an inch wide. In the prime of their lives they had served as packaging for an expensive brand of cigar but they were now being relegated to a more sinister role. He emptied their contents, which was in fact pelleted iron filings, onto a paper tissue and placed it inside the normal loading hatch of the glove box. He took each cigar container and covered them with a thin plastic film, the type that housewives use in their kitchens. These he also placed in the loading port then he closed the outer door. Now he put his arms and hands inside the rubber gauntlets of the glove box and was able to reach the inside door of the loading hatch. This he opened and pulled the black pellets on their tissue paper and the cigar containers into the body of the glove box. Finally he closed the inner hatch door making sure that it was properly sealed.

It was a standard loading operation but for non-standard material. John Grimley flushed hot, a trickle of perspiration ran down his forehead and onto the end of his nose. He desperately wanted to wipe it away but his hands were in rubber gauntlets and to have removed them would have taken time, time which he did not have to spare. He flicked his head and the offending droplet relinquished its hold and crashed ignominiously to the ground. He turned his attention to the four open sachets with the plutonium oxide pellets. Each of these he weighed and entered their weight onto the record card, he then picked up one of the cigar cases, filled it with plutonium pellets from the nearest sachet and screwed down the lid. For these he substituted the black iron filings which he had placed inside the glove box, resealed the sachet in a new polythene bag and returned it to the cylinder from which it had come. He repeated this operation on the second cigar container, as he did so more perspiration ran from his forehead and finished up on the floor. With the substitution complete he turned his attention to the unadulterated sachets and dealt with them in the prescribed manner. Then, via the special underneath loading facility, returned them to the transport container.

The clock on the wall had black featureless fingers and dots around the dial where numbers should have been. It was standard issue, each laboratory had one but for all its utilitarian appearance it accurately portrayed the time. John noticed that this part of the operation had already taken five minutes. He cursed himself for trying to switch two lots of plutonium instead of the usual one. He still had time to complete the operation if all went well, but would it, he asked himself? Almost as if he were psychic he heard the laboratory door open, his heart missed a beat and his stomach turned over. In panic he searched the glove box for somewhere to hide the two illicit cigar holders which now seemed as big as torpedoes. His mind raced, could he send George on an errand. No, that would not work, he would still not be able to get the contraband out of the box unnoticed by the others. The perspiration from his face lay in a small wet patch on the floor.

'Hell,' he muttered to himself as he had visions of being caught red handed on his last run. A voice boomed from the doorway.

'Boss wants a Lab. Supers. meeting in his office, straight after lunch.' It was the unmistakeable voice of Jim Webber that had shaken the room. Jim, from L-03, was the only fellow on site who did not need a telephone, there were enough decibels in his voice to carry far without electronic assistance. The door shut and he had gone, he never waited for a reply for everyone always got his message first time. John Wilberforce Grimley breathed a sigh of relief as his attention returned to the task in hand. He opened the inner door of the loading hatch and placed inside, on a piece of clean tissue, the two cigar containers which now held the plutonium oxide. He replaced the door, removed his hands from the box and moments later, using more paper tissue to prevent contamination getting on his hands, he removed the cigar containers from the hatch, pealed off the plastic film, and put them back inside his walking stick. This he reassembled before dropping the used tissue and cling film into the radioactive waste bin. Finally he frisked himself, his stick and the area in which he had worked, with the RD5 just to make sure that there was no tell tale spread of contamination. He started to walk over to his desk then hesitated for a moment, changed direction and walked to a bench against the wall. From a small heap of plastic bags, he picked one up and walked back to the waste container. Carefully reaching inside, he retrieved the tissue and plastic film that had just been discarded, placed them inside the plastic bag and sealed it with a strip of adhesive tape. This he placed inside his lab coat pocket. The clock on the wall told him that at any moment the others would return. As quickly as possible he made his way back to his desk, sat down, picked up the nearest bundle of papers and went through the motions of reading them. At this instant the laboratory door was thrust open by the returning process workers who took up their positions at their respective glove boxes. John was sweating profusely, he knew it so he kept his back turned to them. He also remembered the damp patch on the floor and successfully willed George not to notice it.

'I've stashed that plut in the container, get on with the next will you?'

'Thank you Mr. Grimley, did you record the weights on the control sheet?'

'Yes,' grunted the Supervisor without turning his head. Inwardly Grimley breathed a sigh of relief, this would be his very last load, by the time it was added to the previous thefts he would have five kilograms of reactor grade plutonium, enough for his purpose. All he had to do now was to get it off the site the same way as he had removed the other. He told himself there would be no difficulty, no one suspected what he was up to, no one would miss the plutonium until after the big day.

CHAPTER 2

Building 301 comprised not only of the assay labs and the Plutonium Stores but also the Health and Safety Department. Their laboratory, situated at the head of the long corridor, was in architecture very much the same at Grimley's and all the others, painted brick walls, grey lino floors and the regulation issue clock on the wall. The Head of Health Physics, who was also Head of Health and Safety, had her offices in the Administration block on the other side of the site, but this morning she was with her assistant in the operational laboratory. They sat together at a desk, at the far end of the room, underneath the clock. The walls were lined with shelves upon which resided a variety of instruments for measuring radiation or radioactivity. The Health Physicist was responsible for "advising" the Laboratory Manager and the Site Directors on all safety matters but had special responsibility concerning radiation and criticality. In theory the Department was advisory and the Management were free to reject any advice although in practise they seldom did. Other departments had a deep respect for the "safety merchants" as they were frequently called, although they would be reluctant to admit it. Ostensibly Health Physics was obstructive, always delaying work for fear of unlikely accidents and they produced nothing. They had no worries about meeting specifications, production schedules, or solving the many technical problems arising from the handling of plutonium. All they did was to make a few simple measurements then don the mantle of the Prophet of Doom and require everyone to follow more and more time consuming, non-productive, procedures in the name of safety. It was a source of irritation to those who worked on the production lines, and also to those involved in maintenance, that such a small group had such an elite standing on the site. Yet for all this outward display of hostility there existed, in the heart of every employee, a warm and welcome corner for these "parasites". Plutonium was a deadly, dangerous material to handle, the consequences of an accident could cause injury or suffering to many, so it was "good news" that a group of their colleagues should be looking over their shoulders, making sure that no one made a mistake. Janice Hardman, a tall slender built lady in her late thirties with a ginger tint in her brown hair which, as always, was done up in a bun, mused over her problems. Her freckles and lack of make up gave an appearance which seemed wholly consistent with her status of a professional woman. She was a career scientist, Head of Health and Safety at Watersthorpe. Her department was efficient and in the short time it had been operational had gained an industry wide reputation. 'I run a tight ship' she would snap at those who belittled her track record by implying that she had been lucky not to experience the accidents and incidents that seemed to dog other nuclear sites. Her approach to safety was not just professional, it bordered on the obsessive. This, without doubt, had its origins in the one tragic event in her life. From a middle class background she had worked her way through university and, by driving herself to the very limits, had managed an upper second in physics. Her first employment had been as a research assistant with the giant Bracken Oil Corporation, but disciplined research had not been her forte and within six months she had quit. It took a further six months for her to find another job, this was with the Nuclear Research Authority. There she worked upon the development of specialised instrumentation for radiation monitoring. This time she was given her head and was able to exploit her inventive flair. She became engrossed in her work giving most of her waking time to it. Then, at the age of twenty seven, she met Ken Wilson. To everyone else he was just a likeable stick-in-the-mud who tended to muddle rather than plan his way through life. Just what she saw in him no one else could ever understand but to her he was Mr. Wonderful and she was madly in love. He also worked for the N.R.A. and was engaged in experiments with plutonium to measure its critical mass under different circumstances. Two years after they first met, and three days before their wedding, there was a terrible accident. Just exactly what happened on that fateful day no one will ever know, somehow too much plutonium had, unexpectedly, come together and caused a criticality accident. Ken received a dose of radiation estimated to be in excess of a thousand rem[6]. Blood transfusions and bone marrow transplants were of no avail, she had to watch helplessly as her sweetheart died in a horrible degrading manner. Six weeks passed between the day of the

---

[6]*A "rem" is a unit of radiation exposure dose. An occupationally registered radiation worker, at the time of the accident, would have a permitted exposure dose of 5 rem in a year although, in practice, most radiation workers received very much less. An acute dose of 500 rem would leave the recipient with only a 50% chance of long term survival. Doses over 1,000 rem would inevitably prove fatal despite the best medical treatment. The "rem" has now been replaced by a unit called the "sievert". One sievert is equivalent to 100 rem.*

accident and his death, six weeks of anguish which were implanted upon her memory for ever. On the day he died she swore a silent oath, the rest of her life would be devoted to safety in the nuclear industry.

She quit her job and started afresh as a trainee health physicist with the Electricity Supply Authority. During the very first week she attended a lecture given by Richard Harry England, this had left a lasting impression. As a safety man, England had been first class but his ability to play the organisation game was well below par. His persistence and interventions in the cause of safety, especially with matters concerning radiation, had caused him to clash with just about every senior manager in the industry. Worse still, when these disagreements occurred, by dint of his irrepressible personality he always won his point. Subsequent events usually proved him to have been correct, but that did not prevent his name being metaphorically entered into many black books. His chance of being promoted into general management, as he occasionally told his friends, might be compared with the chances of a snowball surviving in Hell. He had resigned from the Electricity Supply Authority a few years after Janice had attended his lecture. The last establishment to employ him, where he headed the Radiation and Safety Department, had won the industries "Mac-Triangle" award three years in succession for outstanding safety performance. This had not only brought him fame, it also made many of his colleagues jealous for they considered his results should have been attributed to good luck. His philosophy of 'if you do the same as others you won't do any better' eventually proved unacceptable and he was persuaded to resign with a substantial monetary handshake. Everyone who met England was impressed by his quiet, confident and deep thinking manner. Indeed the central theme of the lecture that Janice Hardman had attended influenced her attitude throughout her subsequent career. Now, as she sat at the desk underneath the regulation clock in the health physics laboratory at Watersthorpe, his words came to her as crystal clear as the day she first heard them uttered.

'Accidents don't just happen, they are caused,' it was not just the phrase but the sincerity with which he emphasised it that stuck with her.

'Every accident has its own harbinger. Identify this, take firm and resolute action, and you will prevent a tragedy.' As Janice mulled over her problem those words echoed through her brain and she saw

England again emphasising his philosophy. 'When you know what needs to be done in the cause of safety, do it and to hell with the political consequences. Your objective is to save lives and to prevent injury, not to make friends with the production departments.' Graham Kindale, her assistant sitting at her side, read her thoughts.

'Jan, those figures are real. I know we haven't proved the gear and it's not been passed by the new Instrument Approval Group, but I'm as sure as hell it is telling us something,' he paused for a moment then went on, 'look, all we've got to do is to re-assay some of that plut. If we've boobed the Brigadier can crow and if we're right the old buffoon will probably get an O.B.E. or something but who cares, it's people that matter,' he said referring to the Head of Laboratories.

'You don't have to tell me that,' snapped Janice, then she regretted the rebuke aimed at her young assistant for he was only following in her wake. 'Okay, I'll put it to Claude Siegfried, but I don't think he will like it or give way, the thing is young Graham,' she liked to remind him of her seniority in years, 'when we take on a mule we have to be sure that we can push hard enough. I'm not convinced that without more evidence we can shift him this time, still as you say we've got to try.'

Half an hour later she was in the Administration building on the opposite side of the site. Armed with a handful of loose papers she marched through the door labelled Head of Laboratories, inside the outer lobby of his office she was confronted by a stern faced secretary.

'Is the Brig in?' she muttered. There was no need to wait for a reply, the expression on Mary Piper's face gave the answer. Janice paused just long enough to give a cursory tap on the mahogany faced door which coincided with the, 'Yes, but I...,' stammered words from the secretary's lips. Janice did not wait for the knock to be answered, she turned the anodised aluminium door handle and made her entry.

'No, don't get up Claude,' she said, settling into a chair in front of his desk, the mahogany of which matched that of the door. 'There's something urgent come up that we must talk about, so if you've got other appointments put them off for half an hour,' she instructed.

The red faced man's blood pressure rose twenty percent, no one else dared speak to him like that but the years of chivalry enshrined in his upbringing prevented him from being rude to a lady. Confound the woman he thought, but forced a gentlemanly smile as he replied, 'Of course my dear, if it's urgent. We don't want any accidents do we?' There was a note of patronage in his voice.

'You're dead right there, but this time it might be more than an accident,' Janice paused for just a moment, 'this time it could be political dynamite if you'll forgive the pun. Someone has nicked some of our, or should I say your, plutonium.' She spat out the word "your" then sat back and waited for the Head of Laboratories to erupt. The Brigadier was a man in his late fifties of medium height and substantially overweight. On his stiff upper lip he sported a short cut military style moustache. His rounded face was red and his nose tainted purple. The waistcoat of his pin stripe suit was straining to encompass his ample girth which, he constantly boasted, had cost him dear in gin and tonics. His father had been a distinguished professional soldier in World War II, Claude was given no choice, he was destined for Sandhurst. As a youth he had been energetic and athletic, the army life had suited him well. With a little help from the old boy network, which more than compensated for his backward and unimaginative qualities, he progressed and by the time he retired he had reached the rank of Brigadier. On leaving the Service, by way of a few words in the right ear, he was helped into an administrative post in the Atomic Energy Agency. When Watersthorpe was set up he was strongly recommended to the E.S.A. for the post of Site Director, it being argued that, despite his lack of technical knowledge, his military career would suit him for such a high security post. There had also been talk on the side that this recommendation was much influenced by Agency's wish to get rid of some dead wood and this was possibly why the E.S.A. resisted pressure to appoint him. In any event he was not one of their proteges and they also wanted to demonstrate their independence of the A.E.A. In the best traditions of British compromise he was made Head of Laboratories and deputy to the Director.

'Rubbish, woman,' the Brigadier exploded, 'our security here is tighter than the Bank of England. I personally see the daily check sheets and I can assure you that all is in order. Last week I even did the count myself and everything was there, you're dreaming, my dear.'

'You might have counted the containers, but you've not checked that the plut is still inside,' Janice responded.

'Come off it, the plut is weighed when it is received by the assay labs, it is analysed and the containers[7] are weighed when they are put into the store. Furthermore we make spot checks on the weight of the containers in the store just to make sure that all the plut is still all there. I tell you everything is in order.' He thumped his desk with his fist and was about to add some stronger language to emphasise his confidence when he remembered he was addressing a lady. Janice tensed a little, she knew all this and so far the interview had gone much as she had expected, now she prepared to play her ace.

'Claude, have you ever thought of the consequences of losing some plut?' she asked. 'Just suppose that someone had beaten your security and then sold the stuff off to a foreign power or even attempted to make a bomb from it. The public reaction would be enormous and could destroy the whole nuclear industry.' She paused for just a moment. 'On the other hand if the loss was quickly discovered and the culprit caught, then public confidence would be restored. Those concerned with the recovery of the material might even get a place in the Honours List.' The Brigadier nodded cautiously as she continued to hold forth. 'Now you are right in as much that all the containers are present, their weight is what it should be, but I am ninety percent sure that not all the containers have the requisite amount of plut in them.' She again paused to let her words sink in. 'Kindale and myself have modified a 1268 so that it can measure plutonium in its primary container...'

'What the Devil is a 1268?' the red faced man behind the mahogany desk interrupted, more in an attempt to disrupt Janice's line of reasoning than in a quest for information.

'It's an obsolete three channel gamma analyser, the power stations used to have them as part of their emergency kit for measuring radioactive iodine,' the Health physicist continued without the slightest sign of being flustered. 'The idea was to hold it against a churn of milk and it would measure the gamma from the iodine and not the other isotopes...'

---

[7] *The Head of Laboratories was not referring to the transport containers in which the plutonium arrived, but to storage containers in the Fissile Material Store. These were cadmium lined polythene bottles in which the plutonium was kept after it had been removed from the transport containers. They were retained in a special vented cabinet and were stacked in horizontal rows a metre apart. The containers and their storage positions were designed to prevent criticality accidents.*

'Surely, if it's obsolete...'

'It was replaced with more sophisticated equipment mainly because milk isn't collected in churns any more,' Janice retorted. 'The stations cleared them out last year and I bagged a couple to play with. We swapped some electronics and re-tuned them to the 13KEV gamma from plut 239. Depending on the geometry we can estimate within plus or minus thirty percent, the amount of plut it's looking at. We tried it out on some of the containers during yesterday's routine survey of the store and some of them, only a few, gave repeated and consistent low readings. I'm sure that they don't contain all they should.' She paused and waited to see which way he would jump. There followed a stunned silence for an endless ten seconds then came the earthquake, he had jumped wrong.

'What the hell do you mean by making unauthorised measurements in my store? Your access authority was for contamination survey not to check the plutonium contents. That is confidential to me not Health Physics. Was this your idea? Did the Store Supervisor know what you were doing, did you lie to him?' The Brigadier flushed an even deeper red, he was suffering from a shortage of breath, Janice wondered if he was about to have a stroke. 'I expect that your young Kindale put you up to this?' He half rose from his chair, then sat down, it gave Janice a moment to interject.

'Brigadier, it was my idea. I take responsibility and I will not have you blame my staff,' she said not giving ground. 'I'm asking you now to authorise the re-assay of the suspect containers. I'll put that in writing to you. Will you do it?' She looked at the Head of Laboratories but he remained poker faced as she continued, 'If not, and if plut is eventually found to be missing, I'll personally see you crucified in Hell for being so stubborn and stupid.' She spoke the last few words in a biting whisper that hissed between her teeth.

The Brigadier was taken aback, he had not expected a counter attack least of all from a woman, he thought for a moment then pronounced, 'To back load a few containers would cause disruption to our programme. We are already under pressure to take the remaining stocks from Windscale. Last week there were questions in the House...,' he looked to the window then returned his stare to the female in front of him. 'No, I can not justify such action on the basis of your unauthorised measurements made with out-dated equipment...'

'You don't have to back load the containers,' Janice persisted. 'Our equipment is crude, but the principle is well established and I am sure that the A.E.A. or the Weapons Group would have something more sophisticated that we could borrow for in situ checks.'

'If that is the case, my dear girl, why does Watersthorpe Health Physics Department not have this equipment?'

'That, my dear Brigadier,' said Janice mimicking his tone 'is explained by what you have already said, it's not my job to look for lost plut, it's yours!' The man's eyes, for one moment, blazed with fury then he composed himself and responded.

'We can not go outside our industry at this stage, we do not want those Atomic Energy fellows thinking that we are at panic stations, could cause all sorts of problems. If there were other evidence to support your suggestion that would be different. I will however, mention the matter to the Director when he comes home from leave next month, but...' His voice tailed off, Janice had risen out of her chair and walked to the door where she paused just long enough to utter,

'In writing within the hour Brigadier!' and with that she slammed the door with such ferocity that she heard the glass jingle in his drinks cupboard.

CHAPTER 3

Back in Laboratory L-05 the big hand of the regulation clock had made two complete circles since John Grimley loaded the plutonium into his walking stick. One by one the glove box operators finished off their work at the boxes. They passed through the wash, change and monitor check routine in the sub-change room then made their way up the corridor in quest of lunch. John was the last to leave, closing the door behind him he gave the security men the nod to lock up. What this man did not notice was the transfer of the small polythene bag of contaminated tissue, as John changed from his amber area lab coat to the one he wore in the green area. Also unnoticed was the rather casual monitoring check that he gave his walking stick, but then who would have suspected the Laboratory Supervisor? John hobbled up the corridor slower than his impediment required, this allowed the others time to get well ahead and clear the main change room before he arrived. There was no one else about as he pushed through the double doors, but he glanced around just to make sure. He took off his white coat and hung it with the others. Carefully, he palmed the polythene bag and slipped it into his pocket, then he moved over to the shoe barrier. He sat down and removed his overshoes, the one on the plaster cast resisting the operation with the tenacity of a Roman Legion. He swung his feet and stick over the barrier and moved across to the grey lockers and opened his own. After removing the sealing tape from the plastic bag, he tipped out the tissue that was inside and watched it fall to the bottom of the locker. He closed the door and turned the key. Routine Health Physics surveys of lockers only took place once a quarter, the last one had been two months ago, so it would be another three and a half weeks before the tell-tale contaminated tissue was discovered. That would be after the big day, he considered the timing could not have been better. Clues had to be left so that the public inquiry, which would surely follow the event, would discover his involvement, but only after the big day.

For what would be the last time, he moved to the contamination check monitors and stepped inside. In dimensions they were not unlike the traditional telephone box, but that was where the similarity ended. They were made from shining stainless steel and had open sides. The floor was a turntable fitted with a grill and the front and backs also had a series of grills behind which lurked sensitive radiation detectors. As John, plaster encased leg and walking stick, moved onto the turntable his weight activated the mechanism. A small red light with the words "Test On" illuminated and there was a slight whirring sound as the floor rotated John through one complete turn. The noise stopped, the red light went off and on came a green one bearing the words "Safe", this was accompanied for audible indication by a few musical chimes. This instrument, as John knew, could have detected the minutest amount of radioactivity on his person, but not the four hundred grammes of plutonium which were sealed inside his stick[8]. He nodded to the guard as he passed into the lobby of Building 301 then he walked out through the door to make his way along the two hundred yards of road which separated it from the office and canteen building.

The canteen section had all the appearance of having been designed by the same architect as the laboratories. Certainly the decor was in the same style, painted brick walls in rather unexciting pale blue. The stainless steel servery, the square formica top tables and the grey plastic chairs were all functional rather than inspiring. John Grimley was one of the last to enter, his eyes scanning the scene in a search for an empty table, as he hobbled over towards the food dispensary. He paid the lady at the till with barely an exchange of words taking place, then made his way across to the table in the far corner. It was not that he had to sit alone, he could have joined George Watkins who was sitting with two of the other Laboratory Supervisors, or Jim Webber who was chatting up an admin clerk, but he preferred to sit alone. He settled down and dawdled through his meal. At a nearby table Janice Hardman and Graham Kindale were in earnest conversation. He could not catch their words, but from the expressions on their faces he guessed that they were discussing something serious. For a moment he wondered if they had somehow stumbled across his surreptitious actions. Could they, he wondered, have already found the contaminated items in his locker or did they suspect that some plutonium had gone missing? He told himself this could not be so, and was reassured when Janice Hardman glanced his way and showed a light and friendly smile which he made no attempt to return. His moments of worry ebbed away and he inwardly laughed

---

[8]*Plutonium emits alpha radiation and this would be stopped by the walls of the hollow walking stick. Its other emissions are so weak that they would not be detected in these checks.*

at the irony of the situation, he was sitting but a few yards away from them with a walking stick loaded with plutonium.

By deploying go slow tactics on his coffee he managed to kill time while the others in the canteen finished their lunches and left. As the big hand of the regulation issue clock reached the vertical, John left his table and limped over to the far end of the canteen where he passed through a double swing door which led to the office accommodation. A casual observer might well have concluded that this part of the building had been designed by a different architect. It had a modern appearance which bordered upon the luxurious. The floor was carpeted with a twisted pile, good quality Wilton which was kind to the feet and the eye. The walls were panelled with wood-grained facia board and the doors leading to the offices were in contrasting mahogany. Grimley hobbled his way along the corridor until he came to one labelled "Brigadier Whatley-Jones - Head of Laboratories". He paused for a moment, and asked himself how a pompous ass like Claude Siegfried Whatley-Jones had managed to reach such an elevated position. It was, he concluded, a typical result of the British class system. The Brigadier lacked all the technical qualifications of his colleagues, but had the overwhelming advantage of an undistinguished military career where, as is not uncommon in peace time, his rank was achieved more by who he knew rather than what he knew. Even as John paused he heard the reverberations of the big man's voice.

'Who told Grimley to be here?' Claude was enquiring of his subordinates already seated around the conference table in his office. 'Why is he not here with the rest of you?'

'He'll be here when he's ready,' boomed Jim Webber's voice. 'I told him 'smorning, he's always late.'

John did not knock, he thrust open the door, walked past Mary Piper and made an entry into the meeting.

'I heard that friend,' he growled as he lowered himself into the one remaining chair. The Brigadier coughed, took command and started his meeting. John had no interest in the proceedings, but tried not to show it. His future at Watersthorpe was about to terminate, but only he knew that. The Head of Laboratories went through the Departments target production figures, discussed the throughput of the assay laboratories and the capacity of the Fissile Material store. He outlined the deliveries that were expected from Windscale in the next three months and held forth at length about the need to meet production line targets. He talked for three quarters of an hour then

Grimley's heart suddenly beat a little faster as he became aware that the subject had turned to security.

'Gentlemen, I can not emphasise enough the need for us all to maintain a constant vigil and the tightest of security. The material that we are handling is not only highly dangerous, it is also politically very sensitive. If some were to go missing it could even jeopardise the entire nuclear programme of this country.' The Brigadier looked round his audience for signs of reaction but received none, they had all heard these speeches before.

'The security here is as tight as the proverbial virgin's ....,' came Jim Webber's reassuring voice which would have been clearly audible in Mary Piper's office. 'I'd lay a pound to a pinch of fertilizer that no one could even get a peanut sized piece of plut out of this site.' The Brigadier winced at Webber's forthright comment, but inwardly felt reassured. He was mindful of Janice Hardman's comments and wondered whether or not to mention them. He decided against revealing her suspicions, such matters should not be discussed with subordinates. He had made up his mind and this he considered to be part of the loneliness of command.

'Is there any reason to think that we may have lost some plut then?' ventured John Grimley in a voice which he contrived to keep casual and not reveal his hidden anxiety.

'Oh no...no..., not really, but you never know, must keep you fellows on yer toes,' responded the Brigadier. Grimley nodded and struggled to stifle a smile at the situation. Less than ten feet away from the old army officer were four hundred grams of stolen plutonium. The meeting continued for another fifteen minutes then broke up. The other Laboratory Supervisors left the office, but John Grimley hung back.

'I want to take a months leave as from Monday,' he announced coming straight to the point. 'Sorry about the short notice, but it's one of those once in a lifetime opportunities,' he said without giving any hint of the subtle meaning of his remark. 'The lab's running smoothly, the charge hand has got things under control and young Jack McKendle is free to cover on the technical side.'

'You seem to have it all worked out, I suppose that I am only a formality?' replied the pompous Whatley-Jones with just one lump of ice in his voice. 'I'll have to consider your request.'

'Please yourself, but I'm not coming in on Monday and I'll be away for four weeks with or without leave. Quite honestly I don't much care whether you say yes or no, I'm not missing this chance for a god forsaken spot like Watersthorpe.' Grimley stopped himself before he said too much.

The Head of Laboratories resented the attitude of his subordinate, it bordered on insolence. His first reaction was to make an issue of the matter, but he sensed that Grimley would go all the way to a resignation, he had seemed rather restless over the past few months and, while the Brigadier would not have shed any tears at losing him, he did not want to do so just yet, Laboratory Supervisors were key people until the backlog had been cleared. He made a face saving response, 'Very well, you can only use your leave once and it will help the rest of us if you take it now, request granted. Let my secretary have your leave sheet for signing.'

'Thanks,' muttered John, as he stumped out of the office leaving a bemused Brigadier who should have known better than bow to such pressure. Grimley did not go back to his laboratory, he passed the remaining part of the afternoon in the library.

The other staff started for home, he too joined the slow moving crocodile making its way to the gate. As on previous occasions when he had been carrying contraband, he felt nervous. So far he had not been searched, but would his luck hold? At moments like these he regretted being an atheist, it denied him asking for divine intervention. He sought reassurance from the fact that the chances of being searched were small. His grade was regarded as senior staff and while, in theory, everyone was liable to search he had never heard of the higher grades being called in. As he approached the inner gate the voice of Joe Kitchen, who was still on duty, interrupted his thoughts.

'Mr. Grimley in here please.' Startled by the order, he looked up from the paving slabs that he had been studying for solace, and noted a process worker leaving the Security Lodge, the man was muttering.

'Third bleedin' time they've done me and they ain't no reason to suspect anythin'. Reckon they're arter somethin' this time.'

Grimley heard these words and reached the point of near panic, his heart thumped and his mind raced. Should he try pulling his rank and protest at being delayed, he dismissed the idea, it would only make them more thorough in their search. He looked at the far gate, it was only opened after clearance from the inner gate, making a dash for the outside would be a disaster. His person was clean, the danger of detection lay with the walking stick. It was noticeably heavier than it should be and if one of the security men picked it up they would, without doubt, want to find out why. They were professionals and good at their job. He gave up the idea of leaving it at the door, that could invite someone to handle it. His only hope, a slender one at that, was to keep hold of it at all time and to make it look natural while so doing. All this flashed through his mind in a split second before he responded.

'Did you want me?' he tried to appear matter of fact.

'Yes Mr. Grimley, just step inside please.' The morning's friendly 'keeper pushed open the steel barred door of the Security Lodge. It took a few moments for John Grimley's eyes to adjust to the change of light, as they did he saw a tall, brawny, Security Officer in his dull blue uniform bearing down on him. Butterflies went rampant in his stomach and his knees went weak.

'Mr. Grimley?' the man asked in a gruff voice.

'Yes...er... what can I do for you?' John countered anticipating that this was the crunch.

'The H.O.L. has been on the blower, says we're to ask for your pass while you're away, just a security precaution. The old boy is getting a bit edgy today, third time he's been on...'

On the bus back to Watersthorpe Village John, as usual, avoided conversation but he did manage a smile and a 'cheerio' as he stepped down from the vehicle and limped off to his flat.

*

Janice Hardman signed her hand written memo to the Brigadier, addressed an envelope and placed her note inside. She flicked it into her out tray, ready for the internal messenger to collect on his afternoon round. She got up from her desk and turned to the large picture window which gave an uninterrupted view across the Lincolnshire countryside. It was then she had the glimmer of an idea, turning back to her desk she reached for the internal telephone.

'Health Physics lab,' the voice responded at the other end of the line.

'Graham Kindale please,' Janice enquired.

'Hold on a sec and I'll get him for you,' the voice said before the line went silent. Janice waited impatiently.

'Kindale speaking.'

'Graham, this is Janice, are you involved in anything at the moment?'

'Nothing that can't wait, what's up?'

'As I said at lunchtime I've had no joy with the Brig, but I have got the glimmering of an idea to discuss. Can you come over to my office now?'

'Sure,' her assistant replied before putting down the phone. Ten minutes later there was a tap on the door and Graham Kindale entered without waiting his boss's invitation. Janice came straight to the point.

'Do you remember a paper by England...about three years ago...?'

'He has written several, which one do you mean?' Kindale replied.

'I don't remember the details, but I'm sure he produced a paper. He argued that plutonium was so easy to detect no one would ever be able to steal and process it without being found out.'

'I don't think it was a paper, wasn't it an off the cuff reply to a question at the I.A.E.A. Plutonium Security Conference in Amsterdam?'

'Could be, I seem to recall that his remarks attracted quite a lot of press interest at the time because the anti-nuclear campaigners had always used the "what if..." argument and his paper demolished that case.'

'I don't think that there is anything in writing Jan, if you want to follow up the idea you'll have to contact Dick England himself,' Graham Kindale suggested.

'I could do just that.'

'Bit risky, he's not with the industry now, it could be regarded as breach of security if you confided in him. It could even constitute a contravention of the Official Secrets Act,' her assistant advised.

'Okay Graham forget it, I was only thinking out loud, but we could do something ourselves. England argued that plut was so difficult to handle that if someone tried to remove it illicitly it would inevitably leave a trail of contamination. Well, what do our routines show?'

'Sod all,' he replied without hesitation. 'The F.M.S. was as clean as a new bog roll at the Savoy, so if England's suggestion is right, it would mean that there hasn't been any lifting from there.' He paused, then added as an after thought 'But if it had been pinched while it was in the labs any contamination spread would be concealed by the contamination from normal operations.' Janice gave a wry smile as she began to see some possibilities.

'You could be right young Graham, suppose one of the process workers or cleaners or anyone else, had somehow taken some of the plut while it was still in the lab, a little at a time, and in such a way that it would not be noticed, it would then be easy to smuggle it off site.' She paused for thought, tweaked the end of her nose which had developed a slight tickle, then continued, 'The odds are that some of their personal gear would be loused up. When was the last routine locker survey?'

Graham thought for a moment then answered, 'Two months ago, we do them quarterly so the next one is due in four weeks time.'

'Right, let's bring the date forward and do one tomorrow.'

'Sorry Jan, but you would need to get the Brig's consent for that. He has an agreement with the Works Committee that personal locker surveys are only done once a quarter and then we have to have one of the Committee present as a witness.'

The Head of Health Physics silently rebuked herself for not remembering the agreement to which she had been party. It had been reached following an accusation that money had been taken from a locker during an Health Physics spot survey.

'You're right, even the Brig could not agree it without consulting the Works Committee and then he would have to say why, that would let the cat out of the bag so as to speak. Daft isn't it? If our hunch is right the whole future of the nuclear industry might be in jeopardy because we aren't allowed to open a locker until next month,' Janice muttered with a touch of bitterness in her voice.

Graham Kindale nodded in agreement as she continued, 'Head of Labs won't heed me without more evidence, yet I can't get that evidence without his connivance, the Director's away for four weeks and the Brig is his deputy. It's a nutty world, isn't it? There is absolutely nothing that I can do while this potential time bomb ticks away.' There was exasperation in her voice and a trace of a tear in her eyes.

'I'll have a word with England on the QT,' volunteered Kindale.

'Like hell you will, it's my responsibility and if anyone sticks their neck out it will be me. I want you to be in the clear, someone has to be around to keep Claude under control if and when I get the chop,' she said with a smile.

'What, you?'

'If I go outside the industry, right or wrong, they will get rid of me, it's about the worst crime you can commit. Maybe half of London is saved from being blown away, but that's irrelevant, it's loyalty to this circus that counts. I'll think on it over the weekend,' she said but this time there was no smile for she realised the deep water into which she might have to enter.

*

John Grimley's flat was one of the custom built, single men's flats which were mainly occupied by the younger generation. Nevertheless as a bachelor, albeit a middle aged one, he qualified for this accommodation. It suited his purposes, the generation gap between himself and the other residents meant he could keep himself to himself. The entrance hall opened into a small but comfortable living room with a table, easy chair, small portable television and radio music centre, all of which were provided with the flat which was industry owned. The hall also led to a modest sized bedroom and bathroom. The kitchen, equipped with fridge freezer and microwave cooker was behind the living room. John enjoyed a love hate relationship with his abode. It suited his purpose and he liked its small size, snug, cosy atmosphere, he despised it because it was a symbol of the industry that he had undertaken to destroy.

For years he had waited but now that part was over, he was already actively serving the cause and the climax of his mission was only a few weeks away. He stumped into his bedroom and from under the bed pulled out a small metal tool box. From it he selected a saw, half an inch wide and six inches long, one end had a moulded rubber handle. He then fetched an old newspaper and laid it out on the floor beside a wooden chair which was positioned near his bed. Inwardly he questioned why he should bother with the newspaper when he would not be the one who had to clear up the mess. Sitting on the chair he stretched out his plaster encased leg and set to work on the cast with the blade. Twenty minutes later the plaster lay in a crumpled heap. He massaged his leg, then started to walk around the room, enjoying a sensation of freedom.

'Three bloody weeks in that concrete,' he muttered to himself. 'The things I do for the cause.' He gathered up the plaster remains, wrapped them in the newspaper and pushed them under the bed. He returned to the living room and gave his attention to the walking stick. After unscrewing the bottom section he removed the two cigar containers with their valuable cargo and selected one of them.

'Now where shall we plant our second clue?' he murmured as he cast his eyes around. A sly smile crossed his face and he added 'Here's to Silkwood,'[9] as he walked into the kitchen and opened his refrigerator. He pierced the thin aluminium with a single prick from a small nail, held the container inside the ice box and gave it a little squeeze. Invisible to the eye, a few thousand becquerels[10] of radioactivity were ejected. He then placed a piece of sellotape over the pin hole to seal the tube. Finally he went over to the sink, washed the cigar tube and then his hands.

The evening passed slowly, he had to wait until the night before he could move. He did not expect visitors, he did not normally have callers, but he felt on edge just in case someone dropped in. Perhaps he should have left the plaster on his leg until the last possible moment? To be found without it could be disastrous. He went into the kitchen, made a sandwich and opened a can of lager. After consuming these he laid down on his bed and dozed. He was in the state of mind which exists between sleep and consciousness when he reviewed the events of the last few weeks. Everyone had been fooled by his plaster leg, how it had been so easy to steal five kilograms of plutonium from under the noses of those who said it could not be done. His imagination was taking him into the next stage of the

---

[9]*Karen Silkwood was an American woman who died under mysterious circumstances after she alleged there were breaches in the safety regulations at the nuclear establishment where she had worked. Subsequent investigation, after her death, discovered traces of plutonium in the refrigerator in her flat. Its origin has never satisfactorily been explained.*

[10]*Becquerel is a unit which indicates the amount of radioactivity. One becquerel is the quantity of material in which one atom splits every second. It is a very small unit for example a common gas mantle would contain many hundreds of becquerels of radioactivity from thorium. Even so normal monitoring equipment would detect surface contamination as low as a few becquerels per square centimetre for alpha radioactivity.*

operation when he was returned to the real world by a voice calling his name.

'John? John, are you there?' There was a short pause. 'We're on our way to the Plough and Partridge, want to come? It's Keith's birthday.'

Adrenaline pumped into his veins, to those outside it would be obvious that he was at home so he had to reply, but he dare not open the door. After a moments hesitation he quickly made his way into the bathroom and called out.

'I'm in the tub and then going to hit the hay. Thanks for the call, but I've got to catch an early train tomorrow.' A second voice from behind the outside door made some comment which he did not catch, but which brought forth laughter from the others as they moved away.

At 2200hrs John put out the light and lay on top of his bed willing the time to pass. It did. At five minutes past midnight he looked at his watch, picked up the 'phone and, by the light of a small pen torch, dialled. After the third ring a female voice answered simply and sharply.

'Research Express.'

'Firewater ingredients are leaving now,' was all John said before he put down the receiver. Everything was on schedule. Using his pen torch he crossed the room and picked up a small suitcase and placed it by the front door. He then returned, extinguished the little beam of light, checked that the doors and windows were closed and drew back the curtains. Finally, having looked all round his flat, John Grimley slipped the catch back on the front door and peered out. One solitary street light interrupted the dark with a ghostly blue twilight, which turned the road and its houses into silhouettes. No-one was about, no person, no car, no cat nor dog, just a deserted empty street. He picked up his suitcase with its illicit contents, slipped quietly out of the door and made his way twenty yards along the pavement to the small garage which housed his car. A few minutes later he was on his way, no one had seen him, no one knew he had gone, no one knew his destination except the female voice at Research Express. With his cover story of an early train and his last minute request for leave, no one would suspect anything sinister about his departure, that is until several weeks had passed and by then it would be too late, too late by far.

CHAPTER 4

It was well into the early hours of Saturday morning when John Grimley reached his destination. He had made only one stop, that was at the all night "Petrorama" filling station just north of Ipswich. It was not that he needed the petrol, but he wanted to make sure that when the time came, the Authorities would be able to trace his journey to Walton-on-Naze. To this end, without being asked, he wrote the car registration on the credit card chit. He asked the young attendant for directions, although he knew the road well. Finally he made a joke at the expense of Her Majesty's Government.

The plain black and white sign, illuminated by two halogen floodlights, was fixed to the eight foot high gate that guarded the entrance to a long shingled drive. On either side of the gate, a fence of equal height, likewise topped with barbed wire, secured the approach which resembled that of a run down farm rather than a dynamic high tech industry. Once more John read the sign and wondered if it was not rather over reacting, perhaps attracting attention rather than discouraging it.

Research Express
Keep Out
Admittance by Appointment only. Guard Dog on Patrol

Grimley stopped the car, got out and in the light of his headlights went to the small grey box which was fixed to the link mesh fence wire a few yards to the left of the gate. He flipped open the lid and lifted the hand set.

'Grimley, alone, for Firewater,' he said simply.

He returned to his car and waited, but not for long. A loud clang, then a whirring sound, indicated that the gates were opening. He drove in and heard them shut behind.

'Bloody Alcatraz,' he muttered to himself.

At the end of the drive stood a large Georgian house which, even a casual glance would have revealed, was somewhat neglected and well past its prime. It had originally been built for Sir Richard Longsands, a wealthy merchant whose source of money was far from public knowledge much to the chagrin of the King's Revenue Men. It stood on the flat Essex lowland and looked towards Horsenose Creek and the Walton Blackwaters. Conveniently, by design or accident, a

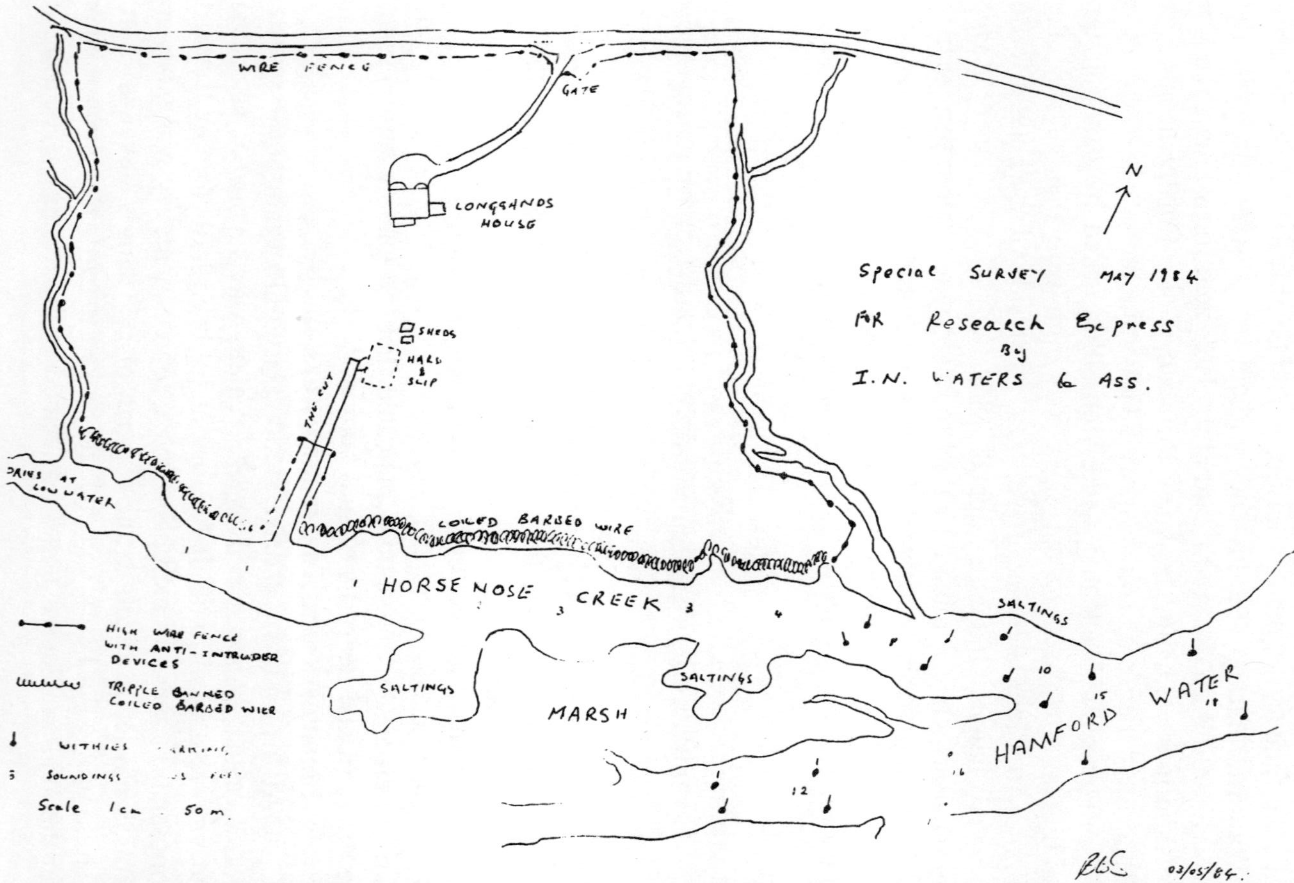

Survey Report of Longsands House site - believed to have been prepared for "Research Express" prior to their purchase of the site.

large part of its boundary coincided with a deep drainage ditch which, together with Horsenose Creek, formed a moat around the property. Not withstanding this a security fence had been added. In late Victorian times the House was sold out of the Longsands family to pay off the gambling debts of one of Sir Richard's successors. It had been bought by a local gentleman farmer who held its title until the Ministry of Defence requisitioned it in 1938. The remoteness of the location made it an ideal site for their secret work. During World War II it was a hive of activity and the locals reckon that it was used by the Special Operations Executive as a training and despatch centre for agents sent abroad. There were many stories of unusual goings on and of sightings of small boats leaving Horsenose Creek and heading out through Hamford water to the open sea.

After the war it was transferred to the Ministry of Supply and some people believe it was associated with another establishment at Orfordness in the development of nuclear weapons. The truth will not be known for many years as Government papers relating to Longsands House have not been declassified under the thirty year rule. Much of its current security systems dated back to those days. It was more than coincidence that as the Atomic Weapons Research establishment pulled out of Orfordness, so Longsands fell into disuse. The House was sold off to a Dutch entrepreneur in 1978 who intended to use it as a workshop for refurbishing expensive jewellery. He successfully obtained planning permission for change of use to light industrial purposes, but the Dutchman's plans never fully matured and after several years, during which time the property was virtually unused, it was again put on the market.

Research Express Limited bought the house and grounds nearly three years ago, they let it be known that the Company were Electronic and Scientific consultants working on computer technology and commercial space equipment. As such they employed few people, none of whom were local, and kept themselves to themselves. Visitors were not allowed past the entrance gates, although electricity and telephone officials did exercise their right of access. They were always escorted and never allowed to stay a second longer than they needed. To these few, the state of the property did not impress them. It seemed far from what one might expect of a modern, progressive, high tech company. What they saw was little short of squalor, but it was none of their business. The house was dilapidated, the blinds were always drawn and the window frames had only the remnants of paint from years ago. The front door was heavy, made from English oak and penetrated with steel studs that made it look as if it, not only could, but already had withstood a siege!

Grimley brought his car to a halt in front of the door, took out his suitcase and locked up before walking up six steps to the oak and steel. He did not have to press the small white button marked "ring", it would not have done any good if he had, for it had long forgotten how to work. The door opened and he was ushered in by a young fellow with a full head of hair and a beard to match.

'Olive will see you in the morning, your room is first on the left at the top of the stairs,' was all he said before securing the barricade and disappearing into the gloom.

Grimley climbed the wide, uncarpeted, wooden staircase, without noticing the dust and grime which had thickened since his last visit. The small 40 watt light bulb, which provided the only illumination, helped to conceal the decay that abounded. Turning left as instructed, Grimley found his room, opened the oak panelled door and turned on the electric light. It would have lost an illumination contest with a Toc "H" lamp. Even so it was sufficient to reveal the peeling paper on the walls, the cracked ceiling festooned with cobwebs and the bare dirty floorboards which showed a lighter shade of black where a carpet had once lain. A camp bed occupied one corner, it was accompanied by a chair, two upturned orange boxes, circa 1970, and a sleeping bag. The curtainless windows were closed with shutters of a bygone age and on the sill a layer of woodworm excrement indicated that they had not been opened for some considerable time. The man from Watersthorpe hardly noticed any of these sights. He was tired and weary after an exacting day and a long drive. He set down his suitcase, took off his jacket and shoes, crawled into the sleeping bag and entered the land of dreams.

Over breakfast, or perhaps more accurately brunch, for it was well past the eleventh hour of the morning, Grimley resumed his acquaintance with Olive who was accompanied by last night's doorman and another fellow. They all sat on four non matching chairs around a bare wooden topped table which bore a basket of bread rolls, a packet of cornflakes, a British Sugar Corporation bag, margarine, marmalade and a heap of crumbs. A between the wars dresser, an old electric cooker and an electric kettle were complemented with the usual kitchen paraphernalia which included a chipped brown crock tea pot loaded with stewed tea. Olive was pouring her third successive mug of the brown liquid as she spoke.

Only Professor Henry Higgins would have guessed her origin to be Moscow. Her real name was Olga, but this she corrupted to Olive when operating under British nationality. Her parents had fought in, and survived, the German siege of Moscow in 1941. On her sixth birthday her mother had been captured by a Wehrmacht patrol, raped, mutilated and left for dead. Somehow she managed to drag herself back to the Russian lines and eventually recovered. Her mother's sufferings remained in her memory as did a bitter hatred of occupation. The defeat of Germany was followed by the Cold War, it was a time of repression and unceasing Russian propaganda against the Western Democracies. This led her to believe in a possible American invasion and further occupation. She swore to serve her country, without question, to the limits of her endurance. She became an entrenched fanatic who saw her mission in life to free the West of war mongering imperialists and replace them by the peace loving communists of the Stalin era. Soon her talents were identified and she was processed by the best of the Russian espionage schools. She became fluent in seven languages including English, she could pass without difficulty as nationals of these countries.

Firewater was her latest assignment and the most ambitious. She was one of the old guard of the Russian Service who were not at all happy with the First Secretary, Mikhail Gorbachev's, ideas on Glasnost and Perestroika. She saw them as a betrayal of the security of her country. If Firewater was successful, the new policies would not be needed, the West would be subjugated by economic means, and the slide in Russian politics would be halted. She might even be made a "Hero of the Soviet Union".

Olive had spent two years in England during which time she had established the present cell, formed Research Express, acquired Longsands and activated John Grimley. She held a near perfect forged passport which showed her as a British born national with an address on the South Coast. Her birth certificate, which was also forged, indicated that her parents were Estonian refugees. They were supposed to have fled to Britain with secret information during the war and had been granted British Nationality together with a change of name to the more acceptable, and anonymous, "Smith". The certificate indicated Olive had been born shortly afterwards. The discrepancy between her real and passport age was not apparent. It was a good cover for it not only evoked sympathy, it also explained the slight defect in her English speech which might just have been detected by an expert.

Most casual observers would have attributed her short dumpy appearance as being due to middle age spread but beneath the slacks and sweater was a body of hardened muscle. Short light brown hair and the suspicion of a moustache did nothing for her femininity, but went well with her image of a self made business woman in a high tech industry. Her true background was unknown to John Grimley and the man who had received him last night. They accepted her at face value and as a Zealot of the British Environmental International Campaign, determined to save the world from its own man made folly.

'John,' she said, 'if you've not already introduced yourselves the fellow sitting on your left is George Brine. His task area is the yacht, its modifications and sailing it to the demonstration area.'

The bearded doorman nodded a 'hi' across to Grimley as they both tried to weigh up each other in the moment of a glance.

'And this is Pete,' continued Olive. John noted the man in front of him. He was about five foot eleven, well built and probably in his early thirties. Like George Brine he wore a blue sweater and jeans, but there the similarity ended. He was clean shaven and had short light brown hair and deep sunk blue eyes.

'Pete is ex-army 'though he doesn't talk a lot about it,' Olive explained. 'He quit them some years ago, got sickened by the things he had to do in Northern Ireland in the name of our, so called, democracy.' Olive Smith continued.

'He's our odd job man, lending a hand whenever and wherever one's required. He takes a special interest in our security and is a pretty useful man to have in a scrap.' She paused for just a moment then added, 'Not that we are expecting anything physical on this job. Well that's the team and now we're altogether I'll outline the overall plan.'

She paused again, this time to sip the mug of stewed tea and allow John time to take a bite at his toast.

'We are going to wake the public up to the real dangers of nuclear power and put paid to the entire European programme for building nuclear stations. This we will do by demonstrating how easy it is to pervert the plutonium that they produce and make it into weapons. John has already lifted all the plut we need from Watersth-orpe and it's here.'

John showed a trace of a smile and looked round for some recognition, but received none.

Olive continued, 'His next task, which starts now, is to go through the motions of processing it into a weapon. This means converting it to a metal, then machining it into weapon shape. He also has to make some explosive, probably one based on nitro. Of course, he won't actually do all that, but when we leave here it will look as if we have. It is central to our plan that the Authorities eventually trace the Watersthorpe plut to here and are satisfied that we did in fact make the weapon. John is a trained chemist and has been handling nuclear materials for several years and knows what he's doing.'

Olive moved her eyes to the beard, 'George has acquired a second hand Surfmaster 32. For the non nautical it's a sailing boat and a rather classy one at that. Unfortunately it was designed before the Australian's won the America's Cup and consequently has one of those old fashioned single keels. We managed to get her up The Cut from Horsenose and hauled her out at the back of the house. The slab keel has been removed and the local engineering works have modified it with specially designed wings to which we will bolt the weapon.'

'Isn't that rather risky?' interjected John Grimley, breaking the monotony of Olive's solo.

'No,' responded Brine. 'We told them that we intended to race her in the summer and that we are doing research on keel design.'

'Did they believe that!'

'Sure, why not? The mod does look like a winged keel and we are a research company, anyhow the technology of these keels is not well understood, there is quite a lot of experimental work going on, so why shouldn't they believe us?' Grimley felt uneasy, but said nothing and Olive continued.

'The modified keel has now been delivered, George has some small jobs to do on it such as drilling the bolt holes for the weapon and then he will refit it to the Surfmaster. As soon as this is done the boat will be launched, taken back down The Cut and anchored in Horsenose. For this we will need plenty of water in The Cut. High Water Springs is in sixteen days time. We then wait for a fine spell before the staff of Research Express go off on their May cruise.'

She allowed herself the luxury of a smile before continuing, 'George has fixed a rendezvous and recognition signal with our Mother ship. When we meet up we simply swap the Watersthorpe plut, which is non weapon grade for a real nuclear device. We then broadcast to all ships telling them to keep clear, set the fuse and make our getaway in Mother. The big bang will happen before the authorities know what to do. Anti-nuclear groups throughout Europe will demand the immediate closure of all nuclear power stations claiming that the plutonium was stolen from a British station. Of course, the Government and Electricity Supply Authority will deny it but soon they will discover the Watersthorpe connection and that will be that.'

'What if they don't?' asked Brine.

'They will, but if they are a bit slow then one of the left wing M.P.'s will be tipped off to raise questions in the Commons,' Olive responded.

'Why not make our own weapon and why strap it to our keel?' queried Pete, trying to think through the process of events. Olive tried not to appear impatient.

'Our plutonium is not sufficiently pure and we can not refine it to make it into weapons grade material. In theory it would be possible to make it explode, but that would be very difficult with our restricted facilities. However, the anti-nuclear campaigners have been claiming for years that a terrorist group could make a weapon from commercial grade plut, but the pro-nucs have poo-pooed the idea. They are probably right, but we will make it look as if they are wrong. We are going to use the winged keel to smuggle the plut out of here, I know it's not likely that we will get stopped by Customs on our way out, but it is just possible. When we meet up with Mother she puts a sling under the Surfmaster, lifts her out, removes our plut container and fits the weapon in its place.' Pete seemed satisfied, but John Grimley looked puzzled.

'I'm having second thoughts about this idea of a switch, why not just proclaim that we have the fissile material and demand the shut down of the nuclear stations on the threat of detonation? We could even make out that we've got it in London.'

'They'd never buy that, they know we couldn't have made a real weapon and there'd be a big risk the Government would call our bluff. The S.A.S. would come shooting and we'd go out horizontal.' Then Olive added as an after thought, 'I don't mind dying for our cause, but I want to be sure it's a success when I do. Few, if any, operations succeed when only threats are made, we have to enter a new era. Action first, with casualties if need be, then follow with demands.' Olive looked at the faces around her, but they were impassive so she continued, 'Doing it this way only a few, or may be no one, gets hurt, but the world gets its most salutary lesson since Nagasaki.'

Grimley didn't give up but pursued his objections. 'I don't like the idea of a swap at sea, what if we miss the Mother ship, the sea's a bloody big place? Suppose we get bad weather, suppose we're spotted, dozens of things could go wrong. Don't forget our time is limited, I've left a trail that will be picked up, it was part of the plan. The Watersthorpe lot should start to suspect something when they monitor my locker in three weeks time, in the unlikely event that they miss the contam there, they will certainly start enquiries when I don't return in four weeks. We don't have contingency time to wait for good weather or hold off because Mother can't deliver on time.'

Olive noted the genuine concern in his voice and hoped he was not starting to crack at this early stage. With operations like these cool nerve and daring were essential.

Grimley continued, 'Why don't we simply take the boat away from here into Harwich or Felixstowe, or even somewhere like Dover, Mother could deliver her little egg to us there, then we could sail out when the weather is right.'

'Come off it John,' chided Olive, 'think it through. Suppose the Customs rummaged Mother, looking for drugs may be and found a nuclear weapon instead? Even if they didn't, how would we transfer the weapon unnoticed, Mother could hardly pull up along side us in a marina? Even if we did the transfer how would we fix the egg as you called it to our keel? If we didn't do that we'd be sitting ducks for a Customs search. All hell will be let loose when they find out they have lost their plut so your suggestion doesn't give us any extra time.' She saw the look on John's face and knew at once he realised just how foolish his comments had been. Olive took the opportunity to belittle him in the eyes of the other two, and continued, 'Every detail of our plan has been worked out, there are contingency arrangements for every possible event, all you have to do is to carry out your instructions to the letter. Please don't waste our time with fatuous comments.'

Grimley cringed mentally and said contritely, 'Sorry Olive, I take your point, where do we meet up with Mother for the swap?'

'That, John, is a secret between myself and George. I have to know to make the arrangements with our friends and George has to navigate us there. No one else needs to know at present and what you don't know you can't talk about, not even by accident.' Olive paused to see if John would come back to her, she was beginning to have uneasy feelings about him and wondered if she should lose him before they took to sea. On the other hand she knew they might need him on the Surfmaster, he had some sailing experience. Grimley sat silent, Olive passed the thought by and changed the subject.

'That's the outline of the plan, now let's have your progress reports. John, you lead.'

'Well, as you said we have the plut. I haven't looked yet, but I presume you've got the glove boxes, nitric acid, caustic soda, magnesium, sulphuric acid, glycerine and all the other chemicals and items I put on the list?'

Olive nodded her assent, 'No trouble, they were falling over themselves to supply Research Express.'

'Good and what about the RD5's?'

'They're here as well.'

'Okay, so now I'll have to set things up as if we were processing and making explosives. I'll splash some chemicals around and let a trace of plut go down the drain. If I don't do that things won't look real. It will start to reach the Backwaters in a few days, but no one will be looking for it. Probably take another week to work its way out and around the coast then...'

Olive interjected with her doubts. 'Why so soon? If it does get noticed before we're ready we have a problem.'

It was now John's turn to make up some of the ground he had just lost.

'Think it through Olive,' he said with a smile, 'when it's discovered, as we want it to be, they will be able to estimate the time of discharge by the extent of the dispersion. It would just not be credible if it turned out that the plut did not escape until a day or two before we sailed. On the time scale to make even a crude weapon, I should start processing now and that means very small traces of plut would be escaping into the atmosphere and the sea. Without very sophisticated equipment total containment is impossible. If the Authorities could prove that we had not processed the plut and made the weapon here, the whole scheme falls flat and could rebound on our cause.'

Now Olive felt a little foolish, but decided to let the matter pass.

Grimley continued, 'I'll also have to rig up a small lathe in one of the boxes and make it look as if we have machined plut metal, that means I will have to process some of the oxide for real however, if you lot have set up the boxes as I asked, then everything should be ready in two weeks, but I'll need help.'

'Yes, Pete will give a hand when you need one,' Olive responded, 'now what about your side of the project?' she asked the bearded George Brine.

'Well...er...er,' he fumbled for words, not used to giving an account of himself. At sea he was Master, decisive and confident, but ashore he was less certain of himself. 'It's like Olive said, we've got the Surfmaster and she couldn't be better for our purpose. The modified slab has been delivered and I've got it in position for fitting. I hope to get the keel bolts in today, then I've got to drill holes for the bolts clamping the bomb on the wings, the actual fittings for the outward journey plut container are due in a few days time. After that there's quite a bit of work to get her ready for the crossing. VHF radio, a Decca Navigator and one or two other odds and ends. I've decided against radar, it's a specialist job to get it fitted, would need a mod to the mast for a special bracket and generally complicate things. The Decca will give us a fix to within a hundred yards so there ought to be no problem finding Mother even if we were to miss her by DR.'

'What's DR?' interrupted Pete a little slow to work things out.

'Dead Reckoning, it's our estimated position from tide, wind and speed calculations. It's what you have to do if you don't have a Decca and anyhow you should still do it even if you have,' Brine explained before continuing. 'Apart from that, should be all systems go, ready in a week. We need High Water Springs to get out of the creek and after that it's up to Olive to say when.'

'Have you got the chart problem sorted?' she responded.

'Oh, that should be okay. I used an old chart to work out the rendezvous for Mother, but when I took it in for updating there were too many corrections and I've had to order a new one. Should be here within a week. It's not all that old, but with the change in buoyage that's been going on there are a lot of alterations. Most would not affect us and anyhow with the Decca buoys are hardly needed, even so I like to be up to date but if it doesn't turn up we still go. I've spoken to the chandlers and they've said that if the new chart isn't in when we need it I can borrow their's and copy any of the changes likely to affect us. It's not a holding item.' The others all nodded as if they understood. Olive cast a glance to Pete, she did not want him to feel left out, even though she doubted that he had anything important to add.

'Security is all satisfactory.' He spoke with a slow hesitant voice which had a strong foreign accent about it that made John Grimley doubt the story about being in the British army, but he kept his doubts to himself. Pete continued, 'The old fence that runs round the grounds has been repaired and I've added simple, but effective, electronic intruder detection equipment. The only way in is through the gate and that is watched all the time by TV and controlled from here.'

'Then how did you get the boat in?' queried Grimley. 'Couldn't anyone else get in the same way?'

'I think that is not very possible. The fence crosses The Cut about two hundred metres from the house and it goes right across, no breaks. We had to undo it to get the boat in and we shall have to do the same when it goes out.'

Grimley was not giving up so easily, having already made a fool of himself he now wanted to show that others were not infallible.

'What about at low water, couldn't someone squeeze under the wire?'

'At low water there is only a few inches of water there and a lot of thick soft mud, impossible to get through. Also I have put microphones and trembler alarms on the wire so that at the slightest disturbance we would know. But no one suspects us, our problem is from hippies and squatters and these people do not come up muddy creeks. They do not like water,' he added in an attempt at a feeble joke.

'Thank you, now let me tell you what I've been doing,' Olive took charge again. 'I've tied everything up with our friends. The weapon will be delivered as soon as we give them the "go". They will need about three days notice to be on standby and then have to be told when we actually sail. I will leave that until the last moment just in case something goes wrong.'

She looked round and saw them all nodding. 'One last word, we don't talk to each other more than we need to, we work independently and we do not go off site unless it is essential. This may sound hard, but it is too easy to let something slip. In ten days time it should be all systems go, if any of you have a problem come and see me. All being well we will all meet up then.'

CHAPTER 5

As the conspirators were discussing their plans around the wooden topped table at Longsands, Janice Hardman was mulling over her problem in her Lincolnshire cottage. She had slept badly which was unusual, for most of the night the problem of the missing plut went through her mind. Was it imagination? Should she really stick her neck out on a hunch? Why not forget it and let events take their course? Could she locate the Director and arrange to see him? Holiday or no holiday surely he would want to know of her suspicions, anyhow he never gave any impression of having confidence in the Brigadier? When not fully awake, while mulling over her options she dozed and became engulfed in confused dreams that meant nothing. As dawn made its arrival she fell into a sound sleep and did not wake until she heard the postman at the gate just before 1000hrs. Over breakfast she made her decision, she would do something and to hell with the consequences. She rejected the idea of trying to contact the Director at this stage and instead settled for taking advice from Richard England, if she could find him.

It was five years since England had quite the Electricity Supply Industry; she had seen him occasionally at scientific meetings so she knew he was still in touch with the technology, but she had no idea where he was working or living. She slumped in an old armchair and her mind went through the possibilities. Wait until Monday then contact the Personnel Pensions Department, they would have England's address. She realised that tack would be fraught with difficulties. The Personnel Officers would not divulge it but offer only to forward any letter, there was clearly not time for that. If she persisted then it might arouse suspicions which would be reported to the Director, or as he was absent, to the Brigadier. She rejected that idea. Perhaps she should contact her colleagues in the Health and Safety Branch at London Headquarters, they might know England's whereabouts. She dismissed that notion as well, mainly because she did not know how to make an approach without making them suspicious, unless she waited until Monday and that meant delay. She had reached a point of despair when something stirred in her brain. Had England retained his membership of the Radiation Protection Society? Now a feeling of excitement came over her as she launched herself from the chair, upsetting the remains of her mug of tea in the process and assaulted her filing cabinet in the corner of the room. She too was a member of R.P.S. and somewhere had last years membership list. After a few minutes searching she let out a whispered 'yippee' and clutching a sheet of paper made for the telephone. She had England's address, directory enquiries found his number, but when she dialled the voice that replied, although it was England's, it was only a recording. All she could do was to leave a message, wait and hope.

*

Dick England was one of those people who were always busy. He hated to waste a moment and maintained that the worst punishment anyone could inflict upon him would be to put him in a room with nothing to do. Even on holiday he would shun idle rest, not for him the lying on sun drenched beaches. He was an early riser and while he readily admitted he was one of those people who needed sleep, he resented having to take it, time in bed is time wasted he would reason. It was not therefore surprising that when Janice Hardman telephoned, in mid morning, Dick England was out.

His passion was sailing and, although most people would regard the end of April as pre-season, his boat was afloat and fitted out. When Janice tried to contact him, he was with his daughter Sally on their yacht *English Lady*, moored off Kyson point on the River Deben. On leaving the Electricity Supply Industry he had set up his own consultancy in Radiation Safety. The Chernobyl accident aroused public interest and his services had been in demand by Local Authorities and other organisations. But with the passing of a couple of years this interest waned and of late his commissions were few and far between. He was not unduly worried, financially with a reasonable pension from the industry he had no problems, and his new found free time had been devoted to *English Lady*. Now, ahead of most, she was afloat and calling for her shake down cruise. This year, just as the climatological text books proclaimed they should, the gales of March had given way to the warmer showery weather of April. This had not been a common event in the past few years. Friday's drizzle was clearing as the shallow depression moved north, giving way to sunshine and a warm south-westerly wind. It was an ideal day for the first of the season's cruises and Dick had decided to make the most of it.

English Lady was a ketch rigged, thirty eight foot, motor sailer. Her design was unusual, but Dick had had it built to his own specification. She had small bilge keels to keep her upright, if and when, she dried out and centre drop keel which enabled her draft to be reduced from seven to four feet. She was a heavy vessel, being constructed in ferro cement, but her sixty horse power Perkins Special gave her nearly nine knots under power. Dick had an aversion to exposed open cockpits at the stern of the boat so *English Lady* was given a centre cockpit with a wind shield and folding hood. Accommodation was in three cabins, one aft, the central saloon with navigator's corner and a miniature laboratory, and the fo'castle. England used the boat as part of his consultancy, his idea of combining business with pleasure, it also meant he could claim running expenses and capital depreciation as being tax allowable. To this end the starboard after side of the saloon, opposite the navigator's desk, had been fitted out as a small mobile laboratory. He had become involved with the problems associated with the dispersal of liquid radioactive waste that had been discharged to sea from various nuclear sites. *English Lady* was used not only to collect samples of sea water and sea bed, but also to carry out preliminary analysis upon them. All in all, she was a strong comfortable boat that could be used for business or pleasure purposes. It was for pleasure that she was now being used.

As soon as the big diesel roared into life, Dick went forward and slipped the mooring while Sally took the helm. Soon they were past Methersgate and approaching the rows of orange buoys at Waldringfield.

'Where to Dad?'

'Take her down to Felixstowe and we'll anchor behind the Horse[11] until there's half flood.'

'But where to after that, let's make a quick trip to Oostende, we can grab a crate of good wine and get our other duty free allowances, then nip back.'

'More like Harwich this time, but we'll see how things go,' Dick said cautiously, but added with a smile, 'I did notify Customs just in case we thought of going over to satisfy your unsatisfiable desire for the Continent, nevertheless I think I'd rather stay close to home until we've put her through her paces.'

---

[11] *"Horse" refers to the Horse Sand which is an area of shoal water approximately half a mile inside the River entrance. At low water it dries forming a bank of golden sand. Many boats moor close to it and it is a good place to anchor while waiting for a suitable tide on which to cross the bar at the entrance to the river.*

England was very fond of his daughter, in fact she was his only family since his wife was killed in a car accident six years back. They had become very close. Sally had qualified with an Upper Second in Physics at one of the provincial universities in the same year her father took voluntary redundancy and set up his own consultancy. She joined him and was now an equal partner. Close as they were, Dick realised that Sally would soon want to get married and leave home. For her sake he looked forward to the happy event. She was engaged to Rodney McDonald, a tough, canny Scot who, after a few years as an insurance assessor, had gone it alone as a private investigator. Normally he would have sailed with them, but had only just returned from crewing as First Mate on a friend's ocean racer in the Nord Hinder. This was the first of the big races in the year and had a reputation for chill winds and hard sailing.

'We'll put the hook down here,' Dick told his daughter as they approached the moorings that surround the Horse. 'Give the flood another couple of hours over the bar then slip out and fetch the Sunk[12]. From there we can either drop back into Harwich although it'll mean punching the tide as the ebb will have set, or carry on to Oostende.'

'Oh, let's go Dad, a night passage will be fun.'

'It might be fun for you youngsters, but us older ones need our shuteye. Anyhow I want the latest weather forecast before making a final decision.'

The conversation was temporarily ended there by the rattle of the anchor chain as Dick let out the CQR on five fathoms. Two hours later the hook was lifted, under a clear sky and assisted by a modest force three south westerly they punched the last of the flood and slipped past the Felixstowe Ferry Yacht Club and along the shore to the transit marks. The small green buoy marking the best depth over the bar was identified and five minutes later *English Lady* was clear into the North Sea. Sally turned her head to wind while Dick ran up the sails, then paid off onto a close reach for the Sunk. The boat gathered speed, heeled ten degrees to port and started pushing her nose through the swell. It was pure magic. Visibility was good and

---

[12] *"The Sunk" is a lightship approximately eleven miles South East of Harwich at the southern extremity of the Shipwash Sands.*

Roughs Towers were in clear view, but a little too tight on the starboard bow.

'The flood is still pushing us south, free her off about fifteen degrees, we should see the Sunk in about half and hour.'

'Aye Aye Sir,' came the response from Sally with enthusiasm and just a touch of irreverence to counter the formality in her father's voice.

As Dick had predicted, the old light ship came up just where they expected and *English Lady*, still carrying all her canvas, closed at six and a half knots.

'Well now's the time for decision, if we keep going with this soldier's wind[13] we'll be in Oostende in the early hours. *Lady* seems to be enjoying herself, okay Sal you have your way and on we go.'

'Great, can I navigate this time?'

Dick nodded and his daughter passed over the helm and addressed herself to the charts and tide tables.

England did not like instant decisions and while he had this one under consideration for some time still had an uneasy feeling that something had been overlooked, of course, weather forecast. He checked his watch, it was coming up to 1700hrs. For a moment he thought of calling up the Coast Guard, but their anytime forecasting had been discontinued a couple of years ago and it was not fair to trouble them for the sake of an hour, anyhow the four hourly ones only extend twelve miles out to sea. The thought of using his VHF reminded him of something else.

'As you've talked me into going foreign I think I'll call up home and see what the ansaphone has to tell me,' he remarked aloud.

'Leave it Dad,' Sally responded. 'It's not yet cheap rate, don't forget Orfordness is only a slave for North Foreland[14] so we'll have to pay the full rate.'

---

[13]*A "Soldier's" wind is one which is on the beam of the ship. It is the easiest and the fastest point of sailing and gets its name from the saying that "even a poor old soldier could manage to sail with such a wind".*

[14]*VHF radio link telephone calls have to be made through a coast radio station. The nearest to English Lady, on this occasion, was Orfordness. This is an unmanned station and operates as a slave of North Foreland. Thus the call would go by radio from the yacht to Orfordness, by land link to North Foreland and then be dialled into the telephone network by an operator, thus making it a long distance call to Suffolk.*

Dick hesitated and Sally persisted. 'We've set our sights on the other side so let's not be put off, what's on that infernal machine can wait until Monday or Tuesday. Anyhow if it does turn out that there's something we should not have neglected, we can always claim that the machine made a hash of the recording.'

'I never thought a daughter of mine would have such a devious mind.'

For a moment Dick paused then made his decision, 'No Sal, we're in business, if someone wants us then we should respond. I will call home, but the odds are against anything urgent, come and take the helm awhile.'

As Sally made an unintelligible disgruntled reply and temporarily abandoned her charts in favour of the wheel, Dick picked up the hand set from the VHF radio, turned to channel 82, listened to make sure that the air was clear, then went ahead.

'Orfordness Radio, Orfordness Radio, this is *English Lady*, one link call please.'

'Station calling Orfordness, your call sign and accounting code please?'

'Two uniform kilo x-ray zulu, accounting code GB one four,' Dick responded and considered himself fortunate that traffic was slack and he was able to get his call accepted without the usual delay.

'The number you require Sir?' Dick gave his home phone number and explained that there would be an answering machine response, but he would like to speak to it. After a few moments he heard the phone ring out then his own voice telling him that he was not at home, but that he could leave a message after the tone. Once these formalities were over he placed a small black box, which emitted a sound signal instruction, close to his microphone and the machine started to play back the calls it had received. The first two were of no consequence, the sort that Dick liked for there was no message at all, then he heard the third bleep heralding another and this time there was a message.

'My name is Janice Hardman. I met you several years ago at a Health Physics meeting, it is very important that I speak to you without delay. Could you please call me urgently on 09842 65281 as soon as possible, it really is most important. Thank you.'

There were no more messages and Dick replaced the hand set with a customary, 'Aw shit!'

'What's up?' Sally enquired.

As Dick explained his daughter looked disappointed.

'Does that put paid to our trip?' she queried.

'No, let's carry on and sod this Janice Hardman, I don't remember her anyway.' Sally was not convinced that her father meant what he had said, she had noticed the way his right hand had tugged at the lobe of his ear, a sign that he was not happy with his decision.

'You're not sure are you Dad? Tell you what, let's get the shipping forecast, then call up this Hardman woman. After speaking to her we can make a final decision? Don't you remember who she is?' Dick smiled and once more thought what an understanding daughter he had sired.

'No, who is she?'

'Health Physicist at Watersthorpe, there was a paper of hers in the Journal on the latest techniques for monitoring of plut.'

'You're able to remember these things better than me, must be your young mind.'

'Not at all, it was relevant to some work I was doing for the Cumbria Council,' Sally replied diplomatically as they sailed on.

Dick looked at his watch and then glanced at the chart, it was nearly a quarter to six and they were three miles past the Sunk, still well within radio range of North Foreland. He could still call the woman from Watersthorpe or he could sail on, he looked up at Sally who was still at the helm.

'You're edgy Dad, so am I. Maybe we'd better abandon the idea of Oostende, after all the season is young. Anyhow it might be another commission and we could use the cash.'

''spose so, but I'll get the forecast anyhow then give the lass a call.' Dick turned and switched on Radio 4 for the shipping forecast. The synopsis reported the depression moving away towards Scandinavia and a ridge of high pressure building from the Azores to North Holland. Thames and Dover were to have a south westerly decreasing overnight then going south east or east later. Sally, at the helm, had also heard.

'Couldn't be better,' she teased, 'a fair wind out and one promised for the return, what a change from last year when all we had were gales. Still want to make that call?'

'Damn, damn, damn,' Dick exploded. Sally grinned for her father had got into a dilemma of his own making, she knew all along that he had been hoping the weather forecast would have been adverse then, if need be, he could have gone back and consoled himself that they could not have carried on anyway.

'Go on, call her up,' Sally urged with a twinkle in her eye that made her father scowl. Dick reached for the hand set and went through the procedure of calling the Orfordness Coast Radio Station, soon he heard,

'65281, Janice Hardman speaking.' He pressed the transmit trigger.

'This is Dick England returning your call, what can I do for you?'

'Oh, thank you Mr. England, I do hope I haven't put you to any trouble...,' she paused waiting for a reassurance that was not forthcoming. 'I have a problem I'd like your advice on and I er... can we speak confidentially?'

'Like hell we can, I'm half way between Sunk and Galloper[15], if that doesn't mean anything to you I'll explain that I'm calling from sea using VHF radio and anyone within twenty five to fifty miles who cares to go onto channel 82 can hear every word, but don't let that stop you.' Dick was being his usual irritable self. He heard the woman go silent, caught a look of reproach from his daughter and regretted his manner. After a pause Janice Hardman recovered from her surprise, 'It is very important,' she said, stressing the word important, 'when can I meet you for a confidential chat?'

'I'm just off with my daughter for a few days cruise, how about next week, I'll give you a call when we get back.' It had taken a lot of heart searching by Janice before she contacted England, she realised that her career was at risk and that in all probability she would be banished to obscurity even if she were right with her hunch. If she were wrong it would be a forced resignation. Now she was being frustrated by the only man she thought could help. Emotion overcame her and quite unintentionally she let slip a sob. Dick swallowed.

'If it is really very urgent we could come back, no great problem really, it's early in the season and anyhow my daughter's getting sea sick,' he lied.

'It is important that I see you very soon, I just can not tell you why now.' Dick had already done the mental arithmetic, they were

---

[15] *"Galloper" refers to the navigational light approximately 30 miles out from Harwich, at the southern extremity of the Galloper bank. The light at the north end of the Bank is, not surprisingly, called North Galloper.*

five nautical miles south west of the Sunk, eighteen miles from Harwich with the ebb against him as he approached Harwich No. 1 Buoy. It would take four hours to Levington which would be the best place to meet up with this woman.

'Is it important enough for you to come and see me now?' he asked.

'Yes,' came the simple reply, then as an after thought, 'I've got a car, you name the time and place and I'll be there.'

'The Marina at Levington, probably in the visitors berth just by the steps where the fuel pumps are. Know it?'

'No, but I'll find it, give me a few clues.'

'It's on the River Orwell, half way between Ipswich and Felixstowe. Get on the A45 and you'll see it sign posted about five miles short of Felixstowe. It's proper name is Suffolk Yacht Harbour.'

'I'll be there Mr. England, bless you.' Dick returned the hand set to its rest and glanced up at Sally. She winked and swung the wheel gybing the boat from through a hundred and eighty degrees. 'Engine?' she queried.

'Yes, two thousand rpm,' Dick responded, then added, 'how about a mug of soup?' Sally grinned and shook her hair in the wind.

'Good idea, pass me up my jacket it's getting chilly up here.'

They left the Sunk to port, headed for Roughs Towers and in the fading light picked up the quick red flashes of Cork Sand. It was quite dark as they passed Landguard Point but they both knew the Orwell and did not even need to get out the River chart as they motored up the channel to Levington and into the Marina.

'Just gone ten,' Sally remarked, as *English Lady* slipped into the visitor's berth. Dick stopped the engine and switched off the steaming lights.

'Customs will think we've had a quick trip,' he remarked. 'I'll give them a ring and let them know that we aborted our crossing.' Sally nodded, it was not strictly necessary but she knew her father always liked to keep them informed.

Not long afterwards Janice Hardman arrived. With the aid of her small torch she stumbled across the yard and down the steps to the pontoons, then she realised that she did not even know the name of the boat for which she was looking. She saw what looked like petrol pumps and called out softly,

'Mr. England are you there?'

'Over here, *English Lady*, hang on I'll put the spreader lights on,' came the unexpected reply followed by a flood of light a few yards away and up in the sky. 'Come aboard, the mysterious Janice Hardman I presume?'

Dick welcomed her into the cockpit with a helping hand and steered her below. Janice was no stranger to small boats, she had sailed on the Norfolk Broads as well as crewed on a friend's motor cruiser. Dressed in sweater, slacks and soft shoes she nimbly stepped down into the cabin.

'I'm Janice Hardman, friends call me Jan, you're Richard England?'

'Friends call me Dick or even Blighty, and this is Sally my daughter.'

They all shook hands and settled round the table.

'Now young lady what's all this about?' asked Dick, after he had fixed up the drinks.

Janice explained about Watersthorpe, her suspicions that some plutonium had been stolen and, despite her efforts, she could not get anyone to take action. To Dick's embarrassment she recalled that first lecture and how she had been impressed with his approach to safety. Her speech had been prepared and rehearsed as she drove down to the marina. She concluded,

'You once maintained that no one in their right mind would steal plutonium because it was so easy to detect. They would not be able to cover up their tracks. This could be the time to see if you are right.'

Dick hesitated, cast a glance at Sally who might have been playing poker for all the indication she gave, then replied,

'If I read you correctly you are asking us to try and ascertain if any plut has been lifted and if so by whom. Moreover we have to do it without the knowledge or co-operation of the Authorities.' Janice nodded and Dick went on, 'I don't want to be mercenary but our time is at a premium, it costs money and we don't skimp on expenses.' The visitor's face flushed.

'I...er...er don't have the authority to make any payments,' she stammered. 'I was really looking to you for advice as well as help after what you said.'

'I'm afraid that advice alone will not help now, you would need the backing of the entire nuclear industry to crack this one and from what you've said you haven't got it.'

'How come, surely there is something that I can do, just point me in the right direction.'

'Miss Hardman, my concept was simple. With common monitoring equipment we can easily detect something like one hundredth part of a millionth of a gram, far less than the weight of a finger print! Now can you conceive that it is possible for anyone, without the sophisticated equipment like you have at Watersthorpe, being able to handle or process plutonium without getting such small quantities spread around?' Janice nodded in agreement as Dick continued, 'Ask how would it spread and where would it turn up? Well, some would probably get out as airborne dust, some would get into the drains, and some on personal items such as clothing, shoes, hands and anything that they touch.'

Janice again nodded, she knew the problems she had in keeping the contamination inside controlled zones and that was when it was being handled by professional staff in a large safety conscious organisation. A back room operator would have no chance.

'But it's not possible to monitor everyone in the U.K.,' she interjected.

'Agreed, we don't have to. The air and sea are already being monitored, drainage systems usually come together at sewage works, people handle common items like money, milk bottles, take their clothes to the laundries and so on. All that is needed is a nation wide survey of all these critical areas. For example money could easily be checked at banks and milk bottles at dairies. Once a positive is obtained it would be elementary detective work to back track it. I need hardly point out all this would need the full co-operation of those involved in nuclear work. Not just the ESI, BNFL and UKAEA, but also universities, hospitals and the military. That's the theory which I give you free of charge, but anything else will cost.'

Janice looked dejected, Sally remained silent and Dick sat back clasping his hands behind his head.

'I just can't offer you any payment. I've already explained that this visit is unofficial. If anyone knew I'd discussed security matters with you I'd get the sack. Of course if you could do something and that led to us finding the plut the industry might make you a ex-gratia payment.'

Dick let out an ironic laugh which caused Janice to pause, but then she continued. 'Mr. England, you always impressed me as a man of integrity who believed in nuclear power for the good of mankind, you did not see it simply as a means of making money, sorry if I misjudged you!'

'My God,' Dick exploded, as he flushed with anger. He was usually an even tempered man, not easily riled unless aspersions were cast on his integrity. 'I give up my leisure time to see you, offer you free advice and you repay me with insults! You get paid for your work, well Sally and I have to live as well. To mount even a modest search on our own would entail an enormous amount of work, cost a small fortune, and would have to be lucky to be successful. If the industry can't, or won't, foot the bill because it's too stuffy to see beyond the end of its nose then let it go to hell.'

'But surely you can see it's because I can't get Watersthorpe to act that I've come to you?'

Dick did see, but said nothing.

'I suppose you think I'm some sort of nut, well maybe I am, I once believed in you! Remember saying, and I quote your own words, "when you know what needs to be done in the interests of safety, do it and to hell with the consequences. The object is to save lives and personnel injury, not to make friends with the Operations Department".' Janice looked across at Dick, but his eyes fell to the saloon table rather than respond, she knew then that she making headway. 'Well, there could be lives at risk now, won't you help save some of them Mr. England?'

'Look lass, it's not that easy, you don't seem to realise what is involved. The stuff could be anywhere in the U.K. or even abroad. Okay, let's assume that it is in the U.K., next question what will it be used for? You say it's not weapon grade, but does the thief know that or will he or she try to make a bomb? Look on the bright side, assume that they do know that, what else? They could just keep it and do nothing, in which case we don't have a chance. On the other hand they might unpack it to do something, like polluting drinking water, then they could be traced but only with a nationwide effort. On our tod we'd have as much chance of finding them as we would of finding an iceberg at the equator! Those words you quoted, yes I said them, I believed them, but they would be more appropriate on my career tombstone. Follow that advice and as far as promotion is concerned you're as dead as a dodo.' Dick drew breath, 'No Janice, you go back to Watersthorpe, be a good girl, try to be nice to your Brigadier and you might just not finish up like me! I owe nothing to that industry of toffee nosed, self centred, pimps who have about as much imagination as a jelly fish. None of them can see beyond their own careers, they are all far too concerned with jostling for their own job prospects than worrying about the long term future of the industry. The more you are right and the more they are wrong, makes matters worse. No thanks, no "well done England" instead they all try and grab your success.'

'The industry still pays your pension Mr. England.' Janice Hardman responded. 'I've been in it long enough to realise that some of what you say is right. Politics, who knows who and all the rest of it, but that happens everywhere. It's a fact of life. There are a lot of good, loyal and devoted people who do a conscientious job to the best of their ability, they need your support. They are your old friends and colleagues, are you going to let them down?'

The remarks stung Dick, he was rapidly coming to the conclusion that the female health physicist from Watersthorpe possessed more determination than he thought. She realised that she was getting through and sought to exploit her opening, she continued, 'Why won't you take up the challenge? There could hardly be a greater one, and when you have succeeded you would have the additional satisfaction of showing up the incompetence you've just talked about? Sort out this plutonium business and you might find that those unimaginative jellyfish would have to take note of your ideas. If I have heard correctly, you left the industry because your ideas clashed with the official thinking on safety organisation. Don't you see, fate has sent you an opportunity to win the day after all?'

Dick swallowed hard, unusually he was lost for words, there was an element of truth in what the woman had said, but she had over stated her argument. Now Sally spoke.

'Come on Dad, let's have a go. We've not got any work on for the next week or so,' she turned to Janice. 'You've put your head on the block by coming here, you must be convinced of the seriousness of the situation and that's good enough for me.' She turned to her father, 'Dad you know the industry, you know what Miss Hardman has said is true, it's not as bad as you make out, you old sourpuss. So it's not perfect, then show me one that is? You know the nuclear plants are the safest method of generating energy, they are the best that we have got. Let us at least try, it might not be as difficult as you have made out, we might turn up something.'

'No, my daughter,' Dick responded. 'It's not as simple as that. Forget the whole idea and tomorrow morning we'll slip our lines and be on our way to Belgium.'

Despite these words Sally knew her father was weakening, it was not so much what he had said, but the lack of conviction in his voice when he spoke. She had listened intently to what Janice Hardman had said, she saw how serious could be the consequences if plutonium had been stolen and she admired the courage of the woman from Watersthorpe for putting her career at stake.

'Dad, if that plut has been stolen, and if it is used in some spectacular way, such as an act of terrorism, then the entire nuclear industry could be forced to close down. Can't you just imagine how the so called environmental groups would exploit the situation. They would make sure there was a massive outcry of public opinion to shut down every nuclear establishment. The media would exploit this with their usual one sided reporting. Look how all the evidence at the Inquiry got distorted and how only the anti's got the media coverage. The lefty trade unions would call for industrial action to stop our nuclear power stations and to go back to burning coal. If we lost our nucs the country, and the rest of the non communist world, would face an energy crisis. It would be back to fossil fuels with a vengeance, back to acid rain, back to the greenhouse effect, but that's only part of the story.' Sally barely paused for breath as she held forth, 'We've already gone past peak production of North Sea oil and within a decade it is unlikely to meet our needs in the U.K. let alone the rest of Europe. No-nucs might give a lift to the coal industry, but the problems of atmospheric pollution is going to restrict our coal burn in the early part of next century. Anyhow, coal stocks aren't all that secure. The loss of nuclear power now would destabilise our long term fuel supplies. It would mean almost complete dependence for most European countries on the Soviet Union and the Eastern Block. It would mean a decline of our industry, a lower standard of living, and unemployment. I don't have to tell *you* all this, isn't it what you have been arguing for for the past twenty years? You understand that if we lost nuclear power then Europe would have to become a Soviet satellite.'

'Okay so I've argued that in the past, and I still think it's true but it won't happen in my life time. When you get to my age you realise time is too short to worry about things that aren't going to affect you.'

'Perhaps not in your lifetime, but it will in mine.' This last remark of Sally's stung her father, he was lost for words. As his brain fumbled for a suitable counter, the verbal onslaught continued.

'Remember when I was in my teens how I helped you in your election campaigns? I thought you were the straightest, strongest, most honest, caring man who ever stood for Parliament. That I thought was why you were not elected. You weren't a quitter then, so why now? Remember the speech you made at your first adoption meeting?' Richard England was reduced to an embarrassed silence, he just shook his head. 'Well I do,' Sally continued. 'I remember every word because they went right to my heart and the hearts of your supporters. If we wanted democracy, you told us, we must all strive to make it work, all of us must take part in the democratic processes, all us give our time and money, and above all we must all be prepared to defend it to the death if need be. Democracy is no natural phenomena, it is one of man's inventions and it has to withstand enormous forces out to see it destroyed. Democratic countries are under pressure all over the world, they exist only through the determination of their peoples, it is so easily deposed. Germany and Italy fell to fascism in the twenties and thirties, in more recent times countries like Argentina and those in the New Commonwealth fall victim to dictatorship. I remember your very words, "*Democracy hangs by a slender thread, many have given their lives to keep that intact, we must not fail them through apathy*". Well our democracy is certainly under pressure and that thread could snap. Are you going to sit there and do nothing?'

Janice Hardman was stunned by the intensity, eloquence and emotion in Sally's speech. Dick England was shamed by it. Now, in his late fifties, he had lost his burning zeal for what was right and just, instead he looked forward to a decade or so of a quiet, slow moving, relaxing, life of leisure which was free from hassle. After Sally had spoken he knew he could not have it.

'You're right Sal. I agree we must try.'

For the next two hours the trio went through the sequence of events and explored each and every possibility. Midnight was near, two hours had passed when Dick tried to bring matters to a close with a chairman's summing up.

'Jan. You are welcome to spend the night here, there's a spare berth in Sally's cabin, but if you're determined to get back then the sooner you hit the road the better.'

'It's tempting to stay, but I ought to go. I don't want people asking where I've been. Anyhow I can probably start some useful work.'

Dick admired her spirit and continued, 'Our first assumption is that the plut has been stolen and not lost or officially, unofficially diverted. If it is missing, and let's face it we are not absolutely sure that it is, then straight theft is the most likely. If it's not missing, well no harm done if we start with the theft premise. All circumstantial evidence points to an inside job, it just does not seem feasible for it to be anything else.'

'Agreed,' muttered both Sally and Janice in unintended unison.

'Your task then, Jan, is to look for clues at Watersthorpe. Check through your records and list the suspect containers. If possible do some more surreptitious store checks to identify as many containers as possible that might be light, but don't attract attention.' Janice nodded assent and Dick went on. 'For each of these check which store keeper booked them in, which lab assayed them, who did the analysis, which store keeper took them back. Look for any traces of contamination, even below the action levels, in areas where it might not be expected. Try and find some common factors, if someone is getting at the plut then that someone must be common to some aspect of handling all the suspect containers.'

'That's not the best of English, Mr. England, but I get your line of thinking,' Janice replied with a touch of humour. 'I'll start as soon as I get back, but it'll be several days before you can expect anything.'

'Second point is motive. It could be blackmail of some kind, but if that is the case then someone is going to get a call fairly soon. It could be for selling to a foreign power, Israel, Iraq or some other. In which case it has probably already gone out in some diplomatic bag.'

'Possibly not,' interrupted Sally. 'Since the Libyan Embassy affair a few years ago diplomatic bags are subject to x-ray checks. Plut oxide is very dense and would undoubtedly show up. My guess is that if it is to be sold abroad, the thief will have to deliver. The question is how?'

'Not by air,' Janice pointed out, 'those travellers and their baggage are also subject to search, what about a Channel ferry in the boot of a car perhaps?'

'Possible,' agreed Dick, 'but not likely, Customs are becoming tighter with ferry passengers and a search is always possible. Last time I went to Holland by ferry several people had their baggage rummaged. You know the best way would probably be in a small pleasure craft like this one. They come and go between countries with only a minimum of control. Sail over to France and you don't even have to report to Customs if you've nothing to declare. Hollow out a bit of keel, pop the plut inside, and the chance of discovery is virtually nil.'

'Come off it Dad, not everyone's like you, most people wouldn't have the slightest idea of what a small boat is like, let alone how to sail it to France.'

'Most people don't steal plut. Jan, it's a long shot, but keep your eye open for anyone who has shown an interest in small boats, especially if that interest has come in the past few months.' Janice nodded and made a note of the request.

'The other motive,' Dick continued, 'and probably the most likely, is that it is to be used for some act of terrorism. Spreading contamination, poisoning water supplies, or injecting it into super market foods, there are numerous possibilities.'

'Or producing a weapon,' interjected Sally.

'No, I don't think that's likely, if they have enough technical knowledge to make a bomb, they would surely realise it is not weapons grade material. They are not likely to be taken in by those stories of weapons made from commercial plutonium having been tested in the States. They will realise that those tests were devices and not weapons. It's one thing to be able to establish some large contraption in a prohibited area and make it explode, quite another to surreptitiously manufacture and deliver a weapon undetected. I think we ought to discard that possibility at this stage, we don't have the resources to follow up everything, we must concentrate on the most likely and hope that we get it right.'

'It would not be easy to spread around in its present form. The oxide particles are heavy and insoluble,' Janice pointed out.

'Yes, but it could be relatively easily dissolved up in acid and then used to contaminate food or water over a vast area. However, if they attempt that our chance of finding the culprits is much greater. Looks as if we have just got to monitor, or get monitored, as many things as we can. All the nuc establishments do routine surveys, it's possible that one of them might pick something up.'

'Suppose,' said Sally, thinking aloud, 'suppose they do have the necessary high tech equipment to contain everything, then we haven't a chance unless,' she paused as her thought process developed and the others held back, curious to hear what was about to be suggested, 'they would have to have bought the equipment from somewhere, there aren't many suppliers of glove boxes, nitric acid, alpha monitors etc, ... if we could check up with those...'

'Good thinking,' interrupted Dick, 'perhaps we, or you, could get Rodney to help, that's much more in his line.'

Sally nodded her agreement, 'I'll ask him, but I think he may be busy at present, he's just had time off for the race.'

Dick knew that what his daughter had said was true, but he was still hopeful.

'We must break up now,' he told the others, 'so let me do a final recap. Miss Hardman will go back to Watersthorpe and have a good ferret around along the lines we've discussed. If she turns up anything worthwhile she'll phone us with the info. Incidentally use my home phone number, if there's no one at home and if it's really confidential, leave a message for us to call back. I don't want to be melodramatic, but just so that you will know a call from us is genuine we will open with the phrase 'volleyball match', likewise when you are calling us your password will be 'prop shaft', agreed?' Janice nodded and jotted down her key phrase. 'Sally and I will look for other possible leads. I will sound out some of my old contacts to keep a sharp eye on their environmental monitoring results, we'll also see what we can do with suppliers.' Dick paused, then muttered as if thinking aloud, 'You know I think there is a good chance that we will sniff out something, but whether it will be enough is open to question.'

They chatted for a few minutes before Janice left to start her long drive back to Lincolnshire, soon after father and daughter retired to their respective cabins and slept soundly.

CHAPTER 6

As the conspirators set about their respective tasks they were not aware of the decision that Janice Hardman had made to call Dick England.

John Grimley surveyed the large room which had long ago been the dining room for the Longsands family, now instead of chandeliers, tapestries and craftsman made furniture, its walls were bare, its floor uncovered and a mass of twentieth century technology lay around. The fluorescent light strips, fixed to the ceiling, were fed with only partly concealed wires which ran down to switches on the wood panelled walls. Cobwebs and spiders festooned the corners and spaces between the lights giving witness to the lack of cleaning over the past years.

'They seem to have done a good job,' Grimley remarked to no one, as he took in the scene before his eyes. Two glove boxes were positioned near to the old fireplace, their exhaust being fed into the chimney. One contained a small model maker's lathe, an electric drill, and a selection of hand tools. The other, a small electric furnace, some graphite crucibles, a balance and a selection of chemicals. In the far corner of the room he noted a large cardboard box, still unopened and in its carriage wrappings, undoubtedly contained the glassware that he had requested. Next to them stood winchesters of fuming nitric and sulphuric acids, as well as ones containing caustic soda, glycerine and toluene. There was a temporary water supply and a sink with a waste pipe passing through the outside wall and into the storm water drain from the roof. This he guessed would empty into The Cut. There were cylinders of argon, nitrogen, and acetylene together with an assortment of cardboard boxes, some of which appeared to contain fire detectors and others, a special type of thickness gauge. Propped in the far corner was a four foot long, decapitated oxygen cylinder. It had steel girders welded along its length.

'Bloody well done,' he muttered again. 'Bloody well done.' At first glance it looked as if everything he had requested was there and waiting for him. 'All I have to do now,' he told himself, 'is to put it together and make if look as if it has been used to make a weapon.' He knew from the timescale that Olive had outlined there was little to spare. He would need to work all the hours he could if he were not to hold up the project. He took off his jacket, searched for, and found, a suitable nail driven into the oak wall cladding, and hung it up, he then set to unpack the glassware.

*

George Brine admired the Surfmaster as the morning sun lit up her canary yellow topsides. He was confident she would be ready in time, and counted out sixteen days on his fingers which took him to Monday fortnight. He turned to Pete, who was standing at his side, 'We'll get her in the water next weekend, rig the mast and test the engine, then bring her out on the Tuesday or Wednesday ready to load the plut, under the keel. That gives us several days in hand.'

'Could we go sooner?

'No, not with the cylinder strapped to the keel. Unless we go on High Water Springs there would be too great a risk of running aground and if we did that, the plut could get left in the putty. Nevertheless we will press on as fast as we can, I'd rather we had time to spare than not enough.' He looked Peter in the eyes and again wondered about his true identity, 'I'll slip out and pick up the injectors, might get them back in this afternoon. If you're free you could slap on some anti-fouling.' Pete grunted and started to walk towards his security fence to make yet another inspection, while Brine continued to admire the yacht.

The Longsands security expert enjoyed his morning stroll around the perimeter. As he went he checked each section of wire, inspected the ground for signs of foot marks or broken blades of grass, either of which would have been tell-tales of an intruder. He wandered past the coiled barbed wire, where the gardens of the house came down to Horsenose Creek, and recalled his training in the forces for getting over such obstacles, but there was no sign of any attempt at entry. He walked along the edge of The Cut and looked at the muddy foreshore. There were a few gouge marks which were made when *Brimstone* had been brought up a couple of months previous. He wondered how many people realised that while the tide scrubs and irons sandy beaches, leaving them clear and unmarked for the next onslaught of small children, the mud of the river banks bears its scars for many months. If anyone did attempt to gain access via the creek, by squeezing under the wire at low water, there would be ample evidence of the intrusion. He checked the trembler devices which, for good measure, he had placed on the wire gate that closed The Cut.

He carried on past the second stretch of barbed wire, then up to the mesh fence and finally finished where he had started. No one had made any nocturnal visits. Pete did not have many responsibilities, he spent most of his time helping out the others, but security was one and he took it seriously. Fortress Longsands would not be penetrated without his knowledge and if he ever caught anyone making an attempt he would shoot first and ask questions later.

*

After the briefing meeting Olive drove her Ford Escort into Colchester and parked in the station car park, a field on a hill which, on weekdays, would be packed with commuters' cars but was now virtually empty. She locked the doors, walked down the grassless track to the road then crossed over to the station entrance.

'Return to London,' she said, pushing a twenty pound note to the ticket clerk.

'Coming back today?' he asked, then, observing her nod, handed over a ticket.

'Which platform?' she queried, just to make sure that if anyone did check up the ticker seller would remember she had headed for London.

However, when the train came she ignored it and caught the next one to Ipswich instead. As she had anticipated there was no ticket inspection on this stretch of line, but she carried a valid return from Liverpool Street in her hand bag as a precaution. At Ipswich there was an open platform, she simply walked out of the station, crossed over the Orwell Bridge and turned into the pay and display car park on the other side. She paused at the top of the steps that lead down to the tarmacadam area below and glanced around to make sure that she was not being followed. It was all an elaborate precaution, there was no reason to suppose that either she, or the contact waiting in the blue Cavalier, were under surveillance but it was vital for the success of Firewater that she must not be linked with the man she was about to meet. He was the Aide to the Military Attache at the Russian Embassy and the person who would send back the message to Moscow that Firewater was, "all systems go". She had to discuss with him the proposed rendezvous where the Watersthorpe plutonium would be exchanged for the nuclear weapon and the place of detonation. The former had been fixed, but the latter was still undecided. One thing was sure, it would not be wasted on a "demonstration" explosion in the middle of the North Sea. What the others at Longsands did not know, was the real plan. It was to cause as many casualties and as much damage as possible, only in this way would achievement of their objective be guaranteed. London, Amsterdam, Copenhagen were top candidates, but the conspirators in Moscow had made a critical evaluation weighing the risks involved in reaching the objective against the weapon's impact. Her gut feeling was to plumb for London, but as it turned out Moscow had different ideas. The clandestine meeting lasted only half an hour after which Olive made her way back to Longsands as anonymously as she had come.

*

John Grimley was more aware than any of the quartet that he was working on the tightest of the time scales. He slept badly on that Saturday night, waking several times as the problems which would face him in the next few days came to the fore of his mind. Sunday morning saw him back at work before the others had risen. On one wall, with the sacrilegious use of drawing pins on the wood panelling, he had secured a piece of paper. It had the title 'Critical Path Plan for Nuclear Device'. If nothing else, John had benefited from the training that he endured while with the ESA. Like most large progressive industries they had insisted their senior staff attend management training courses. John had been on several, generally finding them boring, but one was an exception. It had dealt with P.E.R.T. and Network Planning[16]. Now he had put this acquired knowledge to good use, and had constructed a critical path chart of the work that would have to be completed if a real weapon was to be produced. When the Authorities eventually discovered it, after the big bang, it would help convince them that the device had been made at Longsands. It had another important role, it showed him when the operations

---

[16] *'PERT' is an acronym for Programme Evaluation and Review Technique. It is a practice used in planning major engineering projects. All the essential operations are listed then linked in a sequence network. From this the critical path, ie. the operations which will determine the overall time for the project, can be identified. The network is continuously updated as work proceeds and any departure from the plan is checked to see what effect, if any, it will have on the critical path.*

that would provide subsequent circumstantial evidence had to take place.

Yesterday had been a success and he was on programme. Two glove boxes had been commissioned and the argon purge connected to them, by Monday he would have to make the first small release of plutonium to the chimney and on Tuesday he would get Pete to make the first "test" explosion. He surveyed the planning chart and thought how impossible it would be for him to actually do all that work by himself. The investigators would conclude that there must have been a dozen or so scientists working for the project. On a table, against the wall that displayed Grimley's version of a critical path network, lay a sketch. It showed how a gas cylinder could be converted to form the case for the nuclear bomb that they were supposed to be making, like the chart, it would also be important evidence when the operation was over.

'Oh, it is you Mr. Grimley,' Pete's voice caused John to turn with a start, he had not heard him enter. 'I was just making a security check. Saw a light on, did not think any of us would be at work so early, should have let me know, you might have got shot.'

'What!' John stammered, as he noticed the revolver in the visitor's hand, 'What's that?'

'A Magnum, most powerful hand gun in the world, haven't you seen the Dirty Harry films?'

'I mean what are you pointing it at me for,' said Grimley, starting to recover some composure. 'We don't have to resort to guns.'

'You never know Mr. G., if we have any intruders there's only me to deal with them so I might have to shoot first and ask questions later. Olive would not jeopardise this operation for the sake of snuffing out a snooper if it were necessary.'

John flinched, but said nothing for a moment, then replied, 'Excuse me I must get on with my work.'

'Sure, don't let me stop you.' Pete's gaze moved to the paper on the wall and the sketch below, 'What's that?'

'That, my friend, is the design of the weapon we are supposed to have made, and above, is the work plan of how we produced it. It's called a critical path analysis, all the big firms use it.'

Peter looked suitably impressed and John Grimley, gaining in confidence and in need of an ego boost, added, 'Want me to explain?'

'Please.'

'Our nuclear weapon is made by forcing two pieces of plutonium together, very quickly and very firmly.'

'Why?'

'Well, plutonium gives off neutrons, these split atoms which liberate a lot of energy and produce more neutrons, which in turn split more atoms...'

'Is that what they call a chain reaction?'

'Yes, but it will only happen if the plutonium is larger than a certain size, that's called its critical mass. So we make two pieces that are less than the critical mass and then force them together with a small explosion. The nuclear reaction starts and if the two pieces have been thrust together with enough force it continues long enough to make an explosion.'

Pete took a closer look at the drawing. 'Is that what's going to happen here?'

'That's what we want people to think happened when we let off our device in the North Sea, look this is how it works. We take an old high pressure gas cylinder and have the top cut off...'

'So that's why I took one to Brown's Engineering a few weeks ago.'

'Yes, it's over there now. The rounded end has been reinforced inside with a cup shaped steel filling, this would hold a sub critical piece of plut. At the other end of the cylinder is a plug, it's a sliding fit and tipped with another subcritical lump of plut. Between this and the cylinder end cap, there is a small explosive charge. The whole thing is strengthened with a steel brace and when the charge goes pop the two pieces of plut smash together and, bingo, a nuclear bang.'

'I see, but what is that American source and the ber-y-lee-um foil for?'

'Ah, that's my master stroke. It's to boost the nuclear reaction and make a better bang. Americium gives off alpha particles, it's used in fire detectors and other instruments, that's where we are supposed to have got it from. When these alpha particles strike beryllium they produce a lot of neutrons, we call it an alpha/n reaction, and these neutrons can also split atoms and start a chain reaction.'

'I see, but what's the paper for?' John tried not to appear condescending as he explained what he thought should have been obvious to a two year old.

'We don't want to produce the neutrons until the two pieces of plutonium are brought together, otherwise the bomb would explode as it was being assembled. Alpha particles can't penetrate paper so they don't reach the beryllium until the sliding plunger comes crashing down the cylinder.'

'What are the shear pins for?'

'They hold the plunger in position until the explosion. In fact they hold it for a few micro seconds after the explosion, until the force on it is so great that they snap and the plunger goes hurtling down the cylinder bringing the two pieces of plut together with tremendous force.'

Grimley looked up from the drawing and smiled at the "Heavy" of the team. Pete nodded and tried to look as if he had known that all the time.

'Would it really work? Why do we not make it instead of having to swap it for a military weapon?'

'In theory, yes it might. Exploding under water would be a help, the water would act as a neutron reflector. The first uranium bomb, the one dropped on Hiroshima, was built on this principle, but a different design was used for the plutonium Nagasaki bomb. That's why, when there is a big bang, people will believe that it did work. Olive will make sure the media know about this sketch and there will be no shortage of self opinionated experts to whom they can turn, and who will endorse the view that it would work. You see those who really know the answer are the chaps at Aldermaston and they can not pass an opinion for security reasons. Even if they did claim it would not work who, in the light of our demonstration, is going to believe them? But in practice it's not that simple. It takes years for teams of scientists and engineers to make viable nuclear weapons. I doubt the cylinder would be strong enough in this case, we'd also have to be extremely lucky to get the explosive right. Too little and the plunger stays put or doesn't hold the lumps of plut together for long enough, too much and it blows the whole thing apart! Unlike the Aldermaston boys, we only get one bite of this cherry. For example, we can't make test after test on the explosive like they did at Orfordness when they made the British bombs. There are other uncertainties, such as the critical mass of this type of plut under the conditions we intend to use it in. No, making a back yard weapon is just not on, but a lot of people want to think that it is possible so, as it serves our cause, we'll help them to think it.'

John Grimley turned his attention to the chart on the wall.

'According to our programme you will be making the explosion tests on Tuesday and Wednesday, that's when you blow up the cylinder over there.' Grimley nodded to a modified oxygen cylinder in the corner of the room.

'Are you going to make the explosive here or do I use that which Olive gave me?'

'I'm only going to make it look as if we made the charge here, you will use the stuff that Olive provided.' John pointed to the top row of his chart and continued, 'I shall mix fuming nitric and sulphuric acids and add them to glycerine and toluene. That produces N.G. and T.N.T. so we've got a choice of which to use.'

'I'm not having anything to do with nitroglycerine,' Pete protested, 'it's far too sensitive...'

'Don't worry, you won't have to, Olive's given you a small sample of T.N.T. and Gelignite, which is N.G. stabilised with nitrocellulose plus a few other chemicals thrown in. I shall just make traces and leave them lying around to be found afterwards, it's all part of the hoax.'

'But why make the explosions if they are not needed, as you said we are not going to make a weapon?'

John Grimley tried not to look exasperated and willed himself to accept that Pete did not easily catch on.

'You make a few explosions in the old bunkers on Tuesday and Wednesday evenings. They will be heard as muffled bangs by some of our neighbours. They don't know where they came from or what they were, but they will remember they heard them. When the great investigation takes place and Longsands is discovered they will happily tell the TV cameras what they heard and that will add more credibility to the theory that we did make the weapon here.'

Pete was beginning to understand and he admired the thoroughness with which the man from Watersthorpe and Olive had planned the operation.

'And what does the rest of the chart show?

'The next line represents the extraction of americium from the fire detectors, not a very difficult piece of chemistry, the remainder the conversion of plut oxide to the metal and its machining.'

'Will you have to do that?'

'Yes,' Grimley paused then continued, 'that is the most difficult part of the whole operation, it is also the most important.'

'It looks involved, can you explain it to me?'

Grimley was about to reply when he remembered Olive's warning. Each person is only to be told what they need to know. He had already talked too much, although, on reflection, Pete was going to make the explosions so it would not be unreasonable for him to be told why, otherwise he might not make them look authentic.

'I don't think I ought,' he responded, then changed his mind as he saw the look of anger in Pete's eyes. 'Oh alright, but don't tell Olive.'

'I will not, you can trust me.'

'Well, first I have to get all the air out of the boxes,' Grimley said, pointing to the glove boxes, each of which was now attached to a cylinder of argon. 'Then I mix a small quantity of plutonium oxide, the stuff I nicked from Watersthorpe, with powdered magnesium. Pop it into the furnace and I finish up with plut metal and magnesium oxide. I'm only going to do one crucible, then put the ingot in the other box and machine it to leave traces of plut turnings...'

'...for the investigators...,' Pete interjected.

'...for the investigators...,' Grimley echoed, and continued, 'On Monday I shall make sure a small amount of plut escapes up the chimney, as it certainly would if I were doing a full batch, the filters on these small boxes would be bound to let some pass, they are not as sophisticated as those we have at Watersthorpe...'

'But won't that be discovered?'

'Not unless someone is looking for it and they won't do that until after our demonstration.'

'I think Mr. Grimley, I had better leave you, I think you have a lot to do.'

'Yes, I think so too.' Grimley responded as the other man drifted away. For a moment he mused that in this brief encounter he had come to like the fellow and somehow gained the feeling that he had won Pete's respect, an asset he may need to call upon before they were much older.

*

George Brine also had his work planned out, but not in the same style as Grimley. By Monday morning the modified keel had been fitted and the large circular clips, which would first hold the contraband then later the weapon to the keel, were ready for fixing.

Now he turned his attention to other matters. During the early part of the week he paid several visits to the local boat chandlers where he not only bought the expensive Decca Navigator, VHF radio and Navtex, but also talked freely about his ideas on keel design. He was concerned that in a small community like Walton, not only did everyone know everyone else, they also gossiped. It was quite possible the keel modification, that had been carried out at a local engineering fabricators, was already known to the Customs officer. To talk openly to all and sundry, who might show an interest about how he anticipated the new keel would improve sailing performance, would help allay any suspicions that might arise in the minds of those whose job it was to have suspicions.

The Decca Mk III is an instrument about the size of a small portable radio. It had a LCD display on the front and rows of function buttons below. It clipped into a special bracket which Brine had installed on the bulkhead over the chart table. The aerial was fastened to the boat's pushpit. At the press of the appropriate button it would display the boat's latitude and longitude, speed over ground, course to the next waypoint[17], estimated time of arrival, time and date and even the state of the ships battery! Brine, after fitting the instrument went through the self check procedure and noted there were no rejections. Fitting the VHF radio was not quite so straight forward, the aerial, which would be positioned on the top of the mast, had to be jointed at deck level and while George Brine used the best "dry plug" that he could get, he was still not entirely satisfied. He would not be able to make the final tests until the mast had been stepped and by then time would be running out. The Navtex[18] was the easiest of all to install, it required only a power supply, an aerial and, being about the size of a mini TV set, a small seat on the saloon bookshelf.

---

[17] *It is often convenient to break down a passage into stages, such as navigation marks, or positions where course changes are likely to be made. These are sometimes called waypoints. The Decca Navigator allows for the latitude and longitude of a number of waypoints to be entered into its memory. These can then be recalled to construct a course. The Navigator will display the direction of the next waypoint.*

[18] *"Navtex" is the name of a system of transmitting weather and navigational information in a form that may be recorded and displayed by a special receiver on the boat.*

Brimstone's skipper had other matters which demanded his attention. He was still short of up to date charts and several visits to the local agents did not improve matters. The latest amendments for his Admiralty Pilot had not arrived, but his new Macmillan's Almanac would substitute. He spent hours with his charts working out alternative routes to the rendezvous, each to take account of different weather and tide conditions. From these he selected his waypoints and fed them into the Decca. There were other jobs to be done and some, like swinging the compass[19], could not be tackled until the boat was afloat.

---

[19]*The accuracy of every ships compass is influenced by its position in the boat. Local magnetic effects, such as electric current or iron of the engine etc., can cause the compass to deviate from magnetic North. To overcome this problem a correction card has to be prepared. This is done by allowing the boat to swing through 360° and noting the compass deviation every 5° or 10°.*

CHAPTER 7

Janice Hardman was tired, very tired. She had driven back to Watersthorpe village and not arrived until the early hours of the morning. After a few hours sleep she roused herself and reached for the telephone.

'Kindale!' came the curt response to her call.

'Graham, this is Janice, sorry to disturb you so early on a Sunday morning, but I've seen England and we've got work to do.'

'Christ Jan, don't the wicked ever rest? It's only eight o'clock, can't it wait for a more respectable hour?'

'The trouble with you youngsters is you don't have the stamina of us old timers,' she chided. 'Can you manage to get into work, if so I'll see you there?'

'Are you onto something?'

'Don't know, but I saw England and he gave me some ideas to work on, are you game?'

'You bet, give me half an hour to get a cup of breakfast and I'll see you in the pen. Your office or mine?'

'Yours, we'll need to do some record checking. See you later.'

Janice put down her phone, killed the next twenty minutes then made her way to the Site.

Sunday was much the same as any other day at the Plutonium Facility, some operations continued day in, day out and through the night. Only the administrators and senior staff enjoyed the luxury of Monday to Friday, nine to five employment. While it was not a regular occurrence for Janice and her assistant to come in on a Sunday morning, it was not uncommon. Their presence on site went unnoticed. As arranged they met up in the Health Physics Laboratory in Building 301. The regulation clock on the wall ticked its minutes away as they sat on either side of Kindale's desk.

'Had a long talk with England, he was a bit reluctant to get involved, but his daughter talked him into helping us. However, we are limited on what can be done with our restricted resources.'

'All we need is enough evidence to get the Brigadier to do something, then things will really hum.'

'England wants us to do a detail check back through all our routines. He says it's not the obvious that would shout at us, but the more subtle clues we must look for.'

'Such as?'

'Well, if anyone was taking plut, even if they were very careful with precautions, they would still leave traces of contamination. However, if these were within operational limits we wouldn't have noticed or taken action. I think the sort of thing that England had in mind was to look at our past records and see if any of the PW's ambers were regularly above background, but below an MPL.'[20]

'Christ Jan, that's a hell of a job. Coverall surveys are done at least three times a day, with stores as well as labs and the workshop that makes thirty sets of coveralls checked each day. Say a dozen in each check over three months and we're looking at er...' Graham Kindale hesitated as he wrestled with mental arithmetic. 'er...forty thousand measurements!'

'It's worse than that, we can't restrict our work to coveralls, there are the lab and stores surveys, the corridor, the workshop and reception bay and even here, our own lab. There's also the main change room, maybe we can't survey the lockers now, but we've got past results on the area surveys and overshoe checks. Somewhere there must be a clue in this lot. If there is a thief, even if he has been extremely careful with the way he...'

'Or she,' interjected Kindale.

'Or she,' Janice mimicked with a smile, 'has handled the material, it must have involved non standard operations and left contam levels above what we would have expected even though they were well below an MPL.'

'I think now is the time for me to confess...'

'You're not leaving, young Kindale?'

'No such luck! I didn't tell you at the time, but for the past month or so I've been using my initiative, like you tell us to, I've been working on a computer programme for analysing the area surveys. Most of that data is now on disc so I should be able to get at what we want fairly quickly, maybe a couple of days.'

'Good lad. But all that's only part of the task, we must get data on the containers, when they arrived, who handled them, which lab they went to, who did the transfers to the plastic storage bottles, where they are stored and see if there is any common factors with the ones we suspect. In fact, somehow without the Brigadier or his hench

---

[20] *Jargon meaning process workers amber (contamination) area coveralls being contaminated with radioactivity to a level that was measurably above background, but below the safety limit. Such coveralls would continue in use.*

persons knowing, we must do some more store surveys with the 1268 and see if we can find any more containers that are light,' said Janice referring to the instrument that they had modified for plutonium measurement.

'Is that all, shall I do it instead of my tea break? There are still the routine effluent results to get off to Agg 'n Fish, two lost personnel dosimeters to investigate and I've got to prepare for that debate in Lincoln with the Greenpeace shower. Tell you what, give me a broom and I'll stick the handle up my bum and sweep the floor as well!'

'But how are you going to get the muck into the dust pan?' Janice responded with a smile. They both laughed. Kindale got up from the desk and off a nearby shelf, picked up an armful of lever arch files, these he deposited on the desk in front of his boss.

'You make a start on the coverall surveys, I'll see what compu can do...'

*

Richard Harry England turned over in his bunk and snuggled down inside his sleeping bag. On board *English Lady* there was a sharp Spring chill in the air, this and his late night, provided an added incentive for him to linger. Slowly he opened one eye, then the other and observed a shaft of sunlight that streamed through the port hole like a laser beam. He looked at his watch, but failed to record its message. The fuzzy feeling in his forehead cleared and his mind started to function. Within a minute he was out of his pit and clambering into a track suit.

'Hey Sal,' he called, 'shift yer ass lass, we're burning daylight.'

From the fo'castle, at the other extremity of the boat, his daughter stirred.

'Oh gawd Dad, what's the rush?'

'Don't you remember, you talked me into it? Time isn't on our side so let's shake our feathers, pull out the stops, get our noses to the grindstone and get cracking,' Dick responded deliberately mixing as many metaphors as he could recall, then repeated his favourite phrase which had its origin in an old John Wayne western, 'we're burning daylight.'

By the time he had the kettle in the galley loaded and on the gas, Sally had appeared dressed in her usual jeans and sweater. They settled down to cornflakes and toast.

'Before we burn any more daylight, tell me what we do now?' Sally light heartily mocked her father.

Dick replied in deadly earnest, 'I think we'd better take *Lady* back to Woodbridge and set up HQ at home. Need to get hold of Rodney and see if he is free to help. No doubt if you ask him he will,' Dick teased.

'He might, but he's not a physicist.'

'I know that, but who said we needed another physicist? As you suggested last night if someone has nicked that plut, and quite frankly I have my doubts, then they will need equipment and instruments to handle it. Checking on that angle is detective work which is much more in Rod's line than ours.'

'He's more used to investigating insurance claims and other types of fraud, this isn't exactly his vocation.'

'It sure would result in one hell of an insurance claim if these jokers do something nasty with their loot,' Dick responded, then added in an attempt at humour, 'He'd be close enough to his present work not to have to worry about professional etiquette and straying into other peoples preserves.'

'I'm sure he'll help,' said Sally with a smile.

Dick looked at his watch.

'High water on the bar is about four this afternoon, we could get in anytime after midday, let's say half past one. Couple of hours from here, so if we slip out at eleven, we should get three hours of flood to take us up the Deben, should be picking up our buoy at about half past five this afternoon.'

'That gives us time to 'phone Rodney from here, maybe he'll come and meet us, then we can fill him in as we go home.'

'Good idea, you go and ask the H.M. if you can borrow his phone and I'll get *Lady* ready for sea.'

It was an uneventful trip back, they crossed the bar into the River Deben as Dick had predicted and arrived off Kyson Point just after 1700hrs. Sally had taken the wheel from the time they left Levington and her father had not even appeared as they entered the River mouth. He had found an old map of the United Kingdom among his charts and this had monopolised his attention throughout the trip. On it he plotted all the Nuclear Establishments where he had contacts, which was most of them. He then drew a thirty mile radius around each.

'Will you pick up the buoy?' his daughter's words interrupted his thoughts.

'Okay,' he responded, leaving his chart table and making his way to the bow. 'I've got something to show you down below, it's not good news, let's hook up then I'll explain.'

As soon as *English Lady* was secure, father and daughter went down below to study Dick's handiwork.

'Look Sal, I've drawn a thirty mile circle round each of the establishments where I ought to be able to get the Health Physicist to tip us off if any of their taky-shades[21] or other surveys pick up unexplained plut. There is a chance of finding the source even if it is outside the thirty mile radius, but there is also a possibility of missing a small release within the radius, so I think thirty miles is a fair approximation for estimating probability of detection.'

Sally glanced at her father's work, 'You've missed out the Naval Dockyard at Devonport and what about the Sub bases, surely they do survey work?'

'I know,' Dick muttered, 'but I don't have any contacts there that I could trust. If this were only official we could not only include them, but all the NAIR Scheme participants as well[22]. As it is only about a fifth of the country is covered, moreover we don't know how

---

[21]*Taky-shades were developed by Skelcher et al at Sizewell Nuclear Power Station in the mid 1960's to provide a means of monitoring the environment around nuclear establishments. They consist of a wire frame upon which is stretched a piece of muslin cloth treated with a sticky resin. Minute particles of dust in the atmosphere stick to this cloth and can later be analysed in the laboratory. They are extremely sensitive and can detect, on a semi quantitative basis, very low concentrations of radioactive debris in the atmosphere. They are now used around all nuclear power stations to check that airborne radioactive contamination is not escaping undetected. They are also used by the Ministry of Agriculture Fisheries and Food for qualitative checks on atmospheric contamination.*
Ref. "Environmental Monitoring Around Nuclear Sites", A. Short, Journal Society Radiation Protection, Spring 1984 Sect. 4(1).

[22]*"NAIR" is an acronym for National Arrangements for Incidents involving Radioactivity. It is a scheme whereby establishments throughout the United Kingdom, who have expertise in handling radioactivity, volunteer to be available to assist in an incident in their area. NAIR calls are activated by the police. It involves not only the establishments of the nuclear industries, but also hospitals and universities.*

long we've got or when the shades are changed. Guess our chance of a lead through these routines is only about one in twenty or even one in fifty.'

'Cheer up Dad,' Sally consoled, 'we're not beaten yet, in fact we've not even started, let's see if we can find Rodney.'

Dick made his farewell rounds on *English Lady*, gas off, hatches closed and fastened, all sea cocks closed and the loo flushed through with fresh water. Finally he opened the master switch to isolate the batteries and climbed down into the inflatable dinghy which Sally had lowered from its davits and pulled up alongside.

'That's Rod on the shore,' she said excitedly, as she pointed to a distant figure who appeared to be waving an arm in their direction.

'Okay let her go,' Dick responded, as he pulled the starter on the old, but reliable, *Seagull*. The little engine burst into life and Sally gave the dinghy a gentle push off to help it on its way.

'Hi Rodney,' she called out as they came within ear shot.

'How's my sweetheart? the man in the red anorak responded. The dinghy crunched into the landing hard and Rodney leaned forward, grabbed the painter and with a quick snatch pulled the bow clear of the water as Dick cut the motor. 'What's the panic my lovely? What's so important that you couldn't tell me over the phone? If it's a parking ticket, sorry I can't help,' he joked.

'Don't be a fool,' the girl replied, leaning forward and whispering in her boyfriend's ear. 'All will be revealed when we get home.'

'Now you are exciting me, will you tell me what your phone call was about as well?' he teased.

'Twit,' she replied with a giggle and gave him a peck on his left ear.

'Well England, what's all the flap about,' the use of the surname did not indicate formality, but was part of an ongoing leg pull, the origin of which was lost to both men, said Rodney as he tried another approach to get an explanation.

'We have a problem and need help fast,' Dick said without the usual retaliation that would have been normal under less serious occasions. 'Let's get into the car and high tail it back to the house, I'll fill you in on the way. Sal you take our car. I'll go with Rod.'

'Now I am excited, for an old plod like you to get het up it must be something a wee bitty bigger than normal.'

Rodney McDonald was a handsome looking fellow in his late twenties, blue eyes, light brown hair, and a thick muscular frame. He gave the lie to those charts that would have predicted him as being overweight, for although he only stood five feet ten in height, his thirteen stone was mainly bone and muscle. His education had been in the streets of Glasgow, followed by three years in the army where he specialised in unarmed combat and infiltration techniques. It was only after he had signed on he realised that his independent turn of mind did not fit well with army routine. At the first opportunity he quit and joined a well known insurance company where he was employed as a claims investigator and specialised in the more serious cases of fraud. After two years he wanted independence and set up his own private investigation agency, his clients being the large insurance companies.

'What we are looking for is quite small, and we can't tell anyone that we are searching, that's one of our difficulties,' Dick started to explain as a preamble to the story. He related the full sequence of events, the visit from Janice Hardman with her suspicions, then finally the bad news about there being no money, not even for expenses.

'You sure are a hell of a friend Blighty, and a bloody poor business man. Fancy chasing fairy stories from birds and not even a brass button in it, goes against all my ancestral principles. What you really want is for poor little me to subsidise the entire nuclear industry.' Despite his years in Scotland, Rodney's accent had lost much of its hard Glasweegen brogue and been replaced with a much softer enunciation. He glanced in his rear view mirror then shot a sideways look at Dick, 'Do I have any choice?' he asked. 'What if I say no.'

'Then I reckon your chances of becoming my son-in-law will be pretty slim,' Dick responded with a smile. 'Sally is in on this up to the hilt, in fact she persuaded me to get involved against my better judgement! You know how cynical I am about the nuclear industries, if it had been left to me I'd see those bungling buffoons stew in their own juice.'

'Then why don't you?'

'Because my beloved daughter reminded me of something I had preached years ago. I once made the mistake of telling a public meeting that democracy hangs by a slender thread and can only be preserved by the vigilance and self sacrifice of those ordinary people who enjoy it.'

'That's a load of crap to shoot, I suppose Sally was taken in? Democracy survives because it suits the capitalist system, but I suppose it's better than the alternative. You really think your little problem is so serious?'

'Yes Rod I do, otherwise I wouldn't be involving you and, more to the point, as far as you are concerned, Sally does as well. Quite frankly if the plut has been taken, I don't think the thieves will try making a bomb, but if they were to contaminate drinking water supplies, they could pollute virtually the entire supply in the U.K.'

'But that can be done with other toxins, why go to the trouble of using plut?'

'Because it would catch the public imagination, radioactivity has become a nightmare word for a lot of people who don't understand it. 'fraid we have the media and so called Environmentalists to thank for that misconception, but nevertheless we have to accept that Joe Public is shit scared of radiation yet willingly puts up with far more dangerous things.'

'Okay Blighty, you've convinced me, I'll be another sucker, where do we start?'

'With a cup of tea,' Dick replied, as they turned into the drive of the England's abode.

It was a between the wars bungalow on a half acre plot. The garden was edged with thick hedges and trees, the majority of which had not regained their foliage. At the end of the drive was a double garage and a workshop cum boat equipment store. The original building had been extended in the 1960's when owner occupiers could get tax relief on their building society loans for home extensions. But later it fell into a poor state of repair as an ageing widow lived out her last few years. When the Englands bought the property they had first to spend a good deal of time and money in repair and modernisation. The accommodation was modest, but adequate. After his wife was killed, Dick converted one of the bedrooms into an office and made the lounge double as a conference room. A function which it was to fulfil on this occasion.

The trio made themselves comfortable in the easy chairs and sipped the tea which Sally had conjured up soon after their arrival.

'Quo Vadis?' Rodney asked, to open the conversation with the only piece of Latin he knew, even that he had cribbed from the title of an old film recently rehashed on television.

'I wish to hell I knew,' Dick responded, tugged at the lobe of his ear, then scratched his head in place where hair was in short supply. 'Sal, remember a couple of years ago we did a job for Distoil on the active residues left in their fractionation columns?'[23] His daughter cast a glance of non-comprehension at her boyfriend, then nodded. Dick continued, 'We bought some alpha monitoring equipment for them from NI (Northern Instruments Limited), can you turn up the name of the salesman?'

'No need Dad, we already have a couple of good alpha instruments, they have even got up to date calibration certificates. We can't afford any more, anyhow we don't know where to start looking so we can't do any meaningful survey work.'

'I'm not thinking of buying, right at this moment we need a contact.' Sally went out to the small bedroom that had been converted, without planning permission, into an office. After a few minutes she returned clutching a battered, buff coloured, wallet file close to her ample bosom. She passed it over to Dick then went out again.

'Now where the hell's she gone?' he questioned. 'Women! They never can concentrate on a serious problem, probably gone off to water her plants!'

Sally returned, interrupting her father's comments, with a tray of sandwiches.

'Now what was that you were saying about women?' She scolded her father with a smile as he returned to his original line of thought.

'Rod,' as he spoke he shuffled through the papers that Sally had given him, 'could you go up to Newcastle tomorrow?'

'Sure, a seven hundred mile round trip, no problem, will before breakfast do?' but his sarcasm was lost on his future father-in-law.

'Good,' Dick grinned and left the room, the other two regarded each other with a bemused look. Five minutes and two sandwiches

---

[23]*Some crude oils contain traces of alpha emitting radioactivity. This is left in the fractionating columns during the refining process to such an extent that they exceed the accepted safe levels, thus simple monitoring and protective measures are required.*

later, he returned wearing a smile that would have done credit to a Cheshire cat.

'I've just phoned George Watts, Sales Manager for NI, he's agreed to see you at eleven o'clock tomorrow morning.'

'For what will he see me?' the Scot enquired.

'I've told him you've been retained by the Department of Trade to do some research, confidential of course, on small industries now starting up in the radiation field. Said it was probably something to do with the new Factory Act regs. Develop that line and try and get out of him all you can about the small sales they have made over the past couple of years. He won't be very keen on revealing who his customers are, but he is a bit gullible and I reckon you should be able to hoodwink him. We can then discount the bona fide and see who's left. There are very few firms that make this type of equipment and my guess is that George will know what his competitors are up to. Alpha monitors aren't the sort of things that you can pick up in a supermarket. Jan hasn't missed any of hers so it looks as if these phantom thieves have probably gone and bought something like an RD5, that means from one or another manufacturer.'

'Great idea,' there was scepticism in his voice, 'perhaps I ought to know what I'm supposed to be talking about, what is an RD5?'

'I suggest Sally goes with you, she can officially represent our consultancy and do the intros, what's more George Watts, if I remember correctly, has eyes for a pretty girl, so she might put on her mini...'

'Dad!'

'She can steer the technical discussion,' Dick continued, ignoring the protest, 'and brief you on the drive up.' Sally nodded in agreement, but Rodney had doubts.

'Do you really think it's worth the effort? Of course a trip with Sal is okay by me, but honestly Dick is it likely that the thieves would leave such an obvious trail?'

'I don't see that they have much choice, they will need specialist equipment such as chemicals, instruments, etc. They could import them, steal them, get someone else to buy for them, or set up a legit cover and buy themselves. Now if you were in their position which would you do? All the options except the latter involve an element of risk, but the last is pretty safe.'

'England,' Rodney responded, seeing the merits of his line of reasoning, 'looks as if I am going to marry the daughter of a genius!'

'Who said I am still going to marry you?' Sally interjected in mischief, 'Still,' she pretended to relent, 'I suppose I might condescend to look after a slow coach who doesn't happen to catch on too fast.'

'I've just had another thought,' Dick continued, ignoring the banter. 'Labteck have their offices in Sheffield. You will be going up the A1 so it would not cost too much time if you paid them a visit on the way back. With a bit of luck you'll be there before they close, but I've no contacts so you'll have to feel your way.'

'What, why, and who is Labteck?' Rodney asked.

'As far as I know there are only two manufacturers of nuclear standard glove boxes in the U.K. They're one of them and are probably the biggest.'

'You really are an optimist, surely you don't expect the plut pinchers will go shopping round the country for the best gear, build a lab with it, then go and nick the plut. They must realise what an easy trail they would be leaving.'

'I don't see that they could do anything else. If they have a well thought out plan and they know what they are doing, they will realise that unless they use the best equipment they will spread the plut all over the place and its tell-tale clickerty click would lead straight to them.'

Dick continued, unmoved by his prospective son-in-law's doubts and yet again expounded his way of thinking.

'You can't buy this sort of gear through Exchange and Mart, you can't smuggle it through Customs as hand baggage, and it's too sophisticated to make, so you've got to go out and buy it in a restricted market. The only thing you can do is to set up what passes for a legit front operation. This is why I've always argued that if anyone did steal plut they would be easy to track down in a week or two, specially if there was a national effort with appeals on TV and that sort of thing. However, the way things look at the moment, the thieves do not expect the loss at Watersthorpe to be discovered yet awhile. They have taken care to disguise the loss rather than make it obvious. That means they need time, God knows how much. If the stuff went missing in small amounts, which is likely because it appears to be from several containers, then they might not have finished. Perhaps Jan has stumbled on the plot earlier than they anticipated, but they don't know it yet. My guess is that they are banking on the stolen plut not being noticed until they are ready to make it known.

Remember that the Brigadier said all the containers weighed correctly, that suggests, if Jan is right, something else has been added to make up the weight. They would only do that if they did not want the theft discovered! It could be that we have surprise on our side.'

'So they make glove boxes, it might help if I knew what a bleedin' glove box was.'

'Don't worry, sweetheart,' Sally interjected. 'I'll explain everything as we go.'

'The other company that makes them is Contamination Control, they're North London, I'll pay them a visit and try my hand as a sleuth while you hammer up the A1. Any other ideas?' Dick invited.

'Yes, we go to London and you do the Newcastle trip.' Rodney smiled while Dick searched for some excuse for not reversing the roles he had proposed. Sally winked at the young Scot who relented.

'Okay Blighty, we'll do the trip, it's a long run so let's eat and early to bed, can I stay here?'

'A good idea son,' Dick replied, imitating a well known comedian of his youth, oblivious to the fact that the two youngsters were probably in nappies when it was in vogue.

Monday morning came early for the trio, somewhere around 0600hrs. Sally and Rodney were a length ahead of Dick in reaching breakfast and he was only at the toast stage when the two younger members boarded their sports car and set off for the north. It was a crisp, clear, Spring day, branches dripped with the overnight dew and other surfaces were damp with condensation. Rodney gave a short blast on the twin tone Masseratti style horns as he and Sally left the drive for the public road. Traffic was light, they reached the A45 without delay, then sped along its dual carriageway overtaking the slow moving lorries and keeping a sharp eye in the rear view mirror for police cars. Unusually, there were no road works and in just over the hour they were on the old Roman road which is now the A604 heading for Huntingdon and Ermine Street, otherwise known as the A1. Road works on the Trent Bridge, just north of Newark delayed them for fifteen minutes, but thereafter the way was clear to Blyth where they stopped for fuel and a coffee before entering the Motorway to bye-pass Doncaster. Thereon the road was clear and the TR7 sped up Dere Street towards Scotch Corner with its speedometer needle flickering in the nineties.

'How're we doing sweetheart?' Rodney asked his navigator.

'Well up on schedule, this is Catterick, about forty five miles to go.'

'Good, the young Scot glanced at his watch, then into his rear view mirror.

'Aw shit!' he yelled. 'Shit, shit, shit!'

'What on earth...?'

'Bleedin' police car behind,' he snapped as his hand reached for the brake lever so as not to actuate the tail lights, but he knew it was too late. The white Cortina now had its blue light flashing and headlights on. Rodney slowed and pulled into a lay-by that had just appeared, the police followed.

Rodney wound down the window as the man in uniform approached.

'Do you know what speed you were doing Sir?' the policeman's voice was cold but meticulously correct.

'Er... 'fraid I took my eye off the needle for a few moments, must have crept into the eighties, sorry Officer.' The face beneath the blue cap softened slightly.

'Yes Sir, easily done, you'll need to be more careful in future, can I see your driving licence and insurance?' Rodney breathed an inward sigh of relief as he thought he was about to get off with a caution. He reached into his breast pocket and produced the documents from a brown leather wallet that Sally had given him for Christmas and passed them over for the policeman to examine.

'They all seem to be in order Sir,' the voice was soft, clear and cutting, 'do you know what your stopping distance is at ninety miles an hour?'

'Er...er...'

'Have you ever seen what happens when a car crashes at that speed, ever been first on the scene and had to pull the battered, broken bodies of adults and children alike from the tangled steel?' he paused, just long enough to let his words sink in. 'Ever heard the screams and cries of the dying and those who wished they would? I have and it's not a pretty sight, if I had my way I'd make every speeding motorist serve a spell in one of the accident hospitals that handles these casualties...'

'I have said I was sorry Officer, it was purely accidental, I took my eyes off the speedo for a few moments and the speed just crept up...'

'To ninety two miles per hour, Sir? I am going to book you for speeding, I must warn you that...'

Despite the delay at the hands of the law, they reached the outskirts of Newcastle in good time. The latter part of the journey had been made in subdued silence, Rodney was annoyed with himself for being caught and concerned that this would be the second endorsement on his licence. Sally felt that it was her fault for involving him in what might well turn out to be a wild goose chase. As they left the A1(M) in favour of the A69, Rodney reached for the mike of his C.B.

'One four for directions, any breaker give me directions for Northern Instruments?' His second call brought a Geordie voiced response.

'Breaker for directions, knock her up a couple, come back.'

'Thanks breaker going one six,' he reached down to the set and switched to Channel 16.

'Breaker for directions, what's yer 'andle, I'm Oddjob.'

'Oddjob this is Scotty, glad to catch you, how do I get to Northern Instruments?'

'No problem Scotty, used to work there, what's yer twenty?'

Rodney slowed down to 25mph, glanced to his offside and noticed a public house.

'Just joined the A69, the Jarrow Marchers on the right.'

'Fine, carry on for about half a mile, then turn left at the traffic lights, follow the road for another mile and then left again up Hillside Road. You'll find a large building, used to be a country house, on yer right. That's it.'

'Ten four good Buddy, catch you 'gain sometime.' Rod responded with the usual courtesy. He put down the mike and turned to Sally. 'Some people think C.B.'ers are nuts, but I always find them helpful, especially with local knowledge, Northern Instruments, here we come!'

CHAPTER 8

The Sales Director, George Watts could not have been more helpful. Sally did the introductions and for a few minutes they reminisced over the Distoil contract, then came to the purpose of the present visit. Rodney had taken to Watts and decided to trust him with at least part of the story. He explained that England had a hunch about some mischief that might be going on. He couldn't say what, or who, but they needed information. He promised that it would be kept confidential and destroyed when the project was complete. Watts accepted the explanation at its face value. He had come to respect England's integrity and knew of at least two occasions when unsuccessful attempts had been made to bribe him.

'I'll give you a print out of all our customers over the past two years who have bought alpha monitoring instruments,' he said, as he reached for the computer terminal on his desk. For a few moments he tapped the keys, then the printer at the side of his desk rattled out several sheets of paper. These he tore off, sealed them in an envelope and handed it over to Sally.

'Give these to your father, but make sure they are destroyed, I wouldn't like them to get into the hands of our competitors.'

'Promise,' she responded, then added, 'but you don't have any competitors.'

'You'd be surprised, the French, the Japs, and the Yanks are pushing us hard, but they don't have much of a hold in the U.K. at the moment. There are also several smaller firms who can undercut us on price, but don't offer as good an after sales service.'

'I'd forgotten about them, but don't they just do beta gamma equipment?'

'J.L.D. at Malden and Rayfinder at Devizes have both bought out alpha monitoring equipment in the last twelve months, you might try them but I doubt if they will be as helpful.'

Sally began to realise that the approach they had adopted would not be so straightforward as they had thought.

'Thanks for the advice,' she responded, with a smile. 'I think we ought to pay those folk a visit. It's been nice meeting you again, but we have a long drive back, can I take you to lunch?'

'No, I have an appointment in a few minutes, but thanks for the offer.' They shook hands and were on their way.

‘So far so good, as the man said when he fell off the sky-scraper.’ Rodney muttered as they both settled into the Triumph. He leaned forward and switched on the radio just in time to hear the 12.55pm weather forecast.

The journey back down the A1 towards Sheffield was uneventful at a steady 72mph. They took the M18 turn then slipped off on the Maltby Road at junction 1. Again Rodney used the C.B. and in a matter of minutes were successfully directed to the Labteck car park, it was just 1530hrs.

‘They should be back from their tea break,’ Rodney remarked for no apparent reason as they started over towards the main building in front of them.

‘I don’t expect the Sales Manager has a tea break,’ Sally rebuked him. ‘Don’t be flippant, we are going to need all our finesse to get the info we want, remember here we don’t have any friends like George Watts.’

The industrial estate was an ad hoc collection of brick buildings interspersed with a few portacabins and the occasional, more recent, prefabricated asbestos structure. The site had been a munitions factory during the 1939-45 War and had continued to produce ordinance until 1963. After that it remained derelict while the M.O.D. tried, in vain, to make a decision on its future. The National Coal Board had taken it over with a view to building a gasification plant, but had put that idea on ice when the North Sea gave forth a rival product. They refurbished the buildings and let them out for light industrial purposes. Rodney and Sally walked towards a drab looking, brick crumbling, structure in front of them. At the side of the green painted door was a sign: ‘Labteck Ltd, Registered Office’. Rodney pushed open the door and the duo stepped into the foyer. They were confronted by three other doors. Front left, the entrance to the factory was marked by a battered, but nevertheless, substantial double door. To the right of these was a small counter with a sliding glass window above and a hand written notice advising visitors to press a camouflaged bell push. Further to the right of this was a mahogany faced door labelled ‘Manager’. Rodney approached the window, rang the bell and peered through as he waited.

‘Yes?’ a thin, anaemic, female teenager, presumably on some Government training scheme for the unemployed, was looking at him.

His smile produced no change in the boney poker face, 'I wondered if I could have a word with your Managing Director,' he proffered.

''e ain't 'ere.'

'Is the Sales Director available?' he tried again.

'Don't 'ave one. Bill Child is in, 'e's the Manager, will 'e do?'

Rodney reached into his pocket and took out one of his business cards. It read 'Mr. R. Mackay, Industrial Consultant Agency' followed by an equally fictitious address. He slid it over the counter to the skinny lass on the other side.

'If Mr. Child will see me I would be most obliged.'

''ang on I'll see,' she said, turning her back and making for a side door through which she disappeared. Moments later she returned and for the first time managed an excuse of a smile. 'Mr. Child can spare yer a few minutes, it's that door next t' yer.'

'Thank you,' said Rodney, as he turned to Sally who was trying hard to stifle a grin.

Bill Child was a bluff Yorkshire man who always came straight to the point, 'Well I don't make a habit of seeing folk unannounced, what can I do for you?'

'Sorry about calling cold, we did try to 'phone several times, but kept getting number unattainable,' Sally lied. 'It is very good of you to see us at short notice, we happened to be in the area...'

'Not short notice lass, no notice at all,' the Yorkshire man responded. 'Well, don't muck about with excuses, what can I do for you?'

Rodney cut in, 'My consultancy has been retained to advise one of our established clients on setting up a lab for handling toxic material, my assistant here,' he nodded towards Sally, 'is more familiar with the details.'

Sally stifled her hurt pride at the assistant jibe and resisted the temptation to retaliate, she took up the story. 'I'm not at liberty to give details, but I can say it's to do with genetic engineering, they require some high quality glove boxes and as one of the country's leading manufacturers...'

'*The* leading manufacturer,' Child interjected.

Sally swallowed and continued, '...we were naturally interested in your equipment.'

'Miss Wilkie, you've met her, will give you our catalogue. Look at that then get your clients t' come up and see us, be pleased t' discuss their needs.'

'It's not that simple,' Rodney remarked, trying desperately hard to manipulate the right opening. 'Before making any recommendation to our client, and certainly before revealing his name, we wanted to see your equipment in action, talk to present users and so on.'

'No problem, Aldermaston people use our boxes, I'm sure they'll be pleased to give you an honest opinion.'

'Our client is not in favour of nuclear weapons,' Rodney responded, thinking on his feet, 'perhaps there are some small firms that you've supplied in the past few years who would give us the benefit of their experience?'

The Yorkshire man got up from his desk and walked over to a battered filing cabinet in the corner of his office. Subconsciously Rodney noted that it had no lock as the second drawer was slid open. From it Child took a green coloured file, flicked through the pages then sat down.

'You could try Newcastle or Bristol Universities, they've 'ad some of our boxes.'

'We'd be rather more influenced by the experience of small firms who have commercial pressures and don't have the clout of large industries to get the service they need,' Rodney responded.

'I 'ope by that you don't mean to imply that we don't treat all our customers the same,' Bill Child rebuked, 'any'ow, no offence, there's Newchem at Leicester, Highland Chemicals at Dingwall. That do to be goin' on with?'

It was a start, but Rodney needed the complete list, to have just one name missing could ruin their chances of success. He realised he had played things wrong and to push Child further would start arousing suspicions, instead he formed another plan.

'That's fine, thank you,' he responded, much to Sally's surprise. 'We won't keep you any longer, perhaps we can pick up a brochure from your Miss...'

'Miss Wilkie.'

'From Miss Wilkie on our way out.' They shook hands and left.

As the TR7 pulled away from Labteck, Sally opened the conversation.

'Rod, why on earth did you quit with just two names, we need the whole list.'

'I know that sweetheart, and we are going to get it, but not just now.'

'When?

'Tonight.'

'How, they'll be closed?'

'Correct my dear Watson. I'm going to burgle that office when they are all bye-byes!'

'Rod you can't, you'll get caught, it's not worth the risk.'

'There's not much risk, remember my army training, shame to waste it and if this problem is as important as you thought then it is certainly worth the risk. Let's drive into town, kill a few hours then you'll 'phone your father and tell him we won't be back until tomorrow morning, leave the rest to me.'

'Are you sure?'

'Look, that place is easy, the door we entered is a standard mortice lock, I can pick it in ten seconds. The only intruder alarm is in the girl's office and guards the safe. I doubt if Child's door is locked, anyhow it also had a simple mortice lock and that filing cabinet had no lock at all! Better still there was even a photocopier in Child's office, give me ten minutes and I'll have the complete list.'

*

Dick England waited until 0900hrs before making the first of his many telephone calls. It was to the Health Physicist at Chapel Creek Nuclear Power Station situated on the River Blackwater. The Station's exchange operator put him through.

'Is that Tom Watling? Dick England here, long time no see, how's things?'

'Dick, good to hear from you, how're you making out?' came the reply which ignored the initial question. 'What can I do for you?'

'How d'you know I wanted something?'

'Aw Dick, I didn't work for you for three years without learning your M.O. You always used to say, when you need help go to old friends, so what can I do for you?'

'Well, glad I taught you something, I was only going to enquire about your health, but come to think of it there is a small favour.'

‘So long as it doesn’t cost and I don’t have to break the Official Secret’s Act I’ll try and help.’

‘Tom, you still pull in your taky-shades every two weeks?’

‘Yes.’

‘What do you do on them?’

‘The usual, put them on the gamma spec then ash and do a gross alpha and beta.’

‘Good, tell you what I’m after, it’s only a hunch and I don’t want to say too much at this stage in case I look daft, but...’

‘That would be nothing unusual for you,’ Watling joked.

‘Thanks, didn’t I teach you not to interrupt your elders?’ England countered. ‘Anyhow as I was saying, I’ve got a hunch that you might pick up a bit of alpha in the next week or two...nothing much...probably due to plut. I’m working on a theory that the weapon test stuff does not come down continuously[24], but deposits in clusters, I think conditions are right for a cluster now. If you get any high alphas on any of the shades let me know pronto?’

‘Okay Dick, sounds a screwy idea to me, but I’ll keep you posted if anything turns up, any hurry?’

‘Yes, I must know at once if the results are to be meaningful, even if it’s the middle of the night or Bank Holiday, got to do some other measurements at the same time to tie the theory up.’

‘Won’t be night or Bank Holiday, we don’t work then, but okay if anything does show I’ll tip you off a.s.a.p.’

‘Thanks Tom, do the same for you some day.’

‘That’s okay Dick, I reckon I owe you, cheers.’

‘Cheers,’ Dick put down the phone and then dialled his next number and after that the next, then the next and so on until he had contacted each of the establishments which he had circled on his chart. The conversations all followed much the same lines and he received the same assurances.

Dick looked at his watch, he had already spent an hour, but he reasoned it was well worthwhile. There was one more call to make, but this time it was not to a nuclear establishment.

---

[24]*Although the testing of nuclear weapons in the atmosphere has largely been discontinued, radioactive debris from tests carried out years ago is still suspended in the higher levels of the atmosphere and gradually falls to earth. This debris includes traces of plutonium. It has been estimated that more than 5 tons of weapon plutonium has, over the years, fallen to earth in this way.*

'Contamination Control, can I help you?' a young female voice, with a touch of cockney in it, almost sang out the greeting.

'Could I speak to your Sales Director, please?' Dick responded.

'One moment Sir, who shall I say is calling?'

'England, Doctor Richard England.'

'May I say what it's about?'

'I'm not known to your Director, but perhaps you could tell him it is a confidential matter.'

For a few moments the line went silent, then a middle aged voice with an East End accent cut in, 'Bill Sharp speaking, Doctor England what can I do for you?'

'Mr. Sharp, may I take it you are the Sales Director?' Dick asked, then continued without waiting for a reply. 'There's a confidential matter concerning your self-venting, high efficiency, glove boxes I'd like to talk to you about, could I come over and see you?'

'Sure, can you give me an inkling of the problem?'

'It's not a problem, well I don't think so, but I'd rather not talk over the phone.'

'I'm away all next week, but the middle of May is free, how long will this take?'

'Not very long, half an hour or so, but May is rather late, er...er...any chance today?' Dick said, with deliberate hesitation.

'Sorry, I've an appointment in London later this afternoon, so I'm a bit pushed.'

'I could be at your office by say...eleven...any chance of fitting me in then?'

'Well...,' Bill Sharp hesitated, 'well I could give you half an hour if you promise not to take longer, say eleven thirty?'

'Eleven thirty it is,' Dick confirmed without hesitation, 'Thank you for your cooperation, look forward to meeting you.'

England cast aside his normal laconic approach to matters and, as was his way in such circumstances, went into top gear. Five minutes later he was motoring. The A12 was free from road works and accidents which usually caused delays. Dick wondered how much longer it would be before the new improvements would have to be subject to the road gangs' surgery. As a result of the clear run, despite his strict adherence to the speed limits, he arrived at Contamination Control fifteen minutes early. The factory was on one of those industrial estates that had been established in the 1970's and was strictly functional in design and construction. The building was steel framed with concrete block infill and insulated asbestos roof. The front, which consisted of office accommodation, had a red brick facia that gave some relief to the otherwise austere appearance. A small parking area separated the building from its service road. Dick locked up and made for the only door that presented itself to the visitor. Inside was a painted white door bearing the words 'Enquiries and Visitors' and next to that a blue painted door labelled 'Staff'. For a moment Dick mused on the significance of the different colours then concluded that either the employees could not read or the firm had obtained some job lots of paint. He tapped on the white door and, without waiting for an invitation, entered.

The middle aged woman behind the counter opened the conversation with a touch of cockney which Dick immediately recognised from his earlier conversation.

'Dr. England?'

'Yes, 'fraid I'm a little early.'

The receptionist-cum-secretary glanced at the clock as if to check on the accuracy of England's confession, sniffed, then forced a smile, 'I think that will be alright,' she returned to her desk and spoke into a small black box. 'Dr. England is here, would you like to see him now?'

'Yes, show him in.'

'Dr. England, follow me please,' she said, as she lifted the counter flap and made for the door through which Dick had just entered. They went through the blue door and into a short corridor, at the end of which appeared to be the entrance to the factory. On the right was another white door, half glazed with wire reinforced frosted glass, it bore a polished brass plate: F.W. Sharp - Director.

The secretary gave a courtesy knock and entered, 'Dr. England,' was all she said by way of introduction before scuttling out.

'Pleased to meet you Dr. England,' said the Director, half rising from his seat as he extended the traditional hand for a shake. 'How can I be of assistance?'

Dick relinquished the damp, limp paw and reached inside his jacket pocket, withdrew his wallet and extracted a white business card. It bore the radioactive trefoil sign in the top left corner and his home address opposite. Underneath was printed in italic script:

R.H. England B.Sc, Ph.D, M.Inst.P, M.R.S.C.
England and Associates, Consultants
Radiology, Safety, Environment.

He passed the card to the Director and while it was being read made his response, 'My company has been commissioned by a Government Department, I'm sorry I'm not allowed to say which one as the matter is confidential, to assess the capacity of the Country to handle highly toxic material in the event of an emergency. It means that I have to search out every organisation, no matter how small, which has glove boxes or similar facilities. Of course, the big users are well known, but I'm having difficulties finding all the small companies, those who might be making high purity drugs, electronic components, handling radioactive material, or bacteria etc. I wondered if you would let me have a list of all your recent customers, it would give me a useful start?'

'Surely all that information is already available, held by police and fire services under the Hazchem Scheme, Radioactive Substances Act and so on?'

'Well it is and no it isn't,' Dick said, trying to think of a way forward. 'Those people do have lists of premises which contain toxic substances, but not all have glove boxes and there must be many establishments that do have the boxes, but do not handle toxic material, such as those making high purity materials in controlled atmospheres.'

'Really, such as?'

'Er...er...I can't think of any off the cuff, but I'm sure that there must be some, I mean if I could name them I wouldn't be here asking for your help,' Dick treated the last few words to a forced smile.

'I see. We do, of course, keep a list of our customers and the equipment they have ordered but, quite frankly, I'm not in the habit of making it freely available. I presume the Ministry would pay for the information?'

'Naturally,' replied Dick, wondering if he would have to foot the bill, 'provided it was a small charge just to cover your costs.'

'Information is money Dr. England, if it would save you time in your researches then it must be worth more than just our administration costs. As a consultant your rates are probably around £20 per hour, so let's think, how long would it take you to get the data that I can provide on a few sheets of paper? Lot's of phone calls, several days work, that's going to cost someone well over £500. Tell you what, as I'm as patriotic as the next man and don't want to squeeze the old country too much, you can have the list of our customers for £200.' Director Sharp doodled on his blotting pad as he spoke.

Dick thought fast, if all this comes to nothing then England stood to be out of pocket at the end of the day, even if it did not, there could still be difficulties in extracting the money from the Industry.

'That sounds a bit steep,' he countered, but the other man remained poker faced. 'I'm not sure the budget will run to that, no one else has asked for payment, the other companies we've approached have been only too pleased to help the Government.' Sharp remained unimpressed and continued to respond to Dick with a blank stare. 'Alright,' Dick gave in. 'Invoice England and Associates, can you let me have the info now?'

'Not so fast, I want a written statement that the information supplied is for use by yourself only as part of the Government contract, that means if anyone else gets hold of it I can sue. I also want proof that you are who you say you are and that you are working for Whitehall. I suggest you get the Department to drop me a line then I'll respond with the list you require.'

'You can certainly check on my professional standing. I am well known to the Safety Departments of the various nuclear industries, I have also done contract work for other companies such as Distoil and we have been retained by two Local Authorities, I'm quite sure any of these would vouch for my integrity.'

'Splendid, I know the Safety Manager at Distoil,' Mr. Sharp paused, lifted the hand set off his phone then pressed the call button. 'Judith, get me Fred Wrightman of Distoil please,' he instructed his secretary. 'Now all I need is a note from The Department,' he concluded with a forced smile.

'I'm sorry,' Dick responded, 'but as I've explained, that is out of the question, you see the whole matter is confidential.'

'No, I don't see, if I am to trust you with information that could be very useful to our competitors then I expect you, or the Government Department for whom you claim to work, to trust me.'

'I'm afraid it's not that simple,' Dick started to flounder, but was cut short.

'It is that simple Dr. England, no letter means no information, do I make myself clear?'

'Perfectly,' Dick wondered if he could push this man into a change of mind by bluffing threats about losing Government contracts, being blacklisted and so on. He decided not to try, Mr. Sharp he assessed was not a man to be bullied and further persistence would arouse suspicions. It was, he concluded, time for withdrawal.

'Perfectly,' he repeated. 'I shall need to get the Minister's personal approval, that will take several days. It's possible he won't give it, in which case I will not trouble you again, thank you for your time.'

'You're quite welcome, now if you will excuse me I have other matters which need my attention,' Sharp said as he started to get up and show Dick to the door. At that moment the phone on his desk gave its characteristic chirrup, 'Yes Judith, well thank you for trying, no don't bother again I have a feeling that I will not need to speak to Wrightman after all.'

'Sod it, sod it,' Dick England exploded once he was back in his car, then he calmed down and picked up his RAC road atlas. 'Well maybe I can salvage something out of today.' he muttered to himself and twisted the ignition. It had just occurred to him that there were two small companies, not too far away, that made monitoring equipment. They only had a small share of the market, as they specialised mainly in custom built equipment for the AEA and BNFL, however recently, no doubt prompted by the demand that followed the Chernobyl accident, they had brought out a low cost contamination and radiation monitoring instrument. These were rather simple devices designed for the non-technical members of the public. They would be very attractive to any amateur handling illicit radioactive material. Dick knew the Managing Directors of both and felt sure they would co-operate. The first was Ionic and run by Reg Jones, who at one time had been the instrument engineer at the same station as Dick some years back. He had resigned and started his own business, Dick had been helpful to him in getting his first main contract. Ionic was located at Chelmsford and en route to the second, J.L.D. Instruments, owned and managed by John Luke Dangerfield, at Maldon. Established thirty years ago, it had originally produced specialised instruments for marine engines, it then moved into radar for small boats and, more recently, radiation detectors. Dick had got to know Dangerfield when he bought his radar set. It was one of the first J.L.D. produced and suffered teething troubles. Dick had helped sort out a minor, but irritating, fault. He reckoned that John Luke owed him a favour.

By late afternoon Dick was beginning to feel his luck was changing, as he left Maldon astern he had a list of twenty names of individuals and companies that had been supplied with alpha monitoring equipment by Ionic, he also had assurances that J.L.D. Instruments' alpha monitor was still in the development stage, the three prototypes were with the National Radiological Protection Board for preliminary evaluation. As he drove back to Woodbridge he wondered how the others had fared.

CHAPTER 9

So far things had gone well at Longsands, but by Tuesday morning problems had started to come to the fore. The previous afternoon Olive had a blazing row with John Grimley. She always thought of him as a weak character, being easily swayed by argument or threat, consequently she was taken aback with the determination he had shown in yesterday's disagreement. Notwithstanding she had won, but only by the last resort of pulling rank as leader of the project.

Grimley had wanted to make a small controlled release of plutonium, as originally agreed with Olive. However, when the time came she had second thoughts, she could accept the reasoning Grimley had put forward but, on reflection, considered the risk too great. He had dissented, claiming the chance of detection at this early stage was virtually nil, furthermore, he had pointed out, even if an increase in airborne plut were picked up, as no one was looking for stolen plut it would attract little attention. The result would be regarded as spurious and explained by cross contamination of the sample. Having been over-ruled, not by reason but by prejudice, it was an irritable and, perhaps, a careless John Grimley that set to work early on Tuesday morning. As far as Olive was concerned, her decision had been made and that was an end of the matter, now she had a more pressing problem.

*

Clive Wordman had just passed his twenty fifth birthday and was starting to make a name for himself as an unusual journalist. In fact, it was his ambition to become an entrepreneurial publisher like Robert Maxwell, now he felt he was on the road to success. For two years he had specialised in investigative journalism for a well known national newspaper and, after some revealing successes, decided to start his own monthly. A crusading style against corruption, official bungling, and political humbug soon won popularity with the general public. It was written, edited and, until a few months ago, printed by him. However, last August, with increasing circulation, he had contracted out the printing and distribution. When he first started he feared that following an initial success with easily available material he might find the going got harder as the stories he sought dried up. Much to his surprise he found the opposite. After overcoming initial difficulties such as surviving three libel suits, the public started to supply leads for him to follow.

Wordman was a thin lanky youth, still with a trace of a pimply face and shaving stubble that had not yet hardened. He wore John Lennon glasses and was usually attired in a modest sports coat and brown trousers. His hair was fair and his eyes a pale undistinguished blue. As a writer he lacked much in terms of style, but this was compensated by the intensity and accuracy of his reporting, which in turn was due to dogged and determined research. Now he felt cold and frightened as he cowered in the corner of a dark cellar under Longsands House.

'Who are you?' Olive demanded.

Wordman tried to look up at the harsh female voice that accosted him, his neck ached from the Karate chop that had come from the hand of Pete, his throat was dry with fear, he tried to croak a reply 'Clive Wordman.'

'I said who are you?' Olive repeated. 'I'm not interested in your name, I want to know about you.' The stupefied journalist tried hard to make sense of the question and work out what was wrong with his answer. The delay in his response was misinterpreted by Olive.

'Petya,' she said using his Russian name and continuing in that language, 'loosen him up a little.'

By way of reply the KGB man stepped forward, grabbed Wordman's shirt front in his left hand and drove his right fist into the journalists solar plexus. As Wordman gasped for air, pain sent tears down his cheeks, Pete then brought his knee up as hard as he could into the victims groin, released his grip on the shirt and allowed the whimpering heap to crash to the floor.

Olive gave a short sardonic smile of satisfaction, for she liked seeing men hurt, although she would prefer to have administered the pain herself. The sight of a male at her feet, groaning and clutching at his genitals to try and ease the agony, satisfied that part of her mind which had been warped by the suffering and the rape of her mother. She remembered the project and recovered her composure. Patiently she waited until Wordman's pleading eyes looked up at her.

'Now, tell me who are you? Who are you working for? Who pays you? Don't try to be foolish, my friend is an expert at persuading people to talk, his favourite trick is to insert hot needles under their finger nails...' She paused to let her words sink in. 'Well?'

'Please...please...,' muttered the terrified piece of humanity before her. 'I'll tell you everything...,' Wordman was not a man who could withstand pain or violence. Behind his typewriter he was a fearless Titan, in verbal battles he never flinched, and before the law, in court, when many a stout heart would have turned chicken, he had stood his ground with determination and confidence, but physical abuse he could not take. 'Please...no more...I'm a journalist...I...,'

'Which newspaper?' Olive snapped.

'It...it's my own...monthly...The Iconoclast...,' came the stammered reply.

'Never heard of it, you're lying.'

'No...no...please...it's only a small paper...I own it....,'

'What is it, a girlie magazine?' Olive interjected with disgust in her voice.

'No I...look into scandals...in politics and big business...I was first with the story of the share fraud in the United's takeover bid for Pier Jones Limited...surely you remember that...,'

'Hmm,' Olive hesitated, she did not pay a great deal of attention to the capitalist news, but now she thought she recalled reading something about a city takeover scandal, perhaps the man was telling the truth.

'What brought you here?' she snapped.

'I had an anonymous letter suggesting I look into the activities of Research Express...said that no one was allowed in...suspected...it was a Government base for germ warfare...so I thought I'd pay a visit.' Wordman replied with growing confidence as he regained his breath and composure.

'Your informant was wrong, this is a legitimate business in a highly competitive field, that's why we have tight security, how did you get in?'

'I've been watching for several days, seen some of you come and go. I noticed that to get in you simply went up to the gate and gave a name and a code word, then the gate opened.'

'What name and what code word?'

'I used Brine and Firewater.'

'How did you come to choose those names?'

'I overheard what someone else said.'

'You're lying,' Olive stepped forward and slapped Woodman across his face with the back of her hand. 'You couldn't have overheard, where were you hiding?'

'I...was...behind the hedge on the opposite side of the road,' Woodman sobbed and wiped his smarting face as he looked into the disbelieving eyes in front of him. 'I had a special mike with a parabolic reflector...I could hear everything that was said...'

'When?'

'Early this morning.'

'Could be the truth Olga,' Pete interjected. 'I opened up for George, well I thought it was George, at about eight.'

'How stupid of us,' Olive muttered, then returned to the questioning of the intruder. 'So what have you seen?'

'Nothing much, I looked through a crack in one of the shutters and saw a room with some chemicals and laboratory equipment, then I think something must have hit me, I don't remember...'

'He was looking into Grimley's lab,' Pete interjected.

'I didn't know what it was for...I realise now that you are legitimate, I'm sorry I intruded but I haven't discovered any secrets...I promise not to write about your operation...,' Clive Wordman pleaded like a drowning man clutching at straws.

'I could believe you,' Olive muttered aloud, she considered the situation while Wordman babbled on.

'I never break my word...no one would trust me with information if I did...I've not seen anything to report...,' Olive mulled over the problem oblivious to the journalist's words. She could release him, that would be dangerous, he had been assaulted and would most likely go to the authorities. She could keep him prisoner for the next ten days, or as long as was necessary. Suitably duped, he could be used to add credibility to the story of the bomb being made at Longsands. On the other hand she reasoned that would entail a risk, suppose he escaped? Not likely, but possible.

'Who do you work with?'

'I'm on my own for most of the time, only a printer.'

'You must have a secretary or typist?'

'A local girl comes to help me put the paper together a week before it's published, but then only if I ask her.'

'When is she next due in?'

'I haven't asked her yet, but it would not be before the end of next week.' Woodman was suspicious of this line of questioning, but in his fuddled and frightened state decided to tell the truth.

'Where do you live?'

'In a flat...,' Olive interrupted with a slap across his face as she felt he might be regaining some measure of composure.

'Don't be insolent, I'll ask once more, where do you live?'

'29a Sea Mews, Great Bentley...it's near Chelmsford...I live by myself...It's only a small flat.

'Where's your car?'

'In the sea front park at Frinton, I got a lift part way and walked the rest.'

Olive reached her decision, she turned. 'Petya,' she said speaking in Russian, 'kill him, then go and get his car and drive it into some convenient lake. We will take a chance on him not being missed for the next few days.'

'The body?' queried Pete, also speaking in Russian.

'You are due to do a mock explosion test tomorrow night in one of the old bunkers, make sure the body is close to the explosion, then when the remains are found they will think one of us had an accident.'

'Okay,' Pete moved a step towards their unwanted guest who, not having understood these words, was beginning to think his story and assurances had been accepted, he never even felt the blow that broke his neck.

'Not a word to the others about this, especially Grimley, I don't trust his nerve.' Olive instructed then added, 'I have a meeting this afternoon with the Attache, it should be our final instructions, no doubt I can leave you to clear up this mess.'

'Sure,' Peter replied, with a note of relish in his voice as Olive left the cellar and started on a repeat of her previous journey to Ipswich.

*

Tuesday was not proving to be one of Grimley's better days. In his mind he was seething at being overruled by Olive and as a result was not concentrating on his work with his usual diligence.

Yesterday's argument had cost half a day and he had not fully tested the reduction furnace. After a moments thought he had decided to go ahead, it all seemed straightforward. Now he was starting to doubt the wisdom of that decision. Inside glove box one he watched the temperature in the small muffle furnace. Once the reaction between the plutonium oxide started, he expected the temperature to rise then slowly fall as the stream of argon gas carried away the excess heat to a water cooled heat exchanger before being exhausted through the glove box filter. It was then he realised his first error, the gas supply was not turned on. With two quick paces he reached the gas cylinder and opened the valve, but in his haste the sleeve of his lab coat caught the pressure regulator which controlled the argon supply to the box itself. This caused a gas surge. The gloves inverted and blew outwards, extending into the room like giant udders, and straining at their retaining clips. He was but a split second away from disaster, in another moment the gloves would either split open or tear themselves off the ports and airborne particles of plutonium would come gushing out contaminating his entire makeshift laboratory, if not the greater part of Longsands House. Instinctively he grabbed at the rubber hose that connected the gas bottle to the glove box and pulled. At the instant the gloves were about to fail, the hose came free and gas hissed from both the cylinder and the box.

'Christ,' he muttered to himself as he relaxed. 'That was a bloody near thing.' Then he noticed the furnace thermo-couple reading as the temperature started to race upwards. Deprived of the cooling stream of argon, the inside of the muffle, together with its graphite crucible containing the mixture of magnesium and plutonium oxide, approached white heat. Desperately, he replaced the rubber hose and manipulated both the regulator and a needle valve that controlled the supply of argon to the furnace. To his great relief the temperature indicator steadied, then started to fall. He smiled, wiped the perspiration from his brow and relaxed.

'Crisis past,' he congratulated himself, then a bolt of fear shot through his stomach as he realised his second error. The water supply to the heat exchanger was off, it was ineffective and searing hot gasses were now reaching the glove box filter which was only made from paper. Had oxygen been present it would have burst into flames, the argon prevented that, instead it blackened and crumbled allowing the plutonium vapours to pass directly into the chimney and then to the outside world. He made a dive for the tap and, too late, turned it on. As the cold water hit the now red hot steel, it flashed to steam and the sudden increase in pressure blew off the exhaust hose filling the glove box with a mixture of steam and water. Grimley realised that if the water or steam reached hot metal in the furnace, there would be an explosion. He dare not turn off the water supply as the argon purge had to be cooled, there was only one viable option. He moved forward, reaching for the drain valve on the bottom of the box, he got his shoe caught in the power cable that ran across the floor to the box. It sent him sprawling, his head crashing into one of the steel supports. As he lay dazed, water started to build up inside the box and steam condensed on the cold side obscuring all vision. John's senses slowly returned and, disregarding a thumping pain, he crawled under the box, opened the drain valve and sat back while he regained his strength. The chemical reaction finished, the temperature in the furnace fell and slowly things returned to normal.

Grimley surveyed the mess. 'Well,' he muttered under his breath, 'looks like I've got my way, reckon there's been a good hefty release of plut to both the air and the drain, that old cut is going to be lousy from now on.'

After clearing up and decontaminating himself he went to report to Olive.

*

George Brine was pleased with progress and was convinced that the boat would be ready in good time. Even so he had an uneasy feeling at the back of his mind. He turned his attention to the task in hand. The injectors were now installed after their service and the engine was ready for a test run. He checked the fresh water tank of the primary cooling system, it was well topped up, glancing over the side of the boat he noted that the hose which he had rigged, from a tank of rainwater at the side of the house, to the sea water cooling inlet was still in position. Satisfied he turned the starter switch to the preheat position, counted up to sixty then moved the key to 'start'. On the third turn the engine burst into life, Brine allowed it to run for a few minutes then turned down the throttle letting the engine idle while it replaced the charge into the battery.

'Good, that's another hurdle over,' he muttered to himself as he bowed his head and stepped down into the saloon, lifted the floorboards and inspected the castor oil around the depth sounder transducer. Suddenly a piercing buzzing erupted from the direction of the cockpit and demanded his attention, it was the engine cooling water failure alarm.

'What the...?' he exclaimed as he lurched toward the companion way and grabbed the stop pull. Deprived of fuel the engine died a natural death, while Brine reached forward and turned off the control key. He glanced over the side and to his chagrin saw the end of the hose, which he had wedged into the intake, lying on the ground. The engine had run without its secondary coolant. It had only been for a few minutes, but he knew without looking that it was long enough to have destroyed the neoprene impeller in the water pump. He consulted his watch, it was already past 1500hrs, if he hurried he could just make the chandlers before they shut, on the other hand he doubted that they would carry a spare in stock, more likely than not he would have to get one from a Jabsco agent. He cursed his bad luck and started to strip down the pump.

*

It was Tuesday morning and Dick England waited anxiously for the return of his daughter and boyfriend. He poured another cup of tea and checked his watch. It had progressed only seven minutes since his last glance. He got up from the breakfast table, walked round its perimeter, crossed the floor to the window and gazed out at nothing in particular, again he checked his watch. He fidgeted, walked back round the table and across the hall into the study where he shuffled papers and tried to concentrate on other work, but to no avail. As he approached the depth of frustration the phone rang. Tingling with excitement he picked it up and growled into the mouth piece.

'England speaking.'

'England speaking,' came the mimicking reply from a female voice.

'Sal!' he exclaimed. 'Where the hell are you?'

'Cambridge, thought I ought to let you know, we'll be about an hour and three quarters.'

'Any news?'

'Yes.'

'What?'

'Rodney's got a ticket for speeding,' she teased.

'Oh Christ, nothing else?'

'Yes, tell you when we get back. Bye.'

Dick sighed, at least they had not met with an accident he contented himself as he sat down and tried to curb his impatience.

Sally was right, it did take an hour and three quarters to get from Cambridge to her home. Dick met her at the door.

'Well?' he demanded.

'Quite well thank you,' she replied with a smile.

'Oh for Christ's sake, come on you two what have you found out?'

'Quite a bit,' Rodney chipped in. 'Someone make a cup of tea and I'll tell you all about it in the conference room.'

'We'll tell you all about it,' Sally corrected him as she sidled off into the kitchen to charge up the kettle. 'Wait for me before you start,' she called out, then added almost as an afterthought, 'what about you Dad, any joy?'

'Could have, but I'm not too hopeful, all my gen is rather negative. Come on lass, leave the tea, let's get started, we're burning daylight,' Dick called back.

Sally ignored the request and kept the men waiting until she had a tray with three mugs of steaming hot tea to lay on the conference table.

'Right, you start Dad, age before beauty!'

'Well,' Dick drew breath. 'I managed to get an interview with the Sales Director of Contamination Control, thought I was doing fine but then things didn't gel and I came away empty handed.'

'Tell all,' Rodney invited, which prompted Dick to quickly run through the details of the meeting with Bill Sharp.

'Anything else, did you see any other firms?' Sally asked when her father had finished.

'Yes and I must say I managed rather more success,' Dick responded and, with a modicum of drama, dropped a sheet of paper on the table. It was the list of customers that Reg Jones of Ionic had given him. While the other two looked on bemused, Dick went on to explain that Luke Dangerfield had assured him their alpha monitoring equipment was still being developed.

Dick concluded, 'So that at least ties up all the instrument makers, assuming that you got the goods from N.I.'

'Not quite,' Sally contradicted. 'George Watts mentioned another firm, Rayfinder at Devizes.'

'Damn, well nearly all, so tell me what have you turned up?'

Sally took up the story. 'Found N.I. without any problem and George Watts was a darling, gave us a print out of all his alpha monitoring equipment customers over the past two years.' She reached down into her shoulder bag and produced a brown envelope and tossed it onto the table. 'They're in there,' she added.

'What about Labteck?' Dick asked.

'Well, I don't think Bill Child was taken in by our story. He gave us a few of his customers, but didn't tell anything we didn't already know.'

'So you drew a blank there?'

'Mmm not exactly, seemed a bit unfair that he should keep all his lovely information to himself so we did a little burglary, it...'

'You did what?' Dick exploded, looking his daughter in the face.

'It wasn't risky Dad.' Sally looked round for some assistance from her fiancee, but he was busy staring down at the table examining the micro structure in the wood grain. 'Rod was super, we simply went back at night and he picked the entrance lock. Everything else was open so we ran a photocopy of their order list, relocked the door and came home. Didn't steal a thing.'

'You did,' her father chided, although he could appreciate the motive he would not use the end to justify the means. 'You stole some sheets of copier paper and the use of the machine.'

'I did suggest we left fifty pence in payment,' Sally responded, with a wry smile, 'but Rod thought it wasn't necessary.'

Dick took the stolen sheets of paper that his prospective son-in-law had proffered and laid them on the table.

'Let's see what we've got, pass my gen from Ionic,' he indicated with a nod, 'let's put it all together.' For the next half an hour the trio grouped round the table and sifted through their papers before Dick took the lead.

'So, looks like we've got about eighty percent of all the folk who have been supplied with instruments, but only half of the glove box customers,' he paused for thought. 'Now with a bit of luck our quarry, that is if there is one, will be on both lists so for starters let's shorten up the odds and sort out the names common to both.'

'Then?' Rodney queried.

'Then,' repeated Dick, 'we simply hot foot it up to Company's House and see if they are registered, almost certainly the one we are looking for will be a fake.'

'Doubt it,' Rodney contradicted. 'Firms are careful these days who they supply on credit and they would be even more suspicious of anyone offering cash for this sort of gear. If our friends are smart, and I reckon they are, then they will already have established a legit business.'

'Yes, but it will have to have been founded or taken over in more recent times, it's not likely this venture was planned more than a year or two ago, Watersthorpe is a new establishment,' Sally pronounced. 'So we check for a new company or a takeover.'

'Not just a pretty face, as the saying goes,' Rodney muttered under his breath. 'Well let's get on with it. I'll read the glove box list if you, sweetheart, will search the instrument list.'

'Okay big boy, go ahead I'm all ears,' Sally responded.

Dick sat back and let the youngsters take charge.

'There you are, fifteen names in all,' Sally pronounced as her fiancee called out the last. 'Shouldn't take too long to check that lot.'

'That depends,' her father said with a faint smile, 'on just how soon you can shift your ass and get the next train to the smoke.'

'Aw Dad, I'm whacked out, isn't there some other way?'

'It was your idea that we started this crazy paper chase so you'll have to take the lion's share of the leg work, anyhow there are still some lines that I want to follow up with personal contacts who might just be able to help.'

'Such as?'

'Such as Alf Carter, he only retired from the A.E.A.'s Security Branch a couple of months ago.'

'How can he help?' Rodney queried.

'If I recall correctly he specialised in anti-terrorist precautions and had his finger on most of the known gangs.'

'Can you get him to intervene at Watersthorpe?' Rodney interrupted.

'No, they're not the same industry, but he too has contacts. It's just possible that he might be able to give us a lead, help check out some of those companies or even give us a contact to work with if we ever do uncover anything.'

'That shouldn't take all day, still leave you time to pop up to London,' Sally said without conviction, for she already knew her day had been decided.

'Well I can't go,' Rodney muttered. 'I must get back and tidy up some loose ends before I devote any more of my time to this caper.'

Sally drove to Ipswich, was lucky enough to find space in the car park and a train waiting to take her to London. It even made a small piece of history by arriving on time. Inwardly she smiled to herself and concluded that this was going to be her lucky day.

City Road and the offices of Company's House is only a short walk from Liverpool Street Station and Sally covered the distance with a sprightly stride, arriving just before noon. She entered the Portland stone clad building and glanced at her watch then made her way up a short flight of steps. At the barrier a man in a dark blue uniform checked her hand bag then let her pass through to the index room. As usual it was full of people of different shapes and sizes and clad in a wide variety of dress, all scanning through the microfiches. Sally found one which had just been vacated and set about her task. From her hand bag she took a small note book with the names of the fifteen companies that had been singled out for her attention, they were already in alphabetical order. At the touch of a switch the screen lit up, she rotated the knob on the left and started to scan the 'A' to 'F' indexes. Soon she located Alpha Rad Limited, the first on her list, she noted the company's number then moved on until Dingways Consultancy appeared, she noted its number. For the next twenty minutes, occasionally changing readers, she worked her way through the alphabet until all on her list had been located.

'So far, so good,' she muttered with sufficient audibility to raise the eyebrows of the city gent standing next to her.

In the corner of the room was a small office with a worn pock-marked counter fronting to the public. She picked up the requisite buff form, completed a separate one for each of the companies on her list, then handed them over to the gent in a drab dark blue suit who guarded the rear. He flicked over the corners, counting as he went, then asked for the search fee which Sally duly paid.

'Won't be ready 'til after lunch,' the ageing civil servant declared.

'That's alright, how soon after?'

'Doubt if you'll get 'em 'fore three, lucky we ain't so busy jest now or it would take a while longer.'

'Okay, I'll be back then,' Sally glanced at the wristwatch Rodney had given her on her last birthday and realised she had a couple of hours to kill.

She fed the inner person at a nearby pub, made her way down to the river and strolled along the embankment before returning. It was the same man who again examined her handbag at the barrier. She stepped in to the same corridor, but this time did not turn left, instead she carried straight on to the reading room. There she presented her receipts and a few minutes later a young girl handed over fifteen envelopes. Each contained, on micro film, the statutory returns that every company is obliged to make. These would show the names and addresses of all directors, the Balance Sheet, the date of incorporation and a host of other information which was of little interest to the lady from Woodbridge. She chose one of the several empty tables, sat down and started to feed the negatives into the reader. Twenty five minutes later she shattered the silence with a shout of 'Eureka', gathered up her papers and made off to join the rush hour which was now in its infancy.

*

While Sally was in London Dick, true to his word, was also busy. First he arranged to meet Alf Carter for a pie and a pint at the Goose and Whistle in Manningtree. Alf, also a sailing man, had a Catalac on the Crouch and lived on his own at Braintree. Dick had known him for more years than he could remember, in their younger days they had both raced the same class of dinghy and met up at open meetings. They had been arch rivals at the National Championships, but those were the days when sportsmanship in racing meant more than winning and rivals became friends. They had not seen much of each other in the last two decades, but had kept in touch with the occasional letter and Christmas card. Their last meeting had been at Mrs. England's funeral. Notwithstanding this Dick felt he would be able to trust Alf with the whole story and at the same time get some useful information.

That accomplished he settled down at his desk and started some calculations. He tried to work out how much plutonium would have to be released into the atmosphere and into the aquatic environments before detection was likely. He puzzled over the problem and in doing so digested the top inch of his pencil, he referred several times to reports and books. After an hour he turned on his personal 'micro' and programmed it with standard formula for the calculation of dispersion of aerosols. He fed in the variable data such as atmospheric stability[25], wind speed and direction and possible rainfall. The computer did the rest of the work and soon it was printing out sheets of paper with columns of figures. He reprogrammed the machine for dispersion of solutes in sea water and allowed for different conditions of wind and tide. Dick collected up the printouts and was studying them when he was interrupted by the telephone bell.

'England,' he half growled into the mouth piece.

'Hardman, Janice Hardman,' came the female reply. 'I think we may have turned up some information worth discussing, could we set up a meeting for tomorrow?'

'Sure, but I would rather leave matters until later in the week, unless you have something that solves the riddle now, how about Friday evening?'

The Health Physicist from Watersthorpe hesitated, her impatience for progress urged against delay, on the other hand there was a limit to the time she could spend away from site and while she thought they had discovered some odd coincidences, the mystery was far from solved. If Richard England wanted more time then she ought to agree.

'Well, if you really think we can afford to wait...'

'I don't think we can afford not to, unless you can get that blockhead of a Colonel to move,' Dick said interrupting what she had been saying.

'He's not a Colonel, he's a Brigadier,' she paused then added 'but I wouldn't argue with the adjective. 'fraid he still doesn't want to know.'

'With our limited resources we can't afford to go off on the wrong tack. Give me a couple of days and we should have some definite leads from this end, if we then add these to what you have, we can formulate a plan of action.'

'Okay,' Janice reluctantly agreed. 'When do we meet?'

---

[25]*This is a factor which describes the mixing in the atmosphere. Under "stable" conditions there is very little mixing and the plume, from the point of release, will be narrow and slow to dilute. If it originates from a height, such as a chimney stack, it could travel a considerable distance, perhaps a mile or more, before it comes down to ground level. This is known as the skip distance.*

The opposite applies during unstable or turbulent conditions. Here the plume is wide and rapidly dilutes. From a high level release it could reach the ground in a few hundred yards.

Stable conditions are particularly likely when atmospheric pressure is high, during the evening and early morning when there is little wind.

'Can you make my place on Friday, say seven pm?'

'Wilco, see you then,' and with that she put down the receiver.

In the afternoon Dick went out to *English Lady*, ostensively to give her a check over although he knew full well that she wanted for nothing. It was his usual way of focusing his mind on a problem. He had found from long experience that when pottering on the boat he was far from other distractions and could let his thoughts concentrate on the problem to hand. However, on this occasion there was another purpose, for somewhere at the back of his mind he had a feeling that *English Lady* was destined to be the leading lady in the drama which might unfold. It wasn't so much the boat's own equipment that concerned him, but rather the ancillary gear that she carried. He paid particular attention to the radiation monitors, for although these were limited in scope he had a hunch that they would have some role to play. He checked the portable contamination meter which could measure beta, gamma and alpha radiation against a standard uranium source and made a small adjustment to its EHT[26]. He then turned his attention to two fixed instruments which were designed for measuring radioactivity on air sample papers or swabs[27]. These would also serve to measure the radioactivity on planchets upon which he had evaporated water samples. He calibrated them against small strontium and plutonium sources. As the afternoon slipped by Dick's thoughts were on the missing plutonium. Was it really lost? Were they all on a wild goose chase? After all he knew very little about the Hardman woman, maybe she had imagined the whole thing, perhaps it was some huge practical joke. On the other hand there might be something in

---

[26]*The EHT is the electric potential applied to the sensor which detects radioactivity. Quite small changes in the EHT, such as may be caused by the battery running down, can affect the sensitivity of the instrument and it has to be regularly checked.*

[27]*Loose radioactivity, otherwise known as contamination, is assessed by wiping the suspect surface, over a standard area, with a piece of absorbent paper such as a laboratory filter paper. This is then presented to a suitable detector to measure the activity it has picked up. If the level is high, such as in a working area like John Grimley's laboratory, a portable contamination monitor would suffice. However, if only trace levels are being sought a more sensitive instrument is needed, one which has a low background.*

Airborne radioactivity is assessed by drawing a known volume of air through a filter paper and then, with a low background instrument, measuring the amount of radioactivity it has collected.

it, but who would want to steal plut and for what purpose? The most likely answer that came to mind was the I.R.A. must be involved and they hadn't realised a nuclear weapon could not be made from this grade of material. Perhaps the Irish had infiltrated Watersthorpe, was that what Janice had discovered? Maybe they ought to change their line of enquiry, anyhow it would be something to discuss with Alf Carter in the morning.

Dick spent longer than he intended on board *English Lady* and had only just got back home when he heard Sally's car come up the drive. A key turned in the latch and an over excited daughter rushed in.

'Dad,' she cried out, 'I think we've cracked it.'

'Great, tell me more.'

'Not until I've had a cuppa and something to eat,' Sally teased. 'What's in the freezer?' then before Dick could reply, added, 'anyhow I think Rodney ought to be here when I reveal all, he did a large slice of the work in getting us the gen.'

'Okay, we'll eat,' replied a stoic father.

An hour later, with the dishes stashed in the sink, the trio sat around the "conference" table. Sally produced a clutch of small brown envelopes secured with an elastic band, and her note book.

'It's all on those micros,' she said pointing to the envelopes, 'but I've extracted the info we need.' Opening the pocket size note book she continued. 'I found all the companies on our list without any difficulty and I've checked out their returns. Most have been in existence for a number of years and some have directors who are well known in society. However, there were five smallish firms that caught my eye, four of these had been incorporated in the last two years, and one taken over about nine months ago. In this latter case only one new director had joined the board so it's unlikely that there would have been the drastic change in operations necessary for the company to be used as a front.'

'Not necessarily so,' her father interrupted, 'but the odds are in favour of it being legit, I agree.'

'Good, so let's discount that one, for the time being at least,' Sally continued. 'Now of the remaining four, two have very substantial turnover and major assets, in excess of a million, probably in property, and before you interrupt again,' Sally chided her father, 'I concede that this does not guarantee they are not what we are looking for, but again it does seem less likely. Of the last two, one has employed Godman, Witt and Eversharp as auditors who, as we all know, are a very reputable firm as they also do our accounts. If we can't get an extra postage stamp past them then our "front" company would have an even harder time. On this basis we are left with only one real suspect.' Sally paused to add a little suspense, she was enjoying her star role.

'Go on,' Rodney urged.

'The last one fits like a glove. It was incorporated eighteen months ago and has, not unreasonably, filed only one return. The authorised capital is £50,000, but only £10,000 has been issued. Income for the first twelve months trading was only £5,261. The company has two directors namely, Mr. and Mrs. Smith. Mrs. Smith is also the Company Secretary. It would seem that they are the sole shareholders.'

'What's its name?' Dick asked eagerly, as excitement started to flush adrenalin into his blood.

'International Technical Enterprises,' Sally replied with a smile and continued. 'Now why would a Mr. and Mrs. Smith be trading as an international company with a turnover of five grand?'

'Where is its registered office?' Dick demanded.

'You'll not believe this, it's at Port Bannatyne.'

'Where the Hell's that?'

'Come on Dad, you should remember, where you fell out of the dinghy a couple of years ago.'

Dick looked puzzled for a few moments then slowly a picture developed in his memory, it was one of those incidents he would rather have forgotten, but folk would just not let it rest.

'What! You mean when we took *E.L.* up the West Coast of Scotland in the wettest Summer on record?'

'If I remember correctly,' his daughter teased, 'you'd had too many glasses of wine and tripped over a fender as you were stepping down into the tender. If it hadn't been for Rodney I would have been an orphan.'

'But wasn't that on Bute?'

'Right, Kames Bay, not quite the loneliest spot in the world, but the sheep probably outnumber the humans.'

'There's Rothesay a couple of miles away, but little else. I seem to recall that the word "port" was something of a misnomer for a jetty, a post office and a church.'

'The address is Brea Lodge, Craigmaleish, Port Bannatyne, Nr. Rothesay, Isle of Bute.'

'That's got to be a non-starter, sweetheart,' Rodney interjected, 'why would anyone in their right mind want to take stolen plut to such a god forsaken spot. It doesn't make sense.'

'Agreed,' Dick added his support. 'Looks like you've not done such a good job after all.'

'You two thickies have forgotten something haven't you?' Sally smiled as she addressed the men. 'You've forgotten that there are two nuclear submarine bases only a few miles away.'

'So?' they chorused, almost in harmony.

'Oh come on, motive? You want to scupper plans for Trident or disrupt NATO or something like that. Stage a big leak of plutonium or even a small nuclear explosion and everything goes into turmoil.'

'Good God!' Dick recoiled. 'You might just be right.'

'If I am,' Sally continued, 'we don't have any time to spare. Wonder what they are planning, probably a fairly big conventional explosion on or near one of the subs together with a release of plutonium oxide. Simple really, just wrap the plutonium round some semtex or something like that...devise a means of delivery...shall we say a radio controlled model airplane and...its all happened.'

'Then why the instrument and glove box?' her father queried.

'Mmm...they couldn't be sure the missing plut wouldn't be discovered so they wouldn't want a trail leading back to Bute, especially after the release. They would need all the usual safety facilities to contain the radioactivity while they prepared their device, then they would have to remove all the tell tale evidence before the attack was launched,' Sally suggested.

'Okay, for the want of something better, let's accept your theory,' Dick tugged at the lobe of his ear as he thought aloud. 'If the last batch of plut to go missing was, say, a couple of weeks ago, then they must be damn near ready to strike. Possibly already disposed of the glove box. Might just be in time though...' Dick paused then continued, 'If I remember correctly there are two ferry routes, one from somewhere just south of Gourock direct to Rothesay, the other across the narrows at the north end of the Kyles, that would be a hell of a way round. Think we'd better fly up to Glasgow first thing in the morning, hire a car and make for Bute the best way we can. Bit far to take *English Lady* at such short notice,' Dick added with a faint smile.

'You can't come Dad,' Sally reminded him. 'You've got an appointment to see Alf Carter in the morning, looks like another job for Rod and me, whacko!'

'Shit!' her father exclaimed. 'I'd forgotten that. Still might not be a bad thing. I think I'll put our, or should I say your, theory to Alf, if he has any snippets that tally no doubt he will put a word in the right place and we might get the cavalry after all.'

CHAPTER 10

Unusually, this Wednesday morning the quartet at Longsands House all came together for breakfast, Olive used the opportunity to review their programme. She was perturbed at yesterdays events and concerned that they might involve unacceptable delays.

'Now you've had time to sort out the mess, how much time have we lost?' She shot the question at John Grimley.

'Maybe a day, but it doesn't make any difference, we have plenty of time in hand.'

'What else has to be done?'

'Not a lot, I've salvaged some metallic plutonium and I ought to have enough to turn a bit in the lathe. Only need to leave behind the traces of a few turnings to make it look as if we converted all the stuff into metal for the bomb. I've still got to make some N.G. or T.N.T. so that it will look as if we made our own explosive. That could take a day, or maybe two, but some of this time would be concurrent with the work on the metal so it's two, maybe three days.'

'What about packaging?' Brine asked.

'Pretty well any time once I'm sure I don't need to do any more reductions but as you know I'm waiting for you to provide the the container for fixing to the keel.'

'We're due to meet up with Mother in the early hours of Friday, a week Friday,' Olive clarified. 'That, according to George, means leaving midday on the Wednesday to get maximum depth in the creek.'

'It's not absolutely essential, we could go out in the early hours of Thursday morning and still make the rendezvous, but it would be tight and mean getting through Horsenose and the Walton channel in the dark. Both are unlit,' the *Surfmaster*'s skipper added, then continued, 'the fixings should be delivered on Saturday or first thing on Monday. I am sure the boat will handle okay, but I would like to try it out before we attempt the crossing. Depending on when the straps arrive, I would launch on Sunday or Monday and have a days sailing out at sea. Even if we don't go out 'til Monday, we can come back at midday Tuesday, lift out, load the plut into the cylinder and relaunch in time for the Wednesday tide. Only the weather can stop us and that is not likely.'

'Have you got a direct line to God?' Grimley queried with a touch of scorn.

'Not quite,' Brine replied, 'but I have spoken to the forecasters at the Norwich Weather Centre, they expect this ridge of high pressure to build for a few days then start to weaken by the end of the week.'

'What's that mean?' Olive asked.

'Winds going east to north east for the next few days, probably up to six or even seven during the day and dropping off at night. However, if the Met fellow's crystal ball is reliable, which it often isn't, the wind will move to the south west. An easterly or north easterly would be on the nose and is no use to us, we would have to motor. However, when it goes to the west it would push us in the direction we want to go. Strength depends on how the depression grows, but we should get a day or two before it freshens to a six and that would do us fine.'

'Did you get the chart you needed, and what about the water pump thing that you smashed up yesterday?' Olive enquired.

'Charts still a problem, I'm going to try on Friday but if it's not in then I'll take up their offer of copying in the corrections that are likely to affect us, I presume the ground zero is still the same?' George Brine looked across at Olive who nodded before he continued, 'as far as the water pump impeller is concerned the local chandlers did not have one in stock, but there is one in the post. See no reason why it should not be here by Thursday or Friday and it's only a half hour job to fit.'

'Good,' Olive remarked then turned to Pete and asked, 'What about security, everything still quiet?'

'Sure, no problems,' he lied then continued, 'everything is rigged for the first test explosion tonight, so don't anyone go near the bunker, don't want to find I've blasted a body as well do we?' he warned while inwardly laughing at the irony of his comment.

*

Dick England bade goodbye to his daughter and Rodney a couple of hours before the meeting at Longsands had taken place. They drove to Stansted and caught the early morning flight to Glasgow. By the time most working people were signing in at their offices, the two were already speeding in a hired car towards the Bute ferry.

In contrast Dick had a more leisurely day. He pottered until eleven then drove over to Manningtree and, after a quick shop for essential supplies, settled in a corner of the lounge bar at the "Goose and Whistle". It was an old pub with original oak beams. The tastefully fitted lounge had reproduction chairs and small tables along the walls. From speakers came soft tunes of years ago. Dick bought a pint of shandy then settled in a corner to wait for Alf Carter. He wondered how the other two were making out, could the lonely house on the Scottish Isle really be the object of their quest?

'How's that old lump of concrete which poses as a boat?' Alf Carter's leg pull interrupted his thoughts.

'Better than your box on legs that pretends to be a boat,' he retaliated with a smile. 'Good to see you Alf.'

The two men shook hands, wandered over to the bar, ordered food and then returned to the table with full glasses.

'Well Blighty, what's all this cloak and dagger stuff about? Thought I'd retired from all that?'

Dick told the whole story, starting with the first phone call from Janice Hardman and concluding with his daughter's current dash to Scotland.

'At the moment this is absolutely confidential, not a word to anyone, and I do mean anyone, this is just between the two of us.'

'Sure, I've been keeping secrets all my life, you don't have to worry on that score.'

'I know Alf, but I just wanted to make sure you were aware just how delicate this matter is. Not from my point so much, but at least one person has put her career in jeopardy by coming to me.'

For most of the story Alf had stared at the ceiling, now he lowered his head and looked his old friend in the face.

'Thought it must be serious when you didn't ask about last year's cruise,' he said with a grin. 'Well let's see what I can do to help.' He paused again to collect his words, 'Those directors of International Enterprises, Smith you said was their names, could be a couple from Aldermaston who retired about two years ago. If so, she's a chemist and he's a physicist. They were at A.W.R.E. for years, met them several times and as far as I am aware there was never any doubts over them from the security angle. Quite a few of the older hands took early retirement when it was offered in the mid 1980's, they were among the last to leave. I had heard they'd moved to Scotland, but that's all. Both were keen sailors so I wouldn't be surprised if they had settled on an island. However, people like that always have tabs kept on them so I ought to be able to get an authoritative opinion when I get back.' Alf took another sip from his glass and continued. 'I'm still in touch with my old department, keep my eyes open for them and usually know the general picture. As far as I am aware there are no amber warnings out...'

'What's that?' Dick interrupted.

'Oh sorry, well if the Special Branch mob get wind of any possible terrorist antics they put out general warnings to all the usual targets, our industry in particular. Amber is the lowest level, usually means that some unusual activity has been noted, you know the sort of thing, suspects travelling around, increase in telephone calls and other symptoms that I won't go into. When it's more definite, and they feel that some form of attack is imminent, they give us a red warning. It means going into maximum security. Anyhow, as I said, at the moment all is normal. Furthermore, since Gorby has been smoking the peace pipe, activity from the Ruskie agents is minimal, though a couple of Spetsnaz have been eyeballed making their way to Harwich. Could be returning home as the latest policy seems to be to pull them back in case they rock the new diplomatic applecart!' Alf paused again, but Dick did not speak so he continued, 'Of course there could be a group going to war that we don't know about, sometimes happens but usually we get wind of an operation.' He paused again as the barmaid brought the plated meals and set them on the table.

'Two cheese ploughmans,' she said, stating the obvious, before returning to the bar.

'I think this young girl from Watersthorpe may have you on a wild goose chase,' he carried on, 'but one thing thirty years in security has taught me is never neglect a lead no matter how unlikely it seems. If it's okay by you I'll have a word with my old oppo whose responsible for security there, he might be able to lean on this Whatley-Jones chap.'

'Have a word with him by all means, but no names and don't take it any further just yet, at least not without Janice's agreement.' Dick cautioned.

'As you say, I'll also follow up the Smith's, but I don't really think there's anything there. Incidentally did you get caught out in the eight last August? Came up quite sudden, took the forecasters by surprise let alone us poor yachties.' The conversation turned to boats. They finished eating then went their separate ways.

*

Dick was starting to do his nightly rounds, the doors were locked and the lights out when the phone interrupted his routine.

'Hi Dad, Sal here,' said the voice he knew so well.

'Where are you?'

'Clansman and Sword, Glasgow. Mission complete, but we've drawn a blank. Nothing up here.'

'Oh no, tell me more.'

'I think the details had better wait 'til we get home, but thought you ought to know that as far as we can see our suspicions are unfounded, looks as if we're on the wrong trail.' Dick sighed and his daughter continued. 'Think we ought to have a war council meeting as soon as we get back. Will get the morning flight so it'll be lunch by the time we're home. Do you think you could get Janice Hardman down for a two thirty chin wag tomorrow?'

'I'll try. I'll try,' said Dick, trying to conquer a feeling of disappointment and despair.

CHAPTER 11

More than a thousand miles from Longsands House, in a small Latvian harbour, Captain Petricoff was in the throes of the final preparations for his mission. It was Thursday morning and his instructions were to meet up with a small yacht, in the middle of the North Sea, in the early hours of a day yet to be named, but not likely to be more than a week away. At a pinch he could squeeze 12 knots out of the old converted coaster which now flew the Panamanian flag, but he preferred to cruise at a more comfortable speed. With an anticipated 9 knots the trip would take a little under five days, so a midnight departure would leave time in hand. The *Gulf Queen*, for that was the fictitious name painted on her stern, had a complement of nine. There were four ordinary seamen, an officer engineer, a first officer to assist with navigation, two KGB guard marshals and himself who was not only a Master Seaman with a skipper's ticket, but also a Captain in the KGB. He was the only one of the group committed to the conspiracy. Petricoff tall, bull-necked and well built showed the strain of serving the State throughout his working life. He looked considerably older than his 52 years. Alone he knew the purpose of what lay ahead, but had no doubts that his fellow KGB subordinates would obey commands ruthlessly without question. The others were loyal hand picked members of the Party. He felt no compunction that all of them would be sacrificed when the time came.

The *Gulf Queen* had been built just before the outbreak of World War II, mainly for Baltic trading with occasional crossings to Britain or longer trips along the French and Belgium coasts. She sat low in the water and this made her an ideal convert for the spying purpose in which she had indulged in the 1950's. Her original steel bridge had been replaced by a wooden one with a lowered profile which made her more difficult to see on the radars in use during that time. Her inside had been gutted and filled with electronic eavesdropping equipment which was, at its time of installation, the most advanced in the world. Amidships a platform had been built on top of the original hold covers, it was large enough to accept a small helicopter. In the bow and stern and at a few other places, stubs of tubes protruded through the deck. These housed giant hundred foot, hydraulically operated telescopic aerials. Her real name was *Moscow Star* and she was registered as a research vessel belonging to the hydrographic division of the Russian navy. For the last ten years she had lain neglected and stripped of equipment, but over the past months, since Captain Petricoff had found her, she had been brought to a state of seaworthiness. The engines were overhauled and run up, lights, navigational aids and radio brought up to acceptable standards and below decks crew accommodation had been cleaned and modestly refurbished. A quick coat of paint covered most of her rust stains so that she appeared neither flash nor neglected, just average. Finally she had been given the mythical name of *Gulf Queen*.

As he lounged in the seat behind the chart table on the starboard side of the bridge awaiting the delivery of the final piece of the ship's last cargo, Captain Petricoff ran through the strategy for the next few days. They would slip out in darkness and, keeping in the middle of the Baltic Sea, head south, then east and finally north past Copenhagen and through the narrows at Helsingor where "Hamlet's Castle" commands the straits separating Denmark from Sweden. This would be the worst part of the trip for it would mean the ship was within territorial waters of a foreign power. At all other times the *Gulf Queen* would be unassailable on the high seas. It was the one time he might be required to use VHF radio or have his ship identified. He reckoned to cover the four hundred and fifty miles to the narrows in two days and so take them in the early hours of Sunday morning. After that it would be a matter of keeping a low profile through the Kattegat and Skagerak then into the North Sea. There he would kill time keeping a days sail away from the rendezvous until final date was given by radio. The message would come by VHF from a shadowing submarine and to anyone who overheard the conversation it would sound as if two fishing boat skippers were arranging a get together ashore. Using the Kiel Canal was out of the question for it would leave a permanent record of the ship's passage. The weather forecast for the next seven days lay in front of him, it looked promising although there was a small question mark over a depression developing in the West Atlantic.

The noise of a diesel engine interrupted his thoughts, he got up from the battered wooden armchair and looked out of the side window. On the quay, just aft of the for'ard mooring line, an army truck had pulled up. He saw the driver get out and approach his ship.

'You are on time comrade,' the Captain called out as he came down the ladder from the bridge, 'you had no problems?'

'None Captain Petricoff, I have your sonar tube in the back of the lorry, it is surprisingly heavy. Can your men help lift it on board?' He need not have asked for the two KGB marshals were already conscripting a further two members of the crew to lend their muscle power. Petricoff watched as the six foot long wooden crate, which held not a sonar tube but a tactical nuclear weapon, was carried on board.

'So the General has kept his word,' he muttered to himself. 'Careful how you handle that gear,' he called to the quartet below, 'there's a special rack for it amidships, starboard side, main hold. Leave it crated.'

*

Sally and Rodney's flight from Glasgow to Stansted was on time but from there onwards things started to go wrong. A traffic accident on the A120 completely blocked the road just east of Great Dunmow, the resulting tailback cost them the best part of an hour. Further time was lost with repair work on the A12 south of Ipswich and as a result they arrived home just as Janice Hardman was pressing the front door bell of the England's abode.

'Well timed,' Dick greeted the trio, 'don't just stand there come on in there's work to be done.'

'Hang on Dad,' Sally urged. 'Rod and I haven't eaten for hours, I'm busting for the loo and I guess Jan needs a cuppa.'

'Can't wait, we're burning daylight,' Dick responded with a smile. 'You know where the bog is, there are sandwiches, tea and coffee all on the conference table so let's get cracking.'

Sally sighed and nodded agreement, Rodney smiled and Janice grinned. The group got down to work.

Dick outlined the happenings since they were last together including his chat with Alf Carter.

'Right Sal, what's your side of the story?' he asked.

'As I said over the phone we drew a blank,' his daughter responded and continued. 'No real problem getting to Bute, hired a car and drove to the ferry and that dropped us in Rothesay. Short drive to Kames Bay where we found a pub and dropped in for a spot of lunch. Must have been our lucky day, Rod went to the bar to top up the glasses and chatted up one of the locals, it turned out to be none other than a Mr. Smith, a common name in England but not on Bute, so he brought him over to our table and started talking boats. This fellow was also a keen sailor. From there it was easy to get the conversation on to the Holy Loch, nuclear weapons and radiation. Soon he was telling us about retiring from Aldermaston and his unusual hobby and business. The hobby was collecting radioactive pottery, you know the bright yellow and orange stuff painted with uranium.' Dick and Janice nodded and Sally continued. 'The business was repairing old instruments, particularly those from W.W.2. aircraft. Seems nobody wants to touch them with two barge poles tied together as they are lousy with radium from the luminous paint. Oddly enough he doesn't have to register under the Radioactive Substances Act as, being instruments, they are exempt! However, he has enough sense to do most of the work in a glove box and uses both beta and alpha monitoring instruments.'

'Good story, a cover story?' Janice Hardman asked.

'No way,' Rodney responded. 'Once he discovered that Sally was a health physicist, he took us up to the house and showed all. Even introduced his charming wife.'

'Well at least that is consistent with what Alf told me,' Dick muttered. 'So what now?'

'What we have done,' Rodney started to review the logic of their past thinking, 'is to search through the firms that were common to both lists, but as you said earlier Dick, we only got eighty percent of the instrument buyers and half the glove box customers. The odds are surely on the firm we are looking for being only on one list not both,' he emphasised the "one" and continued with a forced grin. 'What we need to do is check out all the firms on each list, except those that we have already done.'

'Christ love, that must be dozens. I suppose I've got to go back to the smoke again?' Sally said with a note of resignation in her voice.

'Could be,' Dick cut into the conversation, 'but let us hear what Janice has to tell, things can only get better. What's burning a hole in that briefcase?' he asked the lady from Watersthorpe.

She plunged straight in. 'I'm pretty sure now that we are on to something big, but I've not got enough to make the Brig act so we are still on our own.' She reached for the briefcase to which Dick had referred, flipped open the fasteners and took out several sheets of paper. She glanced at them as she spoke. 'We have only used our new instrument on about half the store and out of those checked we found eleven that could be light, when I say light I don't mean light in weight, but short on plut.'

'Understood,' Dick interrupted.

'Two of those, namely numbers AJ/50/64 and AZ/38/79 are marginal. The remaining nine give a strong indication of missing a few hundred grams.'

Dick interrupted with a low whistle.

'You realise that in trying to assess how much material is missing we are, in effect, looking for a straw lost from a haystack so these estimates could be out by a bundle. However, both Graham Kindale and I are convinced that there is some missing so...'

'Who's he?' Rodney questioned.

'My assistant, and a first class health physicist at that,' Janice responded with barely a pause in her stride. 'So the doubt is only one of how much.' She referred to her papers then went on. 'These eleven containers appear to have no common history, they have been handled by different people while at Watersthorpe. Had they been short on arrival it would have been discovered by the assay labs.' She paused to let Dick groan and Rodney exchange a glance with Sally, then continued with a triumphant smile. 'There is one possible exception, the assay labs themselves. Eight out of the eleven all passed through the same lab! Of the remaining three, two are the dubious ones.'

'What about the third?' Dick cut in thinking that if this could not be explained the lab link was barely worth a follow up.

'That's the odd man out I can't explain, unless we assume it to be a spurious result maybe a misreading or a wrong number recorded.'

'Sorry, won't do Jan. We have to explain all the results or they could all be regarded as erroneous,' Dick responded.

'Not quite,' Janice argued. 'There are four assay labs. On a random basis we would expect each lab to have handled two, three or four of the suspect containers. As it is one lab has done eight and the other one. It must be significant.'

'Labs don't steal plutonium,' Sally observed, then added as an after thought, 'but I suppose they could lose it through faulty equipment. Maybe there is not a thief after all, just bad equipment.'

'No way could this quantity be lost accidentally. If you saw the process you would agree it was just not possible.'

'Well, in that case,' Sally persisted, 'it must be that there are two plutonium stealers at work or,' she hesitated thinking aloud, 'or one which switches labs. Is that likely?'

For a few moments there was silence as the significance of her logic dawned on the other three. Janice consulted her notes then looked up with a smile.

'Sally you're a genius. The eight suspects were assayed by lab L-05, the ninth by L-07 but at the time it was done the normal supervisor for L-07 must have been on leave for the completion sheet is signed by the supervisor from L-05. In other words all the nine suspects were processed under the same Technical Officer!'

'Who?' Dick curtly demanded.

'A fellow called John Grimley.'

'What do you know about him?'

'Not a lot, funny sort of chap, keeps himself to himself but I've no reason to doubt his competence. Been with the industry for years. As far as I can remember there has never been any problems with his lab, you know, no spills or cases of contam.'

'What about his politics?' Dick asked as he continued the questioning.

'I honestly don't think he has any or if he does he never gave them voice. I suppose that is a bit odd come to think of it,' Janice concluded.

'I think someone ought to talk to your Mr. G. a.s.a.p.' Rodney cut in. 'Now who would be the best candidate?'

'Not you,' Sally remarked then added, 'unless we want to put him through the third degree.'

'I could,' Janice volunteered, 'but what line would I take?' She paused. 'Come to think of it I haven't seen him around for a few days, hope he's not on leave.'

'Can you find out?' Dick cut in.

'No problem, lend me your phone, I'll give young Graham a ring.'

Dick nodded and Janice left the table and slipped out into the hall.

'This looks promising, what else can we do?' Dick assumed the role of chairman again.

'Better go back to those lists and see if we can uncover the other end of the trail,' Rodney remarked. 'Tell you something though, I'm beginning to think that this lass from Watersthorpe is on to something. I reckon the wild goose chase is over and this is for real.'

'If you mean we start to check out all the firms on our lists, that's one hell of a job,' Sally responded, 'unless we employed a team of professionals it would take weeks and we probably don't...' Her voice trailed off as Janice re-entered the room.

'Graham confirmed that he hadn't seen Grimley all this week so he's going to check. Will phone back in a few minutes.'

'If he is on extended leave,' Dick mused aloud, 'then it could mean we are approaching the climax,' he paused again, tugged at the lobe of his ear and continued, 'in which case we don't have time to work through all those names on the companies list, somehow we just have to make an intelligent guess and get it right first time.'

The other three nodded in agreement and remained silent as they thought around a problem which seemed insoluble. The sound of the telephone brought them back to life.

'I'll get it,' Janice volunteered. 'It'll be Kindale with gen on Grimley.' Again she left the room, then called from the hall way, 'It's for you Dick.'

Richard Harry England wore the grin of a Cheshire cat as he returned from the phone.

'That my friends,' he announced with all the drama of Hercule Poirot, 'that was one of the Health Physicists from Layness. It seems they took in some of their taky-shades late Tuesday afternoon, ran through the prelims yesterday and did the alpha counts this morning, one of them was high, well above normal background.'

'Maybe there had been some release from the station,' Rodney innocently cut in.

'No way, first of all it would probably take a core melt down before any alpha escaped and that certainly hasn't happened, secondly it was one of the controls.'

'What's that mean?' Rodney asked.

'The controls are situated about twenty miles from the site and provide a yardstick against which to measure the background. If the station were to release airborne contamination then the shades nearest the site would pick up the most radioactivity and those furthest away significantly less, by the time you've gone twenty miles the plume would be pretty dilute and the shades would probably not show anything above background. On the other hand if it were due to a passing cloud of radioactivity, such as came from Chernobyl, then all the shades would show roughly the same increase. There are only two possible explanations for one lonesome shade to be high, either the result is spurious, perhaps a bit of cross contamination in the handling process or an error in the lab, or...' Dick paused, 'or there has been a release local to that shade.'

'Do we know that this is not spurious?' Janice asked.

'Not for sure, they're pulling in the backup and other adjacent shades tomorrow. They've also been in touch with Chapel Creek who are pushing their shades through, but nothing unusual yet. Their respective controls almost overlap in the area this high appeared.'

'Where was this shade?' Sally queried.

'Near Wix, that's just south of the Stour. Let's have a look at our list of firms again, any in the...' the phone interrupted. 'Okay, I'll get it. Probably Layness with some more gen.'

'It's for you-hoo Jan,' Dick called from the other side of the door, passing Janice. 'As I was saying...'

'Don't bother Dad,' Sally responded, 'we did a quick scan while you were playing page boy. There's one in Norfolk near Aylesham on the glove box list and one at Raleigh, two near Cambridge and...' Sally paused for dramatic effect, 'and one near Walton at a place called Longsands House that have been buying instruments.'

'Ye gods, ye gods!' Dick exclaimed. 'I think we've got it. Layness told me that they change their taky-shades every month, but not all at once, they are staggered so that adjacent sectors are done on consecutive fortnights. If this is a real pick up then the odds are that it happened in the last two weeks and if you recall the weather we've been having it's been an easterly for part of that time especially in the last few days. The Walton area is pretty well due east of Wix!'

'Sounds too good to be true,' Rodney commented.

'What is?' Janice enquired as she returned and then without waiting for a reply continued. 'That was Graham Kindale, he's checked up on Grimley, seems he's booked out for four weeks, starting last Saturday. He's making enquiries in case anyone knows where he's gone. Apparently had a bit of an argument with the Brigadier, his secretary heard him say something about a 'once in a lifetime opportunity'. Now what conclusions have you reached while my back was turned?'

As Dick finished briefing Janice, Sally looked up from a map she had been studying.

'I've got it Dad, Longsands House is on the Walton Backwaters, just off Hamford Water.'

'What's the name of this company?' Rodney queried. 'I'll make some enquiries?'

'Research Express Limited, that's all we've got.'

'Hold on, hold on,' Dick again took charge of the meeting. 'Let's not all go off at a tangent, we've got to think this through carefully. We are only four in number, time is short and our funds are non existent. We might even be chasing another red herring, but somehow I don't think so. The important thing is we must not cock things up, there will not be another chance.'

'We've got to reccy the House,' Rodney commented, breaking a two minute pause during which each of the quartet had been turning over the problem in their own minds. 'It's a bit late now, so I'll call round first thing in the morning and do my cold canvas insurance salesman act. Once inside I'll have a snoop, find out who runs things then report back.' He shot a glance at Janice, 'What's the Grimley guy look like, might as well know if I meet him?'

'This Longsands,' Dick asked before Janice had time to respond, 'you say it's just off Hamford Water so,' he allowed a short pause, 'so if we took *English Lady* we could also suss it out from the shore, a sort of pincer movement.' He looked at his watch, 'If we slip down River this evening, let go the hook just behind the Horse, then make an early start tomorrow we can be inside the Walton channel for breakfast.' He paused again, tugged at the lobe of his ear and looked towards Janice, 'This ought to be your party too, care to play truant from the old firm and join us for a day or two on the boat?'

'You bet, Hardman started this and Hardman intends to stay with it. I'll get Kindale to cover for me, think it'll have to be something more than a headache this time!'

'What about Rod?' Sally asked.

'No problem, pick him up at Titchmarsh[28] about lunch time,' her father responded.

'Okay by me,' Rodney confirmed. 'Anything else to do in the meantime?'

'I think I'll get on to Alf Carter and put him in the picture. It's as well to keep him primed, if we do need the Fuzz or outside help then he can probably get things moving faster than your Major...'

'Brigadier!'

'I'll also give Chapel Creek a call before they go home for the day and see if they've any alpha in their D.S. samples...'

---

[28] *A yacht marina near Walton on the Naze, Essex.*

'Ask them to take a close look at their sea water samples as well, the Blackwater is only just round the corner.'

At 0530hrs the next morning the sun had risen into a hazy sky and the skipper roused his female crew with a cup of tea.

'Grab a plate of cereal,' he told them, 'then we'll push off. Should make Pye End[29] well before the ebb.'

They did, it was an uneventful trip mainly accomplished under motor through lack of wind at that early hour. Dick was impressed by the way Janice quickly settled into ship routine even on such a short trip, in fact she had been the first to spot the small red and white buoy, which is never easy to see. They counted off the red and green cans and then bore away to starboard into Hamford Water. Just before 0800hrs their hook went down into the mud south west of the entrance to Horsenose Creek.

'That should do fine,' Dick remarked. 'Don't want to get too close, we could have gone into the Creek a cable[30] or two, but that might have got us noticed.'

'But we can't see much from here,' Janice protested. 'What next? Shall I lower the rubber duck and take it up Horsenose for a reccy while there is still water?'

'No!' Dick responded surprised that she had not only dropped into the yachtsman's slang for inflatable dinghy, but also shown an appreciation of tides. For someone who had only a little sailing experience she was adapting remarkably well. 'No,' he repeated, 'remember we are just out for an early season potter around the old haunts. The state of the tide will explain our arrival at this time, but we would be pushing our luck in going unnoticed if the next thing we do is to leap into a dinghy and go charging up the Creek. We'll take our time over a belated breakfast then discover halyard trouble at the top of the mast. You and I can haul Sal aloft and with the small bins she should be able to see quite a bit of Longsands House.'

'Then?'

---

[29]*Pye End is the name of the navigational buoy which marks the beginning of the Walton Channel and the end of the Pye Sand spit approximately a mile South of the entrance to Harwich.*

[30]*Cable is a nautical unit of distance equal to about 200 yards.*

'We take the tender down Kirby Creek, across the Wade and into the Twizzle, meet Rodney at Titchmarsh.'

'Will there be water over the Wade?' Sally asked.

'Should be enough for the rubber duck if we don't leave it too late, but we'll have to come back through the Walton Channel as it will be dead low by then.'

*

The arrival of *English Lady* had not gone unnoticed. Pete, on his early morning rounds, was scanning the perimeter wire when his eye was drawn to the top of a mast gliding along beyond the embankment at the start of the saltings. It did not cause him any alarm, in the summer there were always boats anchored there but, he mused, this must be one of the early birds. Nevertheless he resolved to keep his eye on it. After the affair with the reporter his naturally suspicious mind had been further sharpened. He continued on his way.

It was during the morning break that Olive gave the news to the others. 'I have just heard from our friends, confirming that 'Mother' departed last night, on schedule and everything is going to plan.'

'Where did she leave from?' George Brine shot the question.

'That is not our business, you know the rules George, information is available on a need to know basis only.'

'Well it would be useful if I did know, after all I've got to navigate to the meeting place and to estimate how long she will take, I have to know her departure point.'

'Not so my friend, I have no doubt there is time in hand just in case you foul up the engine again,' Olive responded with a smile. 'So long as we make the rendezvous when we are told that is all that matters. Today is Friday, we should plan to leave on our mission next Wednesday.'

'No problem as far as I am concerned,' John Grimley announced. 'All my essential work is done, a few more days to tie up some loose ends would be useful, could even make the weekend if pushed.'

'Good,' Olive remarked with a patronising note in her voice 'but things will not be pushed, that is how mistakes are made, we will keep to our original timetable. How is the boat George?'

'Oh fine,' responded the bearded skipper. 'Just fine, water pump repaired, reckon we could launch anytime but we are held up on two counts.'

'Yes?'

'The underwater casing that fits on the keel to carry the plut on the outward trip hasn't arrived and neither has the chart I wanted.'

'Mmm...' Olive looked thoughtful then continued, 'we could just pack the plut on board, it's very unlikely the Customs would stop us on an outward trip and you have said you could get by with the old chart, still...I'd be happier with the plut under the keel.'

'Don't worry Olive, the casing will be delivered Monday morning. With luck that still gives us time for a test sail.'

'I'm not worried, but..., her attention was caught by Pete's eyes and she knew he had something to say but not in front of the others. '...but we do not depend on luck,' she concluded forcing a smile. 'Pete, can you give me a hand for a minute?' she added as she walked away. 'What is it?' she asked her loyal henchman as soon as they were out of earshot of the other two.

'We had a yacht anchor off the end of the Creek, came in this morning.'

'So?'

'It was common last season, but it is early for visitors to come on a Friday morning. This time of year we would only expect weekenders, they would arrive in the evening or on Saturday.'

'This must be an exception, I am pleased you are so observant but do not get paranoid. Is that all?'

'No. I have kept it under observation from the attic window, an hour or so after they anchored someone went up to the top of the mast.'

'That is not uncommon on boats,' Olive suggested. 'I saw it happen several times during last summer, it seems that the ropes sometimes get caught up.'

'You do not need binoculars to free a jammed rope,' he responded. 'Whoever was up that mast had glasses and they were trained on us!'

Olive caught her breath.

'That is unusual, I am glad you told me. You know there is an English saying, I think it comes from one of the James Bond books, one is happen-chance, two is coincidence, but three times means enemy action!'

'But this is only once...'

'Not quite, we had an uninvited caller this morning, must have been when you were in the attic. I did not let him in, but he was so insistent that I had to go down to the gate and see him. Said he was trying to sell insurance, but somehow I had my doubts. He was far too interested in what we were doing. It did not strike me at the time, but afterwards, from the way he spoke, I got the impression he knew we had radioactive material.' Pete let out a low whistle and Olive continued. 'Including the reporter we now have three occurrences, I think we need to be extra vigilant.'

'I'm always vigilant. You don't think we have a traitor in our team?' Pete shot the question to Olive.

'No, but I am not happy about Grimley, I think he is a bit soft and does not appreciate the full importance of this mission. Keep an eye on him,' she instructed.

'Do not worry, I will!'

*

As arranged, Rodney met the others from *English Lady* on the hard at Titchmarsh. They strolled over to a nearby grass bank which overlooked the basin of the marina and settled down for a chat.

'Well?' Dick England asked his prospective son-in-law.

'Not much to tell. Called at the gate, no one mans it, you call on a phone. After some hard pushing on my part a woman walked down the long drive and talked to me through the bars. Bit like being at the zoo except I wasn't sure who was feedin' who. Tried the old insurance angle and gave her one of my cards, but it cut no ice. However, I thought I detected a reaction, which she quickly stifled, when I mentioned that we offered cover against accidental spillage of radioactivity. But then she assured me that there was no radioactive material on the site.'

'Now why would a firm that doesn't handle radioactivity buy alpha monitoring instruments?' Sally mused.

'That's what I thought, but I daren't push the questioning.'

'Anything else?' Janice asked.

'Yes, I've never seen such security at a non military establishment, come to think of it there are not many of them that could match up to Longsands House. The wire fence was topped with barbed wire and also fitted with trembler alarms. Any attempts to scale or cut it would be instantly detected. The site appeared to be bounded by a creek or stream on either flank. The fence followed these as well. What about you?'

'They hauled me to the top of the mast,' Sally took up the story with excitement. 'There was a large house, as you say surrounded by wire, but the frontage with Horsenose looked like coils rather than fencing.' Rodney nodded and she continued. 'There was a small cut going off the frontage, about two thirds of the way along to the west. It also appeared to be wired off. I'm pretty sure that there was a small slip at its head and a canary yellow yacht hauled out on a hard.'

'Was the cut fenced off?' Rodney asked.

'I think so, yes I'm sure it was, looked like chain link with something on the top.'

'Probably the same as the road, no doubt with tremblers as well,' Rodney paused then asked, 'was the boat inside or outside the fence?'

'Unfortunately inside, I'm sure.'

'Not unfortunate my love,' Rodney grinned, 'if it's inside then there must be some form of gate which means the fence can not be secured to the bed of the cut, with a bit of luck I could wriggle underneath.' He shot a glance at Dick, 'You're the expert, when's low water?'

'Mmm,' Dick mused. 'Must be about a couple of hours time, say half past one.'

'Twit. I mean tonight, I'm not going to attempt access in broad daylight. Looks like about two o'clock. Sal, I shall need help.'

'Hang on,' Dick cautioned, 'don't want any heroics, this isn't telly where the good guys always win. Anyhow we still aren't sure that we've got the right place.'

'Don't worry, I'll not do anything daft, remember I used to be a professional. If there is any risk at all I won't take it. Trespass is not against the law you know, it's only a civil offence. They couldn't even call the police unless I actually cut their wire!'

'What about the water samples we've just collected?' Janice asked to change the subject.

'Yes, mustn't forget them,' Dick responded then with a gentle tug at his ear continued, 'we could do them on the boat, but it would be somewhat hit or miss, really need a more sophisticated approach with a bit of alpha spec[31] just in case there's any natural about.'

'But if it were due to thorium or uranium there would be beta gamma as well,' Janice pointed out.

'At these very low levels we could not be sure, there will be beta gamma from potassium and we can't do the chemistry to sort that out. No it'll have to be an alpha spec or some other method specific for plut if we are to be sure and get enough to have your General call in the Special Branch.'

'Brigadier,' Janice corrected with a smile.

'Do you know the Layness lot?' Dick asked as if he had not been interrupted.

'Enough to speak to.'

'Good,' he looked at his watch. 'Rod and Sal take Jan back to the boat, let her get her things then pack her off to Layness in the TR7. She ought to make it before they quit even if it is Friday. Then you go back and keep station on *E.L.* and work out the details of your midnight sorties.'

'What about you?' his daughter asked.

'I've just had a thought about that boat, now I want to make some local enquiries. Come back and pick me up about five o'clock. There should be enough water by then, so make it the Yacht Club slip. That'll save me a long walk back here.'

Dick's first visit was to Thames Coastguard Station where he dropped in and chatted up the officers on duty. He had been there several times before and was known to some of them, but not to any of those who were on duty. As a local yachtsman he was frequently in contact with the C.G. for weather forecasts and safety reports[32] and reckoned to try and get to know the men and women who were at the end of his R.T. He got no response to his mention of a bright

---

[31]*Alpha spectrometry is a method of identifying a radioactive isotope from the energy of the alpha particle it emits. In this case it would distinguish between naturally occurring uranium or thorium and plutonium.*

[32]*A voluntary procedure exists in the U.K. whereby a yacht may radio the local coast guard with information concerning its intended passage. This is purely for safety reasons and is often referred to as a "safety report". Should the boat subsequently be reported overdue, or send out a distress call, the coast guards would have some idea of where to organise a search and how many people are involved.*

yellow yacht sometimes seen off Horsenose Creek. He wandered around the local chandlers, renewed an acquaintance with the chart agent and called in at the boat yards. Blighty England and *English Lady* were frequent visitors to these parts and known to the natives. He had no difficulty in chatting them up, but it was only the chart agent who admitted to any contact with anyone from Longsands. Dick knew him tolerably well, and after the usual preliminary speculations about the weather that might be expected in the forthcoming season, edged round to the purpose of his visit.

'We've got a fellow applying for membership of our club who says he lives round here,' he lied, 'bit odd really would have thought he'd have gone for a club at Walton or Harwich. Can't remember his name, but his address was Longsands Mansion or something like that. Know him?'

The chart agent hesitated, 'Don't know of any Mansion but thar's a Longsands 'ouse on the north side of 'amford. Come t' think of it a chap did call in about a week ago an' left that address. Wanted 'is charts corrected. 'ad a beard, looked an 'ardy yachtsman, said his name was Brine from Longsands. Seemed genuine.'

'Could be the same bloke,' Dick conceded. 'The fellow I was thinking of had a beard. Been shooting us a line about planning a long cruise this year. Made me wonder, as most of us don't like to advertise our plans in case they don't come to fruition, 'spose you don't remember which charts he had?'

'I know 'e wanted a 1408 because we ain't got 'em in an' I told 'im so. Got a bit shirty, said 'e was going orf next week,' the chart agent paused to reflect. 'I reckon 'e meant the end of this commin' week cause 'e ain't been back yet.' He picked up a small duplicate book from the counter, flicked through the pages and continued, 'Took a new 1406 an' left 'is 1975 an' 1607 for correction. Mary do 'em last Monday but as I said 'e ain't been back yet.'

'Oh it isn't that important,' Dick tried to sound disinterested. 'Looks as if he might be a blue water man after all. If you've got another 1406 I'll take it, I'm ashamed to admit I've been using an out of date one for the past year!'

The agent grinned, walked over to a special rack of shelves and handed Dick a rolled up chart. Dick paid and left.

He knew the charts that had been mentioned, the 1408 would be a passage chart for anywhere between The Hook of Holland and Texel. The 1406 would compliment it as far south as Dunkerque and the 1975 and 1607 were North and South Thames. As he walked back to the yacht club to await the arrival of his water transport, he turned the information over in his mind. The Thames Estuary charts would not cover London and the two passage charts would not give the detailed information necessary for the harbours of France, Belgium or Holland. It was possible that Brine had got other charts from another source to cover his tracks but somehow Dick thought that unlikely. A picture began to emerge in his mind. If this fellow Brine from Longsands was involved with the plut theft then it looked as if he was going to head for the Continent, but not actually land. Perhaps meet another boat on the high seas and hand over the material before heading back for some place between Walton and Ramsgate. He was standing on the side of the quay and looking down the Walton Channel trying to pick up the tell tale wake of a speeding inflatable when a young female voice interrupted his thoughts.

'Hello Mr. England, not smuggling again I hope?' Dick spun round to a smart young lady in the uniform of Her Majesty's Customs and Excise. She was in her late twenties or early thirties, slender build but taller than average. She wore thin rimmed spectacles and over her shoulder carried the usual Customs bag.

'What brings you here Jane, snooping on us poor yachtsmen again?'

He only knew her as Jane, one of the handful of Customs staff that regularly cleared yachts when they returned from the Continent or issued papers to the visiting French, Dutch and Belgians. It was quite impossible for the Authorities to keep track on the coming and going of small boats. Any skipper with a mind to it could easily bring in the extra bottle of spirits or packets of cigarettes without being found out. By and large this did not happen, the system put yachtsmen on their honour and they inevitably responded accordingly. On the odd occasion that someone was discovered to be abusing the privilege the Customs made their life so unbearable they inevitably gave up boating! More often than not a boat returning from abroad would be allowed the "quick" report procedure, this meant the skipper simply phoned in his arrival and proclaimed there was nothing to declare then waited two hours for a Customs Officer who would probably not turn up. After that the blue copy of the C1328 was posted and everyone was free to go. However, every now and again Jane or one of her colleagues would arrive and go through the clearance procedure. This understanding was not loose or sloppy, it was practical and effective.

It was also supplemented by the Revenue Officers spending some of their time in gossip with the locals when they would often pick up valuable information that lead to important and spectacular capture of drugs and other nasties.

'Now Mr. England as if we'd do anything like that,' the young lady countered with a smile that would have melted an iceberg. 'What caused you to abort your crossing last week? Not like you to miss a trip once you've posted a 1328.'

''fraid it was business that got in the way at the last moment.'

'Oh come on, you're retired.'

'Now you know I do a bit of consultancy, I declare it on my tax form, but this time it was a false start so here I am idling my time away with daughter and her boyfriend.'

There was no significance to this banter, but rather an alternative to discussing the English weather, it gave Dick an idea.

'Your people must have been pleased with that drugs haul from Aldeburgh beach last month, were you involved?'

'Only partly, I spent most of the night hiding in a rose bush and missed nearly all the action.'

'Papers said you had a tip off.'

'You know how it is, we pick up snippets from good folk like yourself, then put two and two together.'

Dick smiled, it was just the opening he had hoped for.

'We've got our hook down just off Horsenose Creek, there's a large house at the end of a small cut,' he paused to watch her eyes, but they gave nothing away. 'Very strange, it's surrounded by barbed wire and has a bright yellow yacht in the grounds. Looks just the set up for a drug smuggling operation, but no doubt you've sussed it out?' He was still watching the young lady's eyes and for a moment he saw she was taken aback and just a little flustered, he continued. 'So I am right, there is something going on, have you got them under observation? Don't want to blow your cover if I happen to meet you under a rose bush one night.'

Jane Seymore hesitated, it was against their procedure to discuss official business with the public, but on the other hand she knew Dick England to be a man with a reputation for integrity. There were times when rules had to be bent, the Service needed the cooperation of the public and that sometimes meant confiding in those who might have valuable information. She looked him squarely in the face, her expression said, 'What I am about to say is not for repetition and is given in confidence in case you can help us,' Dick understood and responded with a nod.

'To tell the truth we don't know much about Longsands, some years ago there was a Dutchman involved in smuggling diamonds. After that it was taken over by Research Express and we've no evidence that they are not legitimate, but...' she hesitated.

'But what?' Dick egged her on.

'We have a fair idea what most companies do, a lot of intelligence comes in through VAT returns. R.E. are not registered! We don't know what they trade in or even who they employ. The Company does not pay wages and there are no PAYE returns. Speculating, it would be an excellent site for bringing in drugs and packaging them, then using small boats to distribute them around the country. However, we have no evidence whatsoever so can't act. I suppose you haven't seen anything we ought to know about?'

'Not really, just seemed an odd place especially as there is this yacht. Don't usually find them on a commercial site. I suppose it is just an ordinary yacht?'

'As far as we know it's a Surfmaster but,' again she hesitated and Dick again judged she needed a little more encouragement.

'They have a reputation for performance and being extremely seaworthy. Don't they have a rather deep slab keel, not very suitable for this part of the world?'

'What's aroused our interest is that the keel has been modified. Had a chunk cut off and wings welded on by a local yard.'

'So? Maybe they've studied the America's cup boats, wing keels are the in thing these days.'

'We know, but our information is that this is not the usual shape, the wings are much longer than on other designs and would make a good base onto which to bolt something. She is a fairly new acquisition and hasn't been outside home waters. If she does go abroad, well, I don't think she'll get the quick report procedure when she comes back.'

Dick grinned, then the sound of an outboard motor caused him to turn back to face the water, his transport had arrived.

'If we see anything suspicious you'll be the first to know,' he promised her as he stepped down into the rubber duck and gave a goodbye salute.

CHAPTER 12

The thirty years that Olga had spent in subterfuge for her country had, if nothing else, developed for her a sixth sense. Intuitively she knew when things were starting to go wrong. She spent the rest of the morning pondering on the events of the past few days then made her decision. As George Brine sauntered into the kitchen to forage for a lunchtime snack, she caught his eye and beckoned him to one side.

'I would like to have a word with you, we can go to my room.'

The Surfmaster's skipper was somewhat taken aback, in all his time at Longsands, Olive had never asked anyone into her inner sanctum. He wondered what fate had in store for him. They climbed the big uncarpeted staircase to a room not far from his own, Olive unlocked the door and bade him enter. It was about twice the size of his own allotted place and much better furnished. A large single bed with duvet and cover dominated one corner. The small cabinet at its side had a vase with fresh flowers which he assumed Olive had managed to find in the grounds. Beneath the window was a large oak desk that looked civil service in style, he wondered if it had been left behind when the Ministry of Supply moved out. The desk was neat and tidy. A tray of papers, a red coloured telephone and an old mug with a selection of pencils and ball point pens were the only items on its surface. Olive went to the green filing cabinet at its side and took out a road map of the Dutch coast which she unfolded.

'As you know Mother is now on her way and our meeting is planned for Friday,' George nodded and shuffled his feet as he tried to focus his eyes on the map and contemplated its significance. Olive continued, 'I want to bring that forward, I want us out of here as soon as possible.'

'We can only reckon on three to four knots with the plut container on our keel, with a hundred miles to the rendezvous we ought to allow a day and a half unless there is a head wind in which case we have problems. If the container does come on Monday we might make it out of the creek on Tuesday, a Wednesday night meeting is just possible, but I really do think we should test sail with the cylinder before we load it, in which case we cannot do better than Friday.'

Olive allowed him to finish before speaking. 'We will not use the container, finish the boat as soon as you can and get her out of the creek on Saturday's tide. Grimley can package the plut for stowage in the bilges.' The surprise that George Brine felt must have shown in his face for Olive continued, 'I am not going into details, but I think we are being watched. No I'm sure it's not MI5, not their style, but could be CIA or I could be wrong but now we have come this far there is no point in taking chances.'

'I agree with that.'

'I have been in touch with our friends and they say, after allowing for the time needed to get a change of instructions to Mother, the earliest we could meet up with her would be just before dawn on Wednesday morning. I have agreed a time of half past one at the Brown Ridge location you already proposed.'

Olive paused and George Brine attempted some mental arithmetic. 'Without the underwater encumbrance we could average five or six knots, the wind is in the east but I think it will get some south in it before much longer, that would make it a reach which is fine. On that basis we would not need to leave Hamford until about one o'clock on Tuesday afternoon, which means the latest for leaving the Creek is high water, say midday.'

George paused and Olive came in, 'Alright, but I do not want to hang on here until then. Could you get her out of the Creek tomorrow? If so do it and we will find somewhere else to lie until Tuesday.'

'I'd better get busy,' the bearded skipper said as he turned for the door, but Olive held out her arm to stop him.

'There is another matter,' she said. 'We are not going to detonate in the North Sea, it would be a waste. This is our target,' she said pointing to the Dutch map.

'But...' George Brine was lost for words, 'but why?' he spluttered.

'We are doing this to try and save the environment,' Olive proclaimed. 'Who has raped nature more than anyone else in this part of the world. The British, French, Germans may all be bad, but by far the worst are the Dutch. They have ruthlessly exploited gas fields without thought for the future. Look at the massive petro-chemical industries around the Hook with all the filth and poisons they spew out.' George nodded and she continued. 'It is not only that, years ago the West Coast was a maze of small islands with tidal waters alive with fish and birds. Now they are barriered off forming static lakes which support only eels and mussels. Look at the old Zuider Zee, converted to vast areas of flat intensively and artificially farmed polders. This is massive corruption of the environment on a gigantic scale. Worse, I understand plans are now being drawn up to seal off the Wadden Zee. They must be stopped.' She placed the index finger of her right hand onto the map, 'That is where we explode the weapon, in the lock gates at Den Oever.' George Brine let out a low whistle and started to speak, but Olive cut in. 'It is all worked out, I will fill you in on the details later, including our escape plans. I am telling you now for two reasons, firstly you will need more charts and secondly,' she paused, 'secondly, I want your support when I tell the others, especially Grimley who I expect will raise objections. Oh yes, I almost forgot to mention it, there is a bonus, the NATO fleet are assembling in Den Helder for an exercise. I suspect it is close enough for the tidal wave to cause havoc with any warships there.'

'But what about public casualties? I'm not a terrorist, I just want to save the environment from the ravages of nuclear power and nuclear war.'

'We will not kill people, there will be a warning in time for the public to be evacuated, I said I would tell you the details later. What we plan will,' she emphasised the will, 'stop nuclear power at one stroke all over the world, it will also lead to a massive call for nuclear disarmament that the politicians of all countries will not be able to resist and it will return the Maas Delta to its natural state. No other single operation could achieve as much.'

'Perhaps you're right, providing there is time to evacuate the public...'

'I guarantee it,' Olive cut in.

'Okay I'll go along with the new plan,' George Brine nodded, swallowed hard and made for the door, he had a lot of work to do.

Olive found her trusty Pete in an attic room observing *English Lady* through a pair of 10 x 50 binoculars. She briefed him fully about the change of plan and, as expected, he raised no objections but took to it with unquestioned enthusiasm. He too had doubts about Grimley and promised to keep a close watch on him. He also reported on his observations of the yacht off Horsenose, Olive listened intently then after a moments thought,

'I think we may be over reacting, but then that is what has kept me alive all these years. They cannot hurt us from where they are, but we do not want to be followed when we slip out tomorrow or Sunday. I think perhaps we should have them disabled...'

'You want me to fix them?' Pete enquired with a grin.

'No, there are a couple of Spetsnaz agents on standby for us. I will have words with them, but not a mention to the others about this, we do not want them to think we are closely linked to Russia.'

For a moment a look of disappointment crossed Pete's face, then he picked up the binoculars and turned back to the window.

'I will say nothing, make sure those boys do a good job.'

John Grimley was in his "laboratory" when Olive told him that she was bringing forward the departure date, she made no mention of the change of target.

'I don't think we should rush things, earlier you told us that we must keep to our plans.'

'We are,' Olive responded. 'We are simply deploying a contingency arrangement.'

'It was always part of our plan to hide the plut under the keel. If we put it in the bilges where the Customs might find it then it is me who takes the rap. I stole it, you only received it. It's too dangerous.'

'I am quite sure that you can package it so that it will be safe and secure. The Customs do not search boats when they leave, only when they return and we will not be coming back.'

Grimley hesitated for a moment, his lips quivered then he reluctantly conceded. 'Alright, but I don't like changing our plans. I may have to work late, but everything will be ready by the morning. I think I have done enough to make it look as if we made the weapon here. I suppose, in a way, I'll be glad to get out of here and on with the operation.'

'Good man,' Olive patted him on the shoulder. 'I knew I could depend on you,' she lied.

'I'll ship some extra ballast to counter the loss of the container weight,' Brine, who had just entered, volunteered.

*

The sky was darkening as it heralded the approach of night, inside the cabin of *English Lady* the quartet were finishing their meal.

'Well now you've eaten, fill us in,' Dick invited the Watersthorpe Health Physicist.

Janice Hardman cut short the move to lift her cup of coffee and responded, 'Nothing to tell, took the samples to Layness as you asked, then came back here and Sally picked me up from Titchmarsh in the rubber duck.'

'We know that! What did the Layness lot say, when will they have the results?'

'Monday afternoon was the best they could offer, oh yes come to think of it there was something else,' she paused.

'Tell,' Sally urged.

'Now let me see,' she teased. 'Yes I think I remember, they have heard from Chapel Creek, one shade near Tollesbury has shown slightly high alpha.'

'Ye Gods,' Dick exploded. 'We must be on the right track, surely two shades can't be wrong.' He looked around the table first at Rodney, then at Sally and finally at Janice. 'You know when you first came to us with your story I really thought it was your imagination out of control, looks as if I was wrong and you were right.' He turned to Rodney, 'This makes a difference to your mission tonight. I was against your going, hoped to talk you out of it, now I think it essential. There must be something at Longsands that will clinch matters. Enough evidence to even convince the...,' he paused for a moment, transferred his eyes to Janice, '...the Brigadier.'

CHAPTER 13

It was the early hours of Saturday morning before George Brine switched off his light and fell on what passed for his bed. He was the last of the conspirators to seek the land of slumber, but the others had preceded him only by minutes. He lay on his back staring into the darkness at an invisible ceiling and his mind rechecked the sequence of events for when daylight came.

High water was at 0930hrs, *Brimstone*, now on the edge of the slip, would be launched at 0800hrs. After the usual checks and engine test he would take her out of the creek sometime between 0900 and 0930hrs, head out along the edge of the Harwich Channel, clear of the Cork Sands, then make north keeping a few miles offshore until the tide turned. After that it would be south, the Wallet, then into the Colne and finally Pyefleet Creek where, he had no doubt, they would find either space to anchor or a spare mooring. There was nothing unusual or suspicious about such a trip, indeed it was a standard jaunt for many an East Coast yachtie, but so early in the season he did not think he would see too many others tramping the same water. They had plenty of time and by first heading north, if anyone did notice them, they would think they were making for Lowestoft or abroad. Everything they needed, including Grimley's plutonium was already on board, *Brimstone* was securely locked and guarded by an intruder alarm.

Although this was an extra trip in a way, he reasoned, it replaced the trial which he had intended and would not only test the boat but also his shipmates. They all claimed to be competent sailors but he had doubts. Pete would be a useful hand for the harder jobs, but doubted if he had any idea of how to navigate. Grimley had admitted having never sailed out of sight of land. Olive claimed to be immune to seasickness and able to handle anything between a dinghy and a sixty footer. He hoped she was not shooting him a line and regretted she would not be coming on this part of the trip, still he saw the sense of her proposals. Someone had to stay at Longsands to give the impression that it was still occupied, to pay off the milkman and to take in the now redundant keel cylinder. Everything must be made to look as normal as possible until the very last moment. She would drive round to Brightlingsea soon after lunch on Monday where he would meet her with the dinghy. The arrangement would also leave him with a car to collect the chart he still needed.

Pete was restless, half asleep and half awake he worried about security. Why had Olive decided to stay behind? He could have handled anyone who turned up and started to make enquiries, he could have paid off the tradesmen, answered the phone and all the other chores that Olive had quoted. Yet she could hardly manage security problems as well as he. Suppose there was a break in and some hand to hand fighting, she didn't have his strength. To Pete it was an illogical decision not to ask him to take the rearguard role, it not only hurt his pride, for the first time it made him question his loyalty to Olga. He tried to figure things out, but could not and as a result never settled into slumber. It just did not occur to him that he lacked the tact and subtlety that might be needed. He looked at the luminous dial of his watch, it was twenty minutes to three.

'Damn!' he muttered to himself, slid off the bed, pulled on some outer garments, picked up his trusty Magnum and set off to do a routine inspection of the perimeter fence.

*

Unlike the Longsands House contingent, the crew of *English Lady* had retired early to their bunks, but that was not surprising. Dick's alarm aroused them at 0130hrs. The sky was overcast and dark, ideal for Rodney's mission.

'Hope you've got the timing right,' Dick remarked as he watched Sally and her boyfriend pull on their wet suits.

'I hope so too,' Rodney responded. 'Should be plenty of water in Horsenose, but I have doubts about the Cut. With a bit of luck there will be just enough to float the duck although we might have to drag it over a few humps. If there's to be any chance of getting under that fence then it has to be done at dead low water. Reckon we'll work our way up and wait 'til low before I slip through. Won't have long on the other side, but I can suss out quite a lot in a quarter of an hour.'

'Are you sure that you want Sal. I'd rather come in her place, I know she's tough, but...'

'But nothing, I'm not sitting in the bottom of the rubber duck waiting for the tide to go out and holding *your* hand,' Rodney retorted with a smile, then added, 'Sal can give all the help I will need.'

Janice, who had been monitoring the conversation, smiled at the worries of an anxious father.

'I'll go if that will help,' she said, almost with a note of mischief.

'No you bloody won't,' Sally asserted. 'I'm not having you hold his hand!'

'Okay, but take the portable C.B. and we'll listen out on 14,' Dick said as he went down below to get the radio while the two got into the inflatable.

Small rubber dinghies do not row well, but Rodney had removed the outboard motor, its noise precluded its use and there was no point in carrying extra weight. With Sally sitting on the transom he slowly pulled away from *English Lady*. As there was still some ebb running he kept close to the shore, his oar occasionally striking silently into the mud. There was water enough for them in Horsenose, but when they reached the Cut it rapidly became so shallow that the dinghy started to touch bottom. Although there was no moon, their eyes had become accustomed to the dark as they gained their night vision. On either side, a shadow in the darkness, they could just make out the coiled barbed wire which gave way to a link mesh fence running along the sides of the Cut. Soon the water reduced to little more than a trickle down the centre.

'Ever seen Bogart in the African Queen?' Rodney queried in a whisper.

'Yes, why?' came the hushed reply.

'Because my love,' he paused a moment, 'you and I are about to do an imitation, it's time to get out and haul. I'll take the bow line and you can do your best to push at the stern.'

'You pig,' Sally snapped back in hushed tones, but without anger in her voice.

The mud was not unduly soft and they only sank in as far as their knees, even so this made every step an effort which was destined to exhaust their reserves of strength. As they heaved and pushed the rubber dinghy half floated, half tobogganed over the slimy mud and foot by foot edged nearer the gate.

'Look,' Rodney commanded in a voice barely audible at ten feet. 'Can just see the fence where it crosses, let's hove too a moment.' He looked at the luminous fingers on his watch. 'There is still an hour to low water, must say I didn't think it would dry so much as this, if access is possible then now is as good a time as ever.'

'Okay if you say so, let's go.'

'Not you sweetheart, you wait here, I'll do the last twenty yards solo. It's just possible there are infra-red detectors on the wire so I'm going to wriggle up the mud, that will absorb most of my body heat.'

'For Christ's sake be careful.'

'I will, but if I'm not back within the hour get out of here as fast and as best as you can and raise an alarm. Cook up some cock and bull story about my falling out of the boat and swimming ashore, that'll get the cops to act.'

With those final words Rodney blew a kiss, rolled over onto his back and lay full stretch in the mud.

By pushing with arms and legs he slowly slithered towards the wire. The mud covered his hair, most of his face and the whole of his wet suit. It was fatiguing work, but his efforts eventually paid off and he could see the fence just an arms length away.

'Looks as if I'm right on several counts,' he muttered to himself as he noticed the presence of anti-intruder devices on the wire. He glanced around, the wire mesh fence that ran along the banks of the Cut terminated in two concrete posts. Off the left hand one of these was hung a tubular steel frame gate, infilled with mesh and barbed wire. The gate extended to the mud but, because of the saucer shaped bottom of the water way, was unable to seal it completely. In the centre there was a gap of about nine inches above a small puddle of water. Rodney rolled over onto his stomach, keeping only his head above the surface and stretched out his right arm. He probed the mud under the gate with his fingers and cursed as he contact something hard and unyielding. He realised that just below the surface of the mud there was a concrete sill. For a few moments he lay still, thinking out what he should do next. As far as he could make out the gate was in good condition, he ran his fingers lightly along the base tubular steel frame, it was smooth and free from rust.

'So the gate is new,' he mused. 'Then why not take it right down to the concrete?' Suddenly the truth dawned upon him, the gate had probably been recently renewed, but the sill was old. If it had sunk more one side than the other then the new gate would only extend to the concrete on the side that had sunk least, in which case there should be a larger gap opposite. He inched up closer to the gate and extended his right arm sideways, feeling the distance between concrete and steel as it went. He rolled over to his right and continued to feel. The gap was reducing. Now he rolled left and repeated the exercise, the gap widened. About six feet from the centre of the gate he estimated the gap to the sill was about eighteen inches, enough for him to squeeze through. Patiently he scraped away the mud until he had engineered a channel which filled with water, but which was large enough for him to wriggle along and under the obstruction. He was in Longsands.

Slithering and sliding he crawled up the bank of the Cut and for a few minutes lay exhausted on the grass.

'As the man said when he fell from the skyscraper,' he muttered under his breath, 'so far so good.' Partly recuperated he started to make his way towards the house itself, but after about fifty yards came upon the Surfmaster sitting cradled on the top of the slip. He unzipped his wet suit, reached inside and took out a hand torch. With the aid of the thin pencil beam of light he inspected the boat, noted its name and colour then moved towards the house. Carefully he felt his way along the walls, noting that each window was closed with wooden shutters. As he turned the corner of the west face he chanced upon a collection of dustbins and other heaps of waste.

'Go no further,' he advised himself. 'If we want to know what is going on then let's take a peep into the dustbins, they always have a story to tell.' He lifted the lid off the first and shone his torch inside. It was full of kitchen waste. He moved to the next, this time the torch revealed several sealed black polythene bags. He reached inside and tore one open, it was full of paper towels. He was about to replace the lid when a thought struck him, he picked up a few at random and tucked them inside his wet suit top. The next bin appeared to be the same and the one after that full of more kitchen refuse. Now he came across a pile of cardboard packing cases, open and half full of more rubbish. He shone his torch along the side of the case and read the manufacturers name. He took a step back to ponder his next move and instantly felt something hard poke in the middle of his spine.

'Freeze!' came the command, or at least it would have been if the word had been completed, but Rodney acted in an instant. He had played out this role many times in training. The man with the gun nurses the element of surprise and does not anticipate any reaction until after his command has been received and understood, then he tenses for the response and the decision to shoot or not to shoot. There is a half second interval when he is relaxed and in that interval Rodney acted. As he spun round his left arm slashed down at an angle of 45° and he felt the impact on the edge of his hand as it knocked the gun to one side. At the same time his right fist struck out and crashed onto Pete's chin, finally the left, having been successful in its first mission, drew back and delivered a clenched fist to the solar plexus. Pete half chocked, started to double as he fought for breath. Rodney took a pace back and, this time choosing his time and place, putting all his weight behind the blow, drove his right fist onto the button of Pete's jaw. Rodney watched him crash to the ground and lie still.

Rodney McDonald did not panic, but he knew he had to get out of Longsands fast. For just a moment he hesitated over inspecting the prone body at his feet then darted back towards the Cut. There was no time to waste for there may well be other men with guns prowling around. At the gate he slithered down the bank and into the mud, then lying on his belly wriggled through the gap and paddled his way back to the waiting dinghy.

'Let's get out of here fast,' he urged. Sally sensed something amiss and kept quiet. She slid over the transom and started to push as her boyfriend pulled from the bow. It was a replay of their arrival, but this time carried out with haste and desperation. Soon the inflatable was floating, they scrambled in and started to row back to *English Lady* with all the energy they could muster. As they eased out of Horsenose Sally spoke for the first time.

'What's all the panic?'

'Tell you later, when we get to *E.L.* we'll slip over the side and remove all traces of mud from ourselves and the tender. You can have the full story when we're altogether, somehow I think we've got the jackpot!' He had just finished speaking when he noticed a light go on in one of the upper rooms at Longsands House.

Down in the snug comfort of *English Lady*'s saloon, Rod briefed the others on what had just happened.

'We must be onto something,' he reasoned, 'ordinary firms carrying out legitimate business don't have men with guns but terrorists do.'

'So do drug runners,' Dick remarked recalling his conversation with the young Customs officer. 'It's also possible they make use of glove boxes, probably the best way of handling some of the more potent drugs, so we still don't know that we've found the plut.'

'Come off it dad, you don't need alpha monitors for drug handling and drugs don't give reading on taky-shades. We must be onto them.'

'We'll soon know,' Rodney responded. 'I saw the lights go on at Longsands just as we got back. Probably means they've found the guy I floored or he's recovered and raised the alarm. Trespass is a civil offence and as I did not do any damage they would have had very little recourse in law, but assault is a different matter. 'fraid I'm guilty of a criminal offence and Sally is an accessory. If the guy dies then all hell will be let loose. Of course, I was justified but it may be difficult to prove self defence. It's only my word that he had a gun, I'm sure all traces of that will be removed before the police are called...if they are called.'

'Oh Rod, what shall we do?' Sally went pale and looked nonplussed. Janice Hardman remained silent and began to wish she had just let matters take their course at Watersthorpe, Dick England tugged at the lobe of his ear.

'It may not be that bad,' Rodney continued with a smile, 'unless I am very unlucky that chap will just have a sore head and an aching body. If they are legit they will simply hide the gun and call in the police. If we keep a watch out we should see any car headlights as they arrive and more lights go on. With a bit of luck they will not realise our entry was from the Cut for quite some time. The tide is flooding and our tracks will be covered until this afternoon. Even if they are spotted there is still nothing to tie them to us respectable yachtsmen. On the other hand if the police are not called it's a pound to a pinch of shit that they are crooked.'

'I think we should get out of here as soon as possible,' Janice Hardman advised with just a touch of concern in her voice.

Sally said nothing, but got up and walked to the corner that served as a mobile laboratory.

Dick spoke, 'We stay put,' he said. 'To move now would arouse suspicion. We are in this up to our necks and have to see it through. Even if we moved out now, while it is still dark, the police would have no difficulty in tracing us. Remember the chat I had with Jane from H.M. Customs? No, too many people know we are here, to clear out could look very wrong. If the police call then we'll just have to brazen it out. If not we keep an eye on what happens at Longsands, Rod's little adventure must trigger something.

'I've got news,' Sally interrupted. All eyes turned, the others had not paid any attention to what she had been doing while Dick was talking. 'Those paper towels that Rod brought back are lousy with plut, or should I say alpha,' she corrected herself, 'and so is the mud that stuck to our wet suits. I put it on to dry out as soon as we came aboard, just checked it with the probe. If we can get these samples confirmed then there should be enough evidence for the authorities to act, even if your Field Marshall,' she looked at Janice with a smile as she mimicked her father's mistake, 'even if he did nothing surely your friend Alf Carter ought to be able to start the action,' she said turning her eyes in Dick's direction.

'That makes it even more imperative we stay put and observe. If they make a move by land or water we must follow, I think that halyard is going to need attention in the morning,' he added with a smile as he shot a glance at Sally.

*

Pete groaned, rolled over onto his side and staggered to this feet. A banging noise in his head gradually eased and he started to collect his thoughts. The gun, his beloved Magnum, where was it? He dropped to his knees and started to grope around until his left hand came across the cold metal lying just an arms length away. He picked it up, struggled back onto his feet and tucked the weapon in his trouser belt. His midriff ached, his jaw was sore and his neck stiff.

'That's the last bloody time I make that mistake,' he said aloud to no one in particular. For a few minutes he wondered what he should do next. Olive would have to be told, she would be furious and he would be the laughing stock of the other two. Perhaps his assailant was still in the grounds or even the house. He decided to have a look round before reporting. He checked the doors and windows of the house, they were intact. He cast an eye over *Brimstone*, but she seemed alright. Then he remembered the bunker where the mangled, decomposing body of the reporter lay spread around the walls. He made his way over and with relief noted the door was still firmly secured. Finally he made a tour of the perimeter fence and, finding nothing amiss, returned to the house and woke Olive.

She cross examined him, 'You are sure that no one got into the House?'

'Yes.'

'Or the outside buildings and there was no damage to the fence and no signs of where an entry had been made?' Pete nodded agreement. 'Surely he could not have jumped the fence without triggering an alarm, there was no noise so it was not a helicopter raid...who was he, who was he?' she repeated in a subdued voice.

'I don't know, but I reckon he was a pro. No amateur would have reacted like that. I didn't even get time to pull the trigger.'

'You fool,' Olive hissed at her henchman, but did not push the rebuke further. She knew that in the not too distant future she might need his loyalty. 'Okay forget it, we all make mistakes. What is done is done, now I have to think out what we should do.'

She was sitting on the chair at the side of her desk and as she finished speaking placed an elbow on the top and supported her chin in a cupped hand. 'If your friend is a pro,' she reasoned aloud, 'then he will know that you are up to something, but if he knew what it was there would have been no need for an entry. You said you thought he had been looking in the dustbins?'

'Yes.'

'Have you checked what was in them?'

'Yes, kitchen rubbish and some of the paper swabs Grimley used in his clean up. They were all bagged, but I think one had been torn open. He probably just wanted to see what was inside.'

'Well paper towels look innocent enough, with a bit of luck you may have disturbed him in time. We cannot call the police, therefore whoever it is out there will come to realise that we do have something to hide, but we have probably got a twenty four hour breathing space. I think we stick to our plan, but make damn sure *Brimstone* sails on tomorrow morning's tide. Do not mention this incident to the others. Let us get what sleep we can, we need to be up at six. Good night.'

George Brine was first up, and before 0600hrs he was itching to go. Once *Brimstone* was afloat he would be master and the operation would be under his control. After a cup of strong coffee and some cremated bread which passed for toast, he made his way out to the Surfmaster. It was just about half tide and the Cut was starting to fill.

'Launch time two hours,' he muttered in a whisper. 'Better check that bloody security gate and make sure it'll still open.' He walked along the side of the Cut up to the gate, it was secured with a padlock and chain, but he noted it was well oiled as were the hinges on the far side. 'Seems Pete's been looking after things alright,' then he saw mud on the side of the opposite bank, he smiled. 'Stupid prat must have fallen in when he was doing the hinge. God, I hope he's not that clumsy when we're at sea.' He turned and walked back to the winch at the head of the slip, started up the donkey engine, flipped over the paul on the ratchet and ran *Brimstone* and her carriage down the slope to await the tide.

Everything went according to the Brine plan. By 0800hrs the boat was afloat and Grimley on board. At the touch of the button the engine sprang into life.

'Open the gate Pete,' *Brimstone*'s skipper commanded as he reached out and let the securing line go, 'jump aboard as we pass through, Olive can close it although I don't see why it's necessary.'

Pete grunted in agreement and obeyed. With one hand still on the tiller Brine turned to Olive, who was still ashore, 'See you in Brightlingsea, Monday at the public hard. If by any chance you don't show by two o'clock in the afternoon we will clear out and try phone contacts, okay?' Olive nodded in agreement as the yellow hull slid out through the security fence.

George kept the helm and coaxed the boat along at only a couple of knots, he felt sure there was enough water but just in case they touched bottom he wanted it to be a gentle affair. There was still a foot of tide to come so in the event of such a mishap they should float off. As *Brimstone* moved slowly towards Horsenose the skipper's eyes scarcely left the echo sounder's repeater which was sited in front of him. Suddenly and unaccountably he remembered the mud by the gate.

'If we do go aground,' he called out, 'it's Pete over the side and push. He won't mind the mud, he's used to it aren't you, old horse?'

'What's that comment meant to mean?'

'Come off it, I saw the marks where you fell in by the gate. S'pose you were greasing the hinges. Might as well own up, even you can make mistakes,' he teased. Pete was not amused.

'Don't know what you mean,' he said without conviction, then the significance of George Brine's comment dawned upon him.

'Turn round we've got to go back, I must talk to Olive.'

'No way old chap, the Cut's too narrow to turn.'

'Well turn when we're outside and come back in, I must speak to Olive.'

'Sorry, if I do that we will be on high water and if we get stranded we might not get off until tomorrow.'

'I must speak to Olive,' Pete persisted.

'Then it'll have to be by phone. I'm skipper and I make the decisions when we're afloat. We're on our way and there'll be no turning back.'

'But they must have come from that yacht,' Pete babbled on, but Brine took no notice. 'Olive must be warned, we must tell her.'

'Who came from the yacht?' This time it was Grimley joining in the argument.

Pete hesitated, Olive had forbidden him to tell the others about last night's intruder. 'Oh...some people we saw in a dinghy...going up the creek.'

George Brine grimaced, 'To think I've got to go to sea with that twit, some bloody folk in a dinghy and he wants to tell Olive,' he muttered to himself and increased engine throttle as *Brimstone* entered Horsenose Creek.

*

'That yacht's coming out,' Sally shouted down from her position at the top of *English Lady*'s mast. 'They're opening the fence that Rod crawled under, what are we going to do Dad?'

'Follow her. No, I've a better idea.' Dick England turned to Rodney, 'Get the bloody anchor up, fast. I'll start the engine. Janice, slack off that halyard slowly and get Sal down here pronto. Can't go to sea with a girl at the top of the mast.'

The crew sprang into action and the big diesel exploded into life. Sally scuttled to her father's side and her boyfriend laboured away at the anchor winch.

'Time you got mechanised and had some power on this thing,' he called back to the skipper who waited impatiently.

'What's it to be?' Sally asked her father.

'If we hurry we can just make the entrance to the Cut and I'll use *Lady* as a block ship to stop them getting out.'

'Anchor free,' called the man from the bow. Dick reached and thrust the single control lever forward. The engine revved, the propeller started to turn and *English Lady* swung to the instructions of the rudder then, quite suddenly, the boat shuddered and the motor died in an instant.

'What the hell...' Dick cursed as he pulled the lever back into neutral and turned the starter switch. Again the diesel came to life, but stopped as soon as the lever went to ahead.

'Looks as if they are through the gate. I can just see the top of their mast,' Sally called to her father. 'What's up?' Dick ignored the question.

'Get that bloody sail cover off, Rod back here and unfurl the genny. We're too late to block her in, but we may be able to follow, there's a good wind.'

The two ladies rushed up onto the deck and feverishly started undoing the ties on the green canvas mainsail cover. In a few large strides Rodney was back in the cockpit and unwinding the jib furling line, he tugged at the sheets and the big sail started to billow out then jammed.

'Christ, Rod what's happened?' Dick called out, but before he got a reply the wind caught the flapping sail and started to turn *English Lady*'s bow towards the saltings. He swung the wheel hard over, but the boat had insufficient way for it to respond.

'The mizzen, get the mizzen up, she won't turn,' he shouted at the females, who promptly abandoned their task and ran aft. It was too late, *English Lady* squeezed her short bilge keel into the soft slimy mud and came to a halt, it was just on high water. The crew of *Brimstone* gave a friendly wave as they motored past.

'Dick, you're not going to believe this, there's a pair of knickers fouling up the winding drum,' Rodney called back from the foredeck where he was investigating the genoa problem.

England turned to the two females who were standing behind him at their mizzen station. Suddenly Janice blushed and burst into tears. 'I did some washing last night, hung them on that line from the foot of the sail. I'm...' she was interrupted by howls of laughter from the others.

'I've never been shipwrecked by a pair of panties before, hope you've got some more.' Dick recovered the situation with a smile. 'Don't worry, it's not your fault. I want to know why that engine failed, could be something around the prop, that lot from Longsands seem to have the luck of the devil.'

'Maybe they're in league with him,' Janice suggested.

'The tide's going fast now, reckon we're stuck but we'll soon be able to see the prop. Oh sod it, let's go and have a cup of char and think out what to do next.'

Down in the saloon the quartet hugged their mugs of steaming tea and took stock of their predicament.

'If we're lucky,' Dick surmised, 'and there's no damage to the prop or shaft, we ought to be able to get her off on tonight's tide, it's a few inches higher than this morning's. If not it will be eleven on Sunday, the tides are making so we should get off but then what?'

'The odds are that yellow boat will be on its way with all the plut and we haven't any idea where. I've never felt so helpless in all my life,' the Health Physicist from Watersthorpe commented.

'Perhaps they've just gone for a trial sail,' Sally suggested hopefully, but the look on Rodney's face confirmed her own thoughts that such an eventuality was too remote to be worth considering so she tried again. 'Dad what about Alf Carter, could he not get a search organised, or Jane from the Customs, why don't we cook up some story about seeing them load drugs onto the boat. She did tell you to let her know if we saw anything suspicious.'

It was Rodney who was responsible for removing the look of scepticism from Dick's face. 'Sweetheart what a splendid idea. Nobody's going to believe a story about plutonium when there's none missing, but drugs is a different ball park. If we could make it sound convincing enough, not only would all our local harbours be put under surveillance, continental police forces would also be alerted. That bloody yacht will soon be found and searched.'

'Probably not searched,' Dick corrected, 'they would only have our tip off to go on so they'd more likely keep it under observation. However, by early next week we should have the confirmation analysis on the paper samples and mud. That would be enough evidence to get action. If they try and get rid of it before then well, the authorities ought to know how and who.'

Dick looked at his watch, 'God, it's an hour since we went on the putty, still that means they're only a few miles away. Sal up to the top again and have a scan with the bins you might just get an idea of the direction in which they are heading. Radar's range is twelve miles so if we can identify their blip we can follow their track a little longer. Jan come with me, I'm going over the side to inspect our prop, you can stay aboard and hand me any tools I may need.'

'That's a relief. I thought you were going to ask me to play mud castles as well,' she replied with a smile.

Dick had just sunk up to his knees in mud when Sally called out from the top of the mast.

'I think I can see them, the yellow hull shows up, looks as if they're heading north.'

'Rod,' Dick called back, 'you know how to use the radar, see if you can pick them up, if so log their course for as long as possible.' A grunt told him that the instruction had been received and understood. 'Sal, stay where you are for a bit, keep the house under observation as well. If all the birds have flown we might risk paying them another visit.'

'Aye Aye Sir,' a voice responded from the top of the main mast.

The following silence was suddenly shattered by the skipper's blaspheming. 'Jesus Christ, I don't believe it!'

Rodney left the cathode ray screen and went rushing up on deck.

'What's up Dick?'

'We've got a bloody length of eight mil rigging wire round the screw and snagged the rudder bracket. The props badly damaged and the rudder has lost part of its support.'

'How on earth did that happen. Those creeps in that yellow boat must have the luck of the Devil.'

'I don't know about that, looks more like the work of the Devil! I'm sure as hell about one thing, this was no accident. Rod my friend, we've been nobbled!'

'Who and how?'

'Don't forget Alf Carter mentioned Spetsnaz agents in the area, maybe they weren't on their way home after all.'

'Can you fix it?' Janice queried, but her question was overruled by another call from the mast.

'I can see movement at the house,' Sally shouted down from her perch.

Once more the quartet assembled in the saloon for a conference.

'Look's like we've lost,' Janice reinforced the note of depression in her voice with a look of dejection. 'Those bastards are clean away by now. God knows what they are up to. Goodbye plut and hello problems! Think I'd better make it back to Watersthorpe and pretend all this never happened.'

'But it has,' Sally asserted. 'Anyhow we've gone too far, there are still the sample results to come, by Tuesday or Wednesday we will have the proof. Hang on 'til then Jan.'

'Not so fast you two,' Dick cut in. 'We are a long way from being beaten, there is still some shot left in our locker. Let's add it up. First they have not all fled, there's still life in the old house. While it means we just can't go and walk in, it also means that there is still something there to guard. Whoever is there has to leave sometime. We can try following them instead of the boat.'

'Yeah, but the plut's on the boat for sure,' Janice countered.

'Maybe, maybe not, but we can still put a spoke in there. Ever heard of 'freephone Customs drugs'? Jan, if you can scramble ashore and find a payphone box do as Sal suggested, put in an anonymous story about seeing suspicious packages being loaded onto that yellow yacht from a dinghy as it slipped out of Hamford Water. Then hitch your way over to Chapel Creek and leave some of our latest samples for the attention of the Health Physicist. I'll give him a bell during the day and warn him what to expect, though it'll be Monday before they can get them on the Alpha Spec for plut confirmation.' Dick paused then turned to the others. 'Rod and Sal, make your way to Titchmarsh and pick up the car then nip round to Longsands House and keep your eyes glued on the gate from some unseen position. We'll keep in touch by C.B. using a bit of double talk just in case there are any eavesdroppers.'

Rodney nodded in agreement.

'It's a bloody long walk from here,' Sally commented, 'but I s'ppse we've nothing else to do.'

'*English Lady* will need a tow and then have to be slipped. As far as I could see she will need a new prop, repair to the rudder bracket and maybe a shaft as well if it's bent. It would have to be Sunday tomorrow.'

'Don't worry Dad, she's done her job, we won't need her again on this case.'

'I wouldn't be too sure about that, somehow I've got a feeling that the old girl might still get in on the final act. Don't forget the "yellow peril" is on the high seas. I'll scramble over to Richardson's, they owe me a favour or two, if young Charlie will bring his big launch and pull her off tonight...'

'On the last radar plot I reckon they were heading north up the coast. Lost them between No. 1 and the Whiting. If they were going south they'd have turned at Pye End for the Medusa, if it was the Continent then there'd be no need to go as far as Harwich No. 1, would have hardened up at Cork Sand.' Rodney contributed, 'Not much to go on, but better than nothing.'

*

George Brine was contentedly happy as he crouched over the chart table. They had only been at sea a few hours, but already the other two showed all the signs of being good shipmates. John Grimley was at the helm and in the long established style of folk who sail small boats, stood feet apart, hands holding raised binoculars and the end of the tiller gripped between the cheeks of his posterior. Pete was in the galley frying up some beefburgers which would make their lunch. *Brimstone*'s skipper tapped the barometer, the black needle vibrated, but held steady, he jotted down the reading on the log sheet.

'One millibar fall in six hours,' he muttered to himself. 'Can't be bad, looks as if the high is only declining slowly. If that means south westerlies by Tuesday I'm not complaining.' He pressed the 'pos' button on the Decca, noted the latitude and longitude then marked their position on the chart.

'Orfordness Light bearing two seven five skipper,' Grimley called from the cockpit. The bearing agreed precisely with the Decca plot, Brine was satisfied. As the morning progressed, a gentle breeze from the east had slowly freshened and the Surfmaster was now on a broad reach making nearly six knots. The ebb had died a couple of hours ago and the south going flood set, it was time to turn.

'John,' he called out to the helmsman, 'take her round through the wind on to one hundred and eighty degrees. Need any help?'

'No thanks, luffing now,' Grimley replied as he started to harden in the sheets and push the tiller to port. Brine noted the new course on the log sheet then plotted his route back to Pyefleet. They would pass through the Shipway between the Shipwash and Bawdsey Banks, then outside the Cork Sands and down the Wallet to the mouth of the Blackwater. For most of the thirty five miles there would be a fair tide, but he reckoned it would turn foul when they were off Clacton Pier. If they made the entrance to the Colne at dusk he would be more than happy. Even if it were dark there were enough light buoys to take him up to the entrance to Pyefleet Creek. The fewer people who noticed them the better.

CHAPTER 14

Olive closed off the entrance to the Cut as soon as the Surfmaster was clear. For a few minutes she watched with satisfaction as it moved slowly towards Horsenose Creek, then she turned and walked back to Longsands House, content that all was going according to plan. She went straight to the attic window from where Pete had observed *English Lady* and was not really surprised to note a figure at the top of its mast. Fascinated, she watched the debacle that followed *Brimstone*'s progress to the open sea and *English Lady*'s inglorious voyage to a mud berth.

'Thank you Spetsnaz,' she said aloud to herself. 'Looks as if you've done another good job.' The lady from the KGB was not prepared to rest on her laurels. She had two days to kill before she could join the others and she knew that was adequate to make not one but many mistakes if she became careless. For the next two days she would have to give the impression that the place was a hive of activity by day and by night. Friday night's intruder was very much in her mind and she would have liked to believe he was from the press, but logic spelled otherwise. The manner in which Petya had been immobilised was not the work of an amateur; finally she concluded that the most likely culprit was the CIA and those fellows would not give up at their first failure. Undoubtedly the yacht must be part of their operation and she deduced that the entrance to Longsands was also likely to be under surveillance. She crossed over to another attic window from which she could command a view of the approach road.

'All clear there, but for how long I wonder?' she muttered.

It was just before midday when she noticed the small sports car almost concealed at the side of the road about two hundred yards from the entrance to Longsands. She watched it for ten minutes, nothing moved.

'So I am under observation,' she told herself in an audible whisper. 'Thought the Agency would have managed something better than that. Think I'll have a bit of fun.' Olive walked down a flight of worn wooden stairs to her office cum bedroom and picked up the telephone.

'Walton and Frinton Police Station,' came the reply to her dial.

'Oh...er...good morning, er...no I think it's good afternoon, oh silly me, I do hope you don't mind my calling,' she babbled on to the impatient sergeant at the other end.

'No ma'am, 'ow can I be of 'elp?'

'I think I may be able to help you,' Olive continued in a disguised voice. 'I don't want to give my name you understand, but I've just seen something suspicious. I was driving along the old road past that big house, used to be a family residence years ago, but that was before the war. Of course, it's not that now, never been the same since the Government took it over, they painted it all grey, still I suppose that was to conceal it from the Zeppelins or were they aircraft, I really can't remember...' Olive was enjoying her performance.

'Yes ma'am, I know where ye mean.'

'Well constable...'

'Sergeant 'all, ma'am.'

'Well sergeant, there was a sports car parked near the entrance to the house. I saw two people, all dressed in yellow like the men wear who go sailing, carrying a black briefcase go up to the car and hand it over. They hid their faces as I drove past. Well we hear such stories about drugs and things these days and this was unusual so I thought I ought to tell you.'

'Yes ma'am, very useful information, I'll git it checked oot. Now when was this and what car were you driving?'

'Oh dear I'm not saying any more, my husband said I wasn't to drive the car. I'll be in terrible trouble if he finds out.' With no further ado Olive put down the phone and sat back to await developments.

*

Richard Harry England looked at his watch, the analogue display which was set to British Summer Time showed it was just past 1600hrs. The small digital window, which he could not read without his glasses, indicated an hour less but then that was set for Greenwich Mean Time. He squelched over the still soggy saltings and climbed aboard his beloved boat. As far as he could assess things could have been much worse. He had found Charlie Richardson at the yard who, after a little persuasion, had agreed to bring the launch and haul *Lady* off on the evening high tide, at about 2200hrs. He also said he thought there was a spare prop in the yard that would probably suit so everything would hinge on whether the shaft had bent.

As Dick wondered how the others had fared something puzzled him, there were specks of mud on the side deck. Someone had been on board while he was away, perhaps it was one of the others. He stepped down into the cockpit, opened up the companionway and entered the saloon. His first action was to switch on the C.B. radio.

'Con Man, Con Man, this is Blighty, do you read?' To his surprise Rodney responded to the first call.

'Blighty, Con Man, knock her up a couple.' Dick reached for the channel selector switch and went to 16.

'Con Man, any news your end?' he queried.

'Yeah, but it's not good. Hadn't been square wheeled long when a smokey buzzed us. Played quiz games for a while but we lost so had to do the decent thing and burn a bit of rubber.'

'Where's your twenty?' Dick asked using C.B. jargon for location.

'Back where we started from, have made several trips past the nest and it looks as if the birds are still there. What now?'

Dick thought for a moment, things were getting complicated. 'I've arranged for the A.A. to come and pull me out of the ditch at about ten this evening, suggest you maintain your present strategy, but meet up with us at the depot when we get in. We don't want the birds scared away do we?'

Rodney understood perfectly and he confirmed, 'Presume it's the firm you named this morning.'

'Yes, will give you a call later when the other passenger returns from her walk.'

'Okay will listen out on one four.' The set went silent and Dick switched it back to the calling channel.

'Mr. England. Mr. England,' a young female voice was calling from outside. It sounded familiar, but he could not place it. Certainly it did not belong to Janice or Sally.

'Yes, who wants me?' he responded as he climbed out of the saloon. 'Oh it's you Jane, not business I hope.' Then as he saw the Custom's launch standing off he realised it was and added, 'Anything I can do to help?'

'Perhaps, may I come on board?'

'Of course, you know you're always welcome on *Lady*.' Jane Seymore scrambled up over the top sides and settled down in the cockpit.

'I suspect there's a joker at work, but we've had some of those anonymous tip offs and they've to be followed up. See you've got a fouled prop is that why you've parked here?' Dick nodded and she continued. 'Have you seen a yellow yacht go past, probably came from Horsenose?'

'Yes, must have been about nine thirty this morning.' Dick responded as he tried to think out just what to say. Clearly Janice had made up a good story but without knowing the details it would be difficult to add to it.

'Notice anything unusual?'

'No, well it passed us just as our prop fouled so I wasn't really paying much attention. Thought maybe it was the boat from Longsands that we discussed the other day.'

'Did you notice if anyone went ashore from it?'

'No, sorry can't be more helpful. Why all the questions?'

'Oh, we had a report that some people in yellow boots were seen scrambling over the saltings, one was carrying a package which they gave to someone in a sports car.'

'You said tip offs,' Dick responded. 'Does that mean more than one informant?'

'Possibly,' the lady from Her Majesty's Customs responded guardedly.

'Come on Jane, out with it. You want our help you've got to tell what's been going on,' he chided.

'Alright, as it's you. There were two phone calls, quite close together and both in a female voice. Could have been the same person, but then it might not. One was to us about a yellow yacht, the other to the local police concerning a car waiting down the road from Longsands House, so it seems likely there is some connection between the two.'

'Not really,' Dick smiled as he realised what must have happened. In addition to Janice's false call, some do gooder had reported Rodney and Sal to the local police. 'The car was my daughter's boyfriend. As we'd got stuck they decided to pop back home, but forgot to take some papers with them. Stopped just up the road by the old house and legged it back here over the saltings. Nothing sinister I assure you and in no way connected with the yellow yacht.'

'Well that clears up part of the puzzle,' Jane conceded, 'but are you sure there was nothing suspicious about the yacht?'

'No...well...' Dick hesitated for effect, 'well...no I suppose...'

'Come on Mr. England, what's at the back of your mind? We can decide if it's important.'

'Well, as I said we were in trouble as they passed, it must have been obvious that we were about to ground yet they just sailed past, no offer to help. Of course, there are a few Hooray Henry's about, but any yachtsman worth that name would surely have offered assistance.'

'Unless they had something to hide?' Jane added. 'I suppose you didn't see which way they headed?'

'As a matter of fact we did,' Dick smiled. 'My friend was playing with the radar and managed to track them down the Harwich channel, after that it appeared they were heading north for the Whiting, but then we lost them.' Jane Seymore looked disappointed so Dick continued. 'Come on cheer up, there's not much north of here. Southwold with a very difficult entrance, Lowestoft or Yarmouth. The latter get quite a few timber ships from Scandinavia, maybe they were going to trade drugs there. On the other hand they could be heading for North Holland, Ijmuiden with its canal link to Amsterdam. Need I say more.'

'I think you've said enough, you seem keen to implicate them in evil just because they didn't stop and offer to come to your rescue, still point taken. I'll put it all to the boss and let him decide whether to target them.'

*

For the Longsands conspirators, the Sabbath was to be a day of waiting. George Brine had taken *Brimstone* as far up Pyefleet Creek as he dared and by good fortune found a vacant mooring. There was no nearby road and no passing yachts. They would be out of sight to inquisitive eyes. The three men lounged down below, reading, playing cards and listening to the radio. Olive also had an uneventful day. At first light she noted *English Lady* had gone. She wondered whether it was back at sea or laid up in a nearby yard. It did not matter, *Brimstone* would have got clear away. Furthermore, as far as she could make out the house was no longer under observation. Perhaps she had overreacted.

*

For Rodney and Sally it was also a day of waiting, but not inaction. They returned to Woodbridge and changed cars then with monotonous regularity kept driving past Longsands. Occasionally they saw a shadow move across a window or a light turn on or off. The house was still occupied. As *English Lady* nestled into the cradle on the slip at Richardson's yard, Dick set about cutting free the tangled wire around the ships screw. He removed the split pin then the castleated nut on the shaft, finally with a borrowed extractor he drew off the damaged propeller. Unfortunately the substitute that Charles Richardson offered was a little too tight on the taper and easing it out took longer than the tide would allow, so *English Lady* had to wait until late evening before launching. It also gave him time to reinforce the damaged rudder segment.

*

On Monday morning Olive did not have to wait long before the lorry arrived with the cylinder that should have been bolted to *Brimstone*'s keel. She opened the security gate and led it up the drive and round to the rear of the house. Once unloaded she escorted the vehicle back to the road and locked the gate behind it.

'Well that's that,' she told herself. 'Now all I have to do is lock up, slip out when no one is about and meet up with Brine at Brightlingsea.' She returned to the attic and scanned all around. The roads were clear, the water was clear, no sports car and no boat anchored off Horsenose, even so she was still not happy about leaving the house. It would probably take some days before the significance of Grimley's laboratory dawned on an investigator, but the mangled body of the reporter would trigger an instant hunt and Longsands staff would be prime suspects. Suddenly she had a thought, blessed the propriety of English law and returned to the phone in her room.

'Walton Police, Sergeant 'all speaking.'

'Good morning Sergeant,' Olive responded, but this time she did her best imitation of an upper class English lady. 'I'm frightfully sorry to trouble you, but I thought I ought to let you know about my works. I am the Managing Director of Research Express...'

'Yes ma'am, I know where yew mean, na what's bin 'appening?'

'Oh nothing, but I thought I would inform you that we will be closing the site for a week as from today. The technical staff and myself are due to attend a conference and it did not seem worthwhile keeping open.'

'Oi see.'

'As you are probably aware we are engaged on some secret Government work...'

'No I weren't, but tha' don't matter.'

'Well we are, and I do not usually allow the site to remain unoccupied, this is an exception. I would like to ask if you could get your men to keep an eye on it for me while we are absent?'

'Tha'al be alright ma'am, jus' leave it to us. I'll 'ave mobile check it over. Jes' mek sure you lock up.'

'I will certainly do that my good man. Thank you very much.' Olive smiled as she replaced the receiver. 'Good old British Bobbies,' she thought. Half an hour later she drove through the formidable gates, secured them and set off in the opposite direction to Brightlingsea. Once certain that she was not being followed she turned back and headed for her meeting with George Brine.

The tide was more than half gone and the public waterfront showed its large expanse of firm dark brown sand. Down near the waters edge George Brine waited with the inflatable dinghy from *Brimstone*. His eyes scanned the road that ran beneath the ramshackle assortment of buildings. He consulted his watch.

'Late,' he muttered, 'but so far by only five minutes. If she doesn't show soon...' He broke off his self conversation as he identified Olive making her way towards the hard. 'Hi,' he called out and waved. She saw him and waved back.

'Everything all right?' she asked in a cold and professional manner.

'Sure, Pete's just gone to the shops for a few supplies to top us up, he'll be back in a minute.'

'I thought I had said you were to keep out of sight,' she chided.

'Damn it, Olive, he'll only be a few minutes, the boat is out of sight and anyhow no one is looking for us or the boat.'

'I know, but we are on the last leg of this operation. In a couple of days it will be all over, I suppose I'm a little edgy.'

'I still need that chart, give me the keys and I'll have a drive round until I get one. Failing that I'll have to take the existing one back to Walton and update it in the agent's office.'

'Yes, of course, here are the keys. The car's in the park over there.'

'Thanks, Pete'll take you over to *Brimstone*, quite a little trip for a rubber duck. Get him to meet me here about six o'clock.'

*

Monday morning also started with another conference in the saloon of *English Lady* as she lay to a mooring off the marina entrance, but this time it was pervaded by an atmosphere of despair and defeat. Rodney and Sally had given up their fruitless watch on Longsands House the previous night and Janice had returned from Chapel Creek on the Saturday evening with the disparaging news that due to pressure of work on their equipment, the analysis of the samples could not be confirmed until Wednesday at the earliest. The only piece of good news was that Dick had managed to effect repairs to the boat, she was afloat and while there was doubt about being able to achieve full power, she was certainly seaworthy and useable. A yacht chugged past and *English Lady* rolled slightly in the wash.

'Suppose I'll be able to enjoy the benefits of a table that stays still,' Janice remarked. 'Not much point in me hanging on here, we seem to be at a dead end. If only we could get those sample results through sooner someone would have to take notice.'

'We don't know for sure it is plut on them,' Dick pointed out, 'but I'd lay money on it. With such evidence, even if your Brigadier wouldn't act I'm sure Alf Carter would get something moving.'

Sally leaned forward and banged both her fists on the table. 'This is bloody ridiculous,' she cried in anger. 'Plutonium, one of the most dangerous substances on earth is being trundled across the North Sea to God knows where and to God knows who. We know how and by who...'

'Whom,' Rodney corrected.

'Whom,' Sally repeated without pause, 'and we can do nothing, absolutely nothing about it!'

'There is one consolation,' Janice added. 'You've proved your point Dick. It is not possible to steal plutonium without leaving traces, but your reasoning did not reckon on the stupidity of British management.'

'English management,' Rodney again corrected, in an attempt at humour. 'I don't think Whatley-Jones is a Scottish name!'

'Oh, what's it matter, we're beaten, we've lost, finished, caput, useless...' Sally sobbed.

'Not quite my daughter, we still have some powder left.'

'What?' Sally snapped.

'Well there's the hope that the Customs have taken to our story, who knows they might even have found that yellow boat and have it under surveillance or even arrest.' Sally said nothing, but shook her head. 'Okay, maybe they haven't, but there's something else, maybe a straw but worth clutching at.' Dick paused again and noted the faces of the two girls brighten for a moment, he continued. 'Remember the visit I paid to the chart agent? This fellow Brine who came from Longsands had not been back to collect his charts and in any case was short of a 1408. That was only Friday; if he was planning a trip he'd have been back before then for the corrections. There's something else as well, that boat has had a new keel fitted, well no good seaman would take a yacht that had been modified on a long trip without a sea trial first. I think we've been too pessimistic, that boat will be coming back or might even have come back. I guess the plut is still in the big house, that's why they didn't all go.'

'If that's the case why did they try to disable us?' Rodney asked.

'I can't answer that, but there's probably some reason we don't appreciate at the moment.' Dick replied.

'Let's get off and go and have a look,' Sally said.

'Right, but not in *E.L.* we don't want to advertise that she is operational. You two love birds take the rubber duck and have a picnic on Stone Point. Have a peep at Horsenose on the way, if they are not back, go over to the Point where you will command the entrance to Hamford. We'll keep in touch by C.B. Jan give it another day, stay here with me in case we need *Lady* in a hurry. I'll call Layness this afternoon to see if they have any sample results. If nothing turns up then we'll put you ashore tomorrow morning and you can go back to your General,' Dick concluded with a smile.

*

George Brine was on high when he returned to Brightlingsea and chatted away to Pete as they ferried the long trip back to *Brimstone*. He had the charts he needed, although he had had to drive to Walton to get them. They were all corrected up to date, furthermore the weather forecasters had told him what he wanted to hear. The patchy visibility would clear by late morning and the wind shift to the south west as the ridge of high pressure gave way to an incoming shallow depression. From Tuesday afternoon until at least Thursday he could expect light to moderate south westerlies, after that it did not matter. He was more elated once back on board. The other three seemed to have settled in well. Their kit was properly stowed and the boat looked in good shape. For once there was no suggestion of any friction between them and his fears that they might not weld into an efficient small boat crew evaporated. They all felt the sense of destiny that pervaded the small craft.

'I think, George, it is time to put everyone in the picture,' Olive announced as she won the attention of Pete and John Grimley. 'Lay the chart on the table.'

Brine unrolled the 1408 that he had just bought from the agents and weighed down each corner with a shoe, a pot of jam, binoculars and a hand bearing compass. Olive leaned across and ran her finger diagonally upwards from the Blackwater.

'We meet up with Mother here,' she said pointing to Brown Ridge, a small bank with a least depth of eight fathoms some forty five miles west of the Dutch coast. 'It is not marked,' she continued, 'but George is sure he can find it even if the Decca is out of action, the echo sounder will tell us when we are there. It is away from the shipping lane and clear of gas rigs.'

'Is that where we detonate?' asked John Grimley with a note of excitement in his voice.

Olive hesitated then decided it was time to tell the others of the new plan. 'No, we exchange our plut for the weapon and then sail on to a small place called Den Oever where we lock into the Ijsselmeer, that is where we explode the weapon.'

'But...,' the man from Watersthorpe stammered.

Olive continued, 'It is about sixty five miles from the Ridge and we will allow fifteen hours which means we arrive about seven o'clock in the evening. High water is at eight o'clock. The force of the explosion will vaporise the lock and rip out part of the sea wall. It will send a tidal wave right across the Ijsselmeer swamping a large part of the reclaimed land and damaging the entire water way system as far as Amsterdam. A much bigger wave will sweep out into the Wadden Zee.'

Olive moved her finger to the stretch of water between the mainland and the offshore islands of Texel and Terschelling. 'These will partly contain it and create a minor Niagara Falls in the sea gaps. There is a NATO meeting in Den Helder so we can count on most of those boats finishing up in the High Street.'

She smiled with satisfaction. 'The weapon has a two hour delay device. As soon as we have tied up *Brimstone* in the waiting area at the lock entrance, we will scramble ashore to four bikes that have been left for us. In ten minutes we will meet a car which will then rush us across the Ijsselmeer dam, through North Holland and into Germany. After that there can be no problems.'

'But this is not what I agreed to,' a sullen John Grimley objected. 'People will get killed, there will be no warning, the damage will be enormous.'

'There will be a two hour warning,' Olive corrected, 'it will be given out as soon as we confirm our arrival.'

'That will not be enough,' Grimley persisted.

'Our experts have estimated that complete evacuation from the danger area is possible within that timescale, there need be no loss of life,' Olive lied.

'Sounds a great idea to me,' George Brine feigned surprise. 'After the way the Dutch have raped the environment it would be sort of poetic justice that the sea should reclaim the old Zuider Zee.'

Grimley still looked doubtful, Olive cast a glance to Pete.

'Don't see that it matters, we let off the bomb in a way that will teach the world it must get rid of weapons and nuclear power stations, anyone object to Olive's plan?' He slid his hand inside his jacket towards the butt of his Magnum.

'I do not think anyone dissents,' Olive said as she looked Grimley in the face. He diverted his eyes and nodded agreement.

'Good. George run through our duties while on board and gen us up on how everything works.' Olive looked at her watch. 'Gentlemen, there are only twenty hours left to our departure time!'

*

Time dragged slowly on *English Lady*. At first, Dick and Janice talked over the age old health physics problem of the uncertainties in estimating the effects of low level radiation. While the establishment took the view that the studies of the effect of radiation on the survivors at Hiroshima and Nagasaki could be applied to long term exposure at low dose rates, Dick was surprised to learn that Janice tended to share his view that such assumptions were unjustified and low dose radiation was probably much less dangerous than the official figures suggested. When that subject was exhausted they talked about themselves, about their holidays, about *English Lady* and her predecessors. They sipped endless cups of tea and waited. Every time the C.B. made a noise as the squelch opened in response to some other operator's transmission, Dick's heart skipped a beat. At one stage some children took over the all important channel 14 and saturated it with pop music. It seemed to last for hours and Dick was convinced that Sally was trying to get through, but after ten minutes when things returned to normal, there was still no call from the rubber duck. Dusk had just fallen and Janice was making a start on preparing a mixed grill for the evening meal when the sound of an outboard motor, followed by a slight bump, announced that Sally and Rodney had returned. Dick at once rushed up on deck, Janice turned out the gas and followed.

'Well?' he queried. 'What have you seen?'

'Boats, kids, swimmers, sand, seaweed, but no sign of that bloody yellow yacht. I think we've lost this one.' Rodney responded in despair.

Dick grimaced then turned to Janice and said in a quiet sombre voice. 'Looks as if I was wrong Jan, let's go and eat. I'll put you ashore in the morning and drive you back to Woodbridge where you can pick up your car. Sal and Rod can sail *Lady* round. Sorry, but it looks as if we've done all we can. As soon as the sample results come through, if they're what we think they are, you have a go at your Brigadier and I'll tackle Alf Carter. However, by then I think it will be a case of closing the door after the horse has gone!'

CHAPTER 15

George Brine reached out from inside his sleeping bag and picked up a small transistor radio. Looking up from his bunk in the fo'c'sle, through the translucent hatch cover, he saw the sun starting its relentless climb into a sky which carried a hint of grey cloud despoiling the otherwise unblemished blue. The pale yellow rays of the new day were still too weak to dry the night's condensation.

'Not bad, not at all bad,' he muttered as he switched on for the early morning broadcast.

As the strains of Rule Britannia died away the announcer proclaimed that Radio Four was about to start the Tuesday morning with another Shipping Forecast, followed by News Briefing and Farming Today. He closed his eyes and waited as the voice droned on ... 'high pressure will move slowly to south east and decline ... a shallow depression 1001 millibars expected Forties by 0500 hours tomorrow ... area forecasts for the next twenty four hours ... Dogger, German Bight; south to south east three to four, later variable then southerly three. Humber, Thames; south to south west, three, later four, locally five. Dover ...' George Brine had heard enough and silenced the set.

'Well that's it, we go,' he shouted in jubilation to the others. Pete, on the opposite bunk, grunted, rolled over and pulled his head down inside the red bag.

In the saloon John Grimley slept on, only Olive gave a positive response. 'Good,' she said raising to one elbow, 'What time do we want to leave?'

'No rush, get a bit more shut eye, we'll be short of it before we're through. Slip off a bit earlier than I originally intended. We can always kill time if we're early, but not make it up if we're late. How about midday?'

'Okay, Olive agreed, 'but I need to get ashore to make the final confirmatory phone call, will you run me across after breakfast?'

'Sure, about ten do?'

'Fine.'

'Good, nothing can stop us now, so let's get a bit more kip.' George Brine temporarily terminated the conversation and the boat lapsed into silence.

*

The skipper of *Brimstone* wedged himself alongside the chart table to counter the roll of the boat, plotted their Decca position and measured off the distance to the southern end of Brown Ridge. With the sun already set and the sky darkening he was about to hand over the watch to Pete and John, but wanted to set the final course to the rendezvous. Grimley had been sick, but now appeared to have found his sea legs and Brine was happy to hand over for the next four hours while he and Olive got some sleep. It would mean they would be fresh for the actual meeting.

He reflected how well things had gone. Olive had come back from her phone call and announced all was in order. A message would have been relayed to Mother for a meeting in the early hours of tomorrow. They had passed a handful of other boats as they made their way down the Colne and out of the Blackwater, but none paid them any attention. There had been no sign of the yacht which anchored off Horsenose Creek nor any police and customs launches.

The weather was perfect with a fair wind giving them more than five knots. All the others had settled into ship routine and they were up to schedule. He estimated the tidal set over the next six hours, made due allowance from the rhumb line and jotted down the required course in the boat's log.

'You'll need to come south by ten degrees, John,' he called up to the cockpit where Grimley was already at the helm. 'I've logged the new course. If I'm not up on deck in four hours time come and give me a shake.'

'Right,' came the economical reply from the Watersthorpe Laboratory Supervisor.

'And don't hesitate to call me if there are any problems. Keep a lookout for the big ships, they don't always see small yachts. You've got a deep water shipping lane to cross. I don't think it will be too busy, but it only takes one ship to sink us! Don't insist too strongly on our rights, give way in plenty of time so that the other fellow, if he has seen you, will understand your intentions.'

'Yes skipper. You get your sleep, Pete and I won't cock things up at this stage.'

George Brine smiled to himself, then crawled into his sleeping bag on an adjacent bunk.

*

Captain Petricoff leaned over his chart table and marked off his latest Decca position, then ran the dividers from the cross he had just made to the southern tip of Brown Ridge.

'*Gulf Queen, Gulf Queen ... Sea Harvester, Sea Harvester,*' the VHF radio broke into his thoughts. He reached out, turned the power down to one watt and responded.

'*Sea Harvester* this is *Gulf Queen*, try channel eight.'

'Going eight.'

'*Gulf Queen*, this is *Sea Harvester*, glad to have caught you Ken.' The conversation was in good English though the accents dubious, the respondents did not want there to be any suggestion of a Russian boat in the area. 'Wanted to confirm the arrangements for our retirement party.'

'As you previously indicated, same time and place?'

'Roger, I understand that those with the greatest distance to travel have already left and should meet up with you as they arranged.'

'Good, well thanks for your chat. If you get a chance tell Dad that there are no problems this end, have a good watch.'

'Wilco, good fishing. Out.' The conversation ended as abruptly as it had begun. Having delivered its message the shadowing submarine dived and continued its mission. Petricoff returned to his chart, looked up at the ships clock and smiled, there would be no problems.

'Same course, eight knots,' he ordered the helmsman.

*

There was no great rush by those on board *English Lady* to welcome the new day. The mood of depression and feeling of failure that they all suffered confined them to their berths until after the Eight O'clock News had started. It was one of the few occasions when Dick had been on board that he had not woken for the five to six shipping forecast. Breakfast was a sombre affair with conversation restricted to only the essential instructions necessary for its completion. As things were being cleared away Dick spoke out.

'Get your kit together Jan, I'll take you back to Woodbridge for your car. Can I trust you two with *Lady*?' he cast his glance at Rodney.

'Sure, but it would be pushing it to get over the Bar before next high, we'll come in on the afternoon's tide if that's okay?'

'Might as well, there's no hurry. Give a shout on the C.B. as soon as you pick up the mooring, I'll be listening out on one four. Sal are you going to come to bring the duck back?'

'When you're ready,' she replied.

Despondency had turned to lethargy and as a result it was near midday before Janice tore herself away from the *English Lady* and boarded the inflatable for her trip back to Watersthorpe. They landed at the marina and after bidding farewell to his daughter, Dick led Janice across the yard to the car park. On their left was one of the few surviving old red telephone boxes.

'Hold on a minute, Dick, I'll give Kindale a ring and find out what's been happening back at the ranch while I've been enjoying your company. Never know, there's always a faint hope that something may have turned up.'

'Okay, I'll wait here,' came the despondent reply. He watched with vacant eyes as Janice walked over to the kiosk and struggled, as millions of her predecessors throughout the United Kingdom had done in previous years, to open the heavy cast iron door. As the Health Physicist from Watersthorpe talked, he paced to and fro, tugging gently at the lobe of his ear.

'Fool, fool, England you're a bloody fool,' he exploded.

'Don't tell me, let me guess,' Janice was back at his side, her call complete. Dick failed to notice her smile, she continued, 'I suppose you've left the car keys on the boat,' she suggested.

Like someone coming out of a trance Dick returned to the real world. 'No, nothing as bad as that, but I've just had a thought. I...what are you grinning about?'

'A ray of light has appeared, Graham has just told me the Brigadier ordered a full check on our plut stocks this morning. Seems it's to be given top priority. They've already started the prelims in the store and pulled out a couple of suspect containers. These'll be back loaded tonight and then assayed tomorrow.'

'How long before the results come through?'

'Well, it depends, but they'll be lucky if they find anything before tomorrow or Thursday. Something's made the Old Man change his mind.'

'Could be Alf Carter's been whispering in some ears,' Dick muttered then continued. 'Look while you were in that phone box I realised we'd missed a trick.'

'We?'

'Well I. The chart agent, I should have gone back there yesterday to find out if that fellow from Longsands had returned to collect his 1408. We know he hadn't on Friday and their boat sailed on Saturday, presumably with him on board, so he couldn't have collected it then. If he needs it for his passage, and presumably he does otherwise he wouldn't have ordered it, then they either laid up somewhere on Sunday and collected it yesterday, or they still haven't left for their final destination.'

'Or they got the chart elsewhere,' Janice interjected. Dick ignored the comment.

'If they haven't yet departed, and if your boys show that the plut is missing, then there's a good chance of catching up with them. Look, the shop is almost on our way. Let's call back and renew our enquiries.'

'Okay by me.'

The bell on the shop door had hardly stopped ringing as the agent came scurrying out of the rear room.

''allo Mr. England,' then he noticed Janice who had followed Dick in. ''allo miss.' Turning back to Dick he continued without pause. 'That chappy Brine you were asking about on Friday, 'e came in yesterday an' took 'is 1408 an' other charts, so reckon 'e is a proper cruising man after all.'

'Yesterday,' Dick repeated. 'Oh Christ.'

'Eh, sommat wrong Mr. England?'

'Er no, no.' Dick thought fast. 'Think I'd better take a 1408,' he said.

'I'm sorry, I ain't got one left. Well that ain't strictly true. I got an old un. 'e left 'is when he got the new un. Said 'e brought it in case I still ain't got 'em in in the 'ope of correcting it, but didn't need to see 'cause I 'ad got 'em. But I ain't got 'em now see..'

'If I could have the old one it would be most helpful,' Dick said for no particular reason, except perhaps to humour the man.

They were back in the car when Janice started to question her companion.

'What are you getting so excited about Dick?'

'Look, if the fellow from the large house collected his charts yesterday then they haven't high tailed it with the plut after all. It was as I speculated, Saturday's outing must simply have been a trial. They are here...somewhere not far away.'

'But they didn't come back...'

'You mean we didn't see them come back...maybe they slipped in when we weren't looking...maybe they're anchored in the Stour...or the Blackwater...or the Colne. None of those places are far from Walton by road.'

'But...'

'Sorry Jan. I'm not going to have time to take you back to Woodbridge just yet, must get out to *Lady* before she leaves. You take the car...'

'No way, if there's a chance we can still find them I'm staying. Watersthorpe can wait a few more hours, how do we get out to your boat without a rubber duck?'

'Easy, a drink for the yacht club boatman should do the trick, let's go.'

The bright red launch came gently alongside *English Lady* and Dick let out a loud 'ahoy there' to give the couple below fair warning that they were about to be boarded.

'Thanks Willie,' he said turning to the almost barrel shaped boatman wearing a navy blue jersey emblazoned with bold red R.N.L.I. letters, 'that's a scotch I owe you.'

'Don't 'e worry about that', I'll catch you in the club som'time,' he replied with a grin on his beetroot red, weather beaten face. 'Mind 'ow you git aboard missy,' he said turning to Janice, then with a wave he eased the boat away and was headed back.

As Dick and Janice stepped down into the cockpit, Sally appeared at the hatch.

'Good God, Dad, what brings you back?

'Well I could say Willie Waters, but more to the point I think we've turned something up that could give us a lead. Looks promising enough for Janice to decide to stay. Let's go below and I'll explain.'

Once more the quartet sat round the saloon table, Dick briefly reviewed their visit to the chart agents and repeated his reasoning.

'So you see there's a good chance they're still in the area, all we have to do is start looking.'

'Oh come off it,' Rodney objected. 'There must be thousands of places they could be lying, we'd need a lot of luck to spot them. Anyhow it was yesterday they collected the charts so they're probably away by now.'

'It's possible,' Dick conceded, 'but I still think it's worth a try, we can reduce the possibilities by the application of reason.'

'How?' Sally asked.

'Well it's unlikely that they're in anywhere that's restrictive on leaving. That eliminates the Deben, the Ore, Southwold and possibly Shotley Point Marina.'

'Great thinking Dad, that only leaves Lowestoft, Yarmouth, The Orwell, The Stour, The Blackwater, The Crouch, Bradwell Creek, Brightlingsea, Pyefleet, need I go on?' Sally countered with sarcasm.

'It's not that bad,' Dick persisted. 'Most likely they are fairly close to Walton because they went back for the chart.'

His daughter looked sceptical, so did Rodney, Janice looked bored then her eyes caught sight of the still rolled up chart Dick had deposited on the table.

'I suppose their old chart won't tell us anything?' she interjected.

'Doubt it,' Dick replied as he unrolled it on the table and weighed the corners with an assortment of handy objects. 'Looks a bit dog-eared.' Four pairs of eyes scrutinised it.

'What are all those pencil marks and lines on it?' Janice queried.

'They're old courses, trips the owner has already done and not rubbed them out.'

'I don't think that one is,' Rodney made the comment with a note of excitement in his voice, 'look there are no hourly plots, just the one lay off, I think that is a planned route rather than a trip completed.'

'What are those figures there?' Sally asked pointing to a faint smudge in the middle of the chart. Dick picked up a magnifying glass and studied them closely.

'Looks like 03.30 or 83.30.'

'If it's an E.T.A. then it has to be 03.30,' Rodney pointed out the obvious and the four lapsed into silence. Sally was the first to speak.

'If I'm thinking the same as you are, then hadn't we ought to be moving?'

'You mean that smudge at Brown Ridge is a meeting point or something,' Janice asked.

'Could be something like that,' Dick conceded, 'but if it is we don't know the date, only the time.'

'Dad, look at it this way. If the plut is still at Longsands then the security people will know where to look. By late Wednesday or Thursday not only will the first results of the check at Watersthorpe be available, so will our sample analysis. There will be enough evidence for prompt action and the material will be recovered. However, if it has been moved, as we suspect on that yellow yacht, then it could be out of the country by then only if the boat has sailed yesterday, today or will sail tomorrow. After that their chance of escape will be very small. In a nutshell the best thing we can do is to hot foot it to Brown Ridge and hang around there for forty eight hours. We can keep in touch with link calls.'

'We might just get Scheveningen from there, it's forty five miles to the nearest coast radio, I reckon they won't pick up our transmission so we can't count on the telephone, but I think Sal is probably right, what have we got to lose?'

'Can we make this Brown Ridge by half past three?' Janice asked.

Dick looked at his watch, then laid the dividers over the chart. 'Eighty five miles, we don't get much help from the tide and we've got fourteen hours, fifteen if that is G.M.T.' He paused, tugged the lobe of his ear and continued, 'Normally *Lady* will motor at seven but with this makeshift prop we may have to settle for five and a half or six knots.' He turned to the chart table and picked up a pocket calculator. 'Somewhere between fourteen and sixteen hours. If the wind stays fair, yes we can, but we must leave right away.'

'Let's go,' Sally said firmly.

'Agreed,' Rodney and Janice said in unison.

*

Although the sun was not yet visible the sky had lightened. The wind had gone, leaving an oily swell and wisps of sea mist which reduced visibility, in patches, to about half a mile.

George Brine put aside the binoculars and, with a hint of a smile of satisfaction on his face, turned to Olive who was clutching the tiller.

'She's there, about a mile and a half off our bow, another ten degrees to starboard should do.' Olive peered into the gloom, at first she saw nothing but a grey dull mist, then as her eyes adjusted to the light, she could just make out the shape of a ship.

'How do you know that is Mother?' she asked.

'Got to be, bang on station. Anyhow there's not likely to be anything else out here except perhaps a fishing boat and that's too large to be one of them. What now?'

'Wake the others and bring a signalling lamp or large torch, we have to make an identification signal.'

The skipper did as he was bid and returned shortly with a powerful hand lamp, an excited John Grimley and a stoic Pete. For the next ten minutes four pairs of eyes strained across *Brimstone*'s deck at the indistinct shape in front. As the distance reduced so the visibility improved.

'Signal F W,' Olive commanded then in response to Brine's hesitation added, 'dit dit dar dit, dit dar dar.'

'I bloody well know F W.'

'Then why hesitate?'

'I wasn't sure they would know what it was,' the bearded mariner responded with a smile as he flashed out the two letters several times. From the dark shape in front a pin point of light gave reply.

'That is it, O L G A, the correct response, congratulations George.'

'Thanks, but Decca should really take the credit, I could hardly have missed with that, good job our chain wasn't out on maintenance.'

The gap between the two boats closed rapidly, soon they could read the name *Gulf Queen* then, when only a cable apart, a man appeared on the freighter's deck and motioned the yacht to the starboard side. As he did so a boom swung out and started to lower the lifting harness.

'Welcome to my ship comrade,' Olive looked upwards at the face above.

'Captain Petricoff? I trust you have our package?' she replied.

George Brine, aided by Pete, slipped the straps under *Brimstone*'s hull and then signalled the deck hand at the winch to start lifting. The yacht was kept suspended some three feet above the *Gulf Queen*'s deck, but secured by four lines, one on each quarter and on each side of the bow.

'Aren't we getting out?' John Grimley queried.

'I have to go and see the Captain,' Olive responded, 'but there is no need for anyone else to leave. The experts on the boat will bolt the weapon onto the keel and give you the firing instructions. It is activated by an ultrasonic pulse so there are no wires passing through the hull. You will be provided with a small black box which looks like a portable radio. I will not be long.'

'Are you coming with us to Den Oever?' Brine queried.

'But of course, it will be the climax of our operation, I would not miss it for anything.' As Olive spoke, one of the deck hands placed a ladder against the side of *Brimstone*. 'Not only that, you could not manage the trip without me, we still have nearly seventy miles and fifteen hours at sea in front of us.'

'I could do it without you, in fact I could do it single handed,' Brine boasted, 'but I'd rather have a crew. It will be daylight all the way, two would be adequate, three better and four luxury!'

'George, I am coming with you, that is definite, now give me a hand over the side onto this ladder,' Olive terminated the conversation and climbed out of the cockpit and onto the side deck. George was just thinking that Olive was quite nimble for her age and build when he heard a cry of anguish and a dull thump. She had slipped off the last rung of the ladder and lay sprawled across the deck.

'Are you okay?' he called to the figure that was just starting, with the aid of a deck hand, to get to her feet.

'I...I think so, the ankle hurts a bit, expect it will be alright in a minute.' Olive turned to the man who had come to her assistance. 'Lend me your arm for a minute and take me to the Captain's cabin,' she commanded.

George Brine looked on bemused then turned to the others. 'Somehow I've got a feeling we shall be three on this trip!'

'No way, Olive will come,' Pete responded with confidence.

'If you don't mind,' John Grimley said, changing the conversation, 'I'll go for'ard and crash out, didn't get my full share of shut eye in the night.' The other two hardly took any notice as the man from Watersthorpe stepped into the fo'c'sle and closed the door. They were too busy removing the extra ballast and the Watersthorpe plutonium.

CHAPTER 16

Dick England had been right about the replacement propeller. With assistance from the moderate south westerly, *English Lady* had made nearly seven knots over the first part of her course, but as the evening closed in so the wind died and under power alone she would make no more than five and a half. Excitement was running high and, contrary to normal practice, they had not kept set watches but simply taken it in turn to cat nap. Now as the dawn approached, six eyes strained into the shadowy mist in search of their quarry, the other pair were glued to the radar screen.

'That blip we've been shadowing for the last hour or so is now about ten miles ahead and ten degrees to starboard. Looks like a yacht from its speed and size of signal, but it's right on the limit of our range.'

'Anything else about?' Dick called down from the cockpit.

'Only those two tankers in the D.W. behind us,' Rodney replied referring to the deep water channel they had just crossed.

'Wish I had a fix, with only DR and an out of date chart we could easily be several miles out.'

'Told you we should have bought a Decca,' Sally commented unhelpfully, 'but you would insist on waiting to see whether it was going to be superseded by Loran or Satnav[33]. Why not try a DF?[34]

'Don't think there's anything out here we'd pick up.'

---

[33]*Decca was a system developed during the war, and continued afterwards, as a navigation aid to position finding. It works from a series of transmission stations sending out radio signals and mainly covers the North Sea. In the mid 1980's there was considerable speculation over the long term continuation of this system and it seemed likely that it might be superseded by a similar, but more universal system known as Loran. Also navigation by satellite, ie. SATNAV, was coming to be used in small boats. This was based on American military satellites.*

[34]*D.F. is jargon for radio direction finding. A few navigation buoys and some coast and aero beacons emit radio signals in morse code. By using radios with directional aerials the bearings from these can be established. If more than one can be received at any position then a fix can be obtained from where the bearings intersect. Unfortunately these radio beacons are often limited in range and number. While some transmit continuously it is more common for them to be grouped with others on the same frequency when they only transmit for one minute in six.*

'Amsterdam has a range of seventy five miles, we ought to get that. Goeree is fifty and we might just hear that under these conditions.'

Dick looked doubtful, Sally continued. 'I looked them up in the Almanac a few minutes ago.'

'Worth a try, but at this distance I reckon any such fix would be no better than my DR, see what you can do,' her father suggested.

Sally went below and switched on the DF radio. She set the tuner to 381kHz and slowly rotated the aerial. The morse letters SPY started to come through clear then faded at the null point. She noted this bearing. She then retuned to 287.3kHz and again rotated the sensor, but heard nothing. She looked at the ships clock and realised that as Goeree was grouped it would not be transmitting for another three minutes. She waited then heard the letters morse GR, very faint but clear. Again she found the null point and noted the bearing. She squeezed past Rodney and settled at the chart table where she plotted the fixes.

'Got it Dad, the DF seems to think we are more or less where your DR put us! About ten miles west sou' west of the southern end of Brown Ridge. We're right on the edge of the shipping lane.'

'Dick,' this time it was Rodney calling from below. 'Dick come and have a look at this.' The skipper passed the wheel over to Janice and made his way below to the radar set.

'What?' he asked.

'That,' Rodney said pointing to a blip on the extremity of the screen, 'is the boat we've been following for the past two hours.'

'So?'

'Well, it's got bigger. Just took my eyes off it for a few minutes to look over Sal's shoulder and I swear it got bigger.'

'Hmm...' Dick pulled a face and tugged gently at the lobe of his ear. 'I suppose it could be a change in conditions, but I think not. The other explanation it that we now have two ships close together. The set would not be able to resolve them at this distance. I wonder if our friends have met up with another vessel? Is the blip much larger?'

'Quite a bit.'

'Then it must be a bigger ship, a coaster or large trawler perhaps. If it is then they will almost certainly have radar and have us under observation. Also...,' Dick was thinking aloud, 'this second ship hasn't crossed our screen,' Rodney nodded in agreement, 'so it must have approached from the north or north east.' Dick went to the companionway, 'Jan alter course to north east.'

'What's that for?' Rodney asked.

'If we continue as we are we will attract attention long before we can get close enough to see what is going on. Somehow we've got to close without being spotted.'

'Let me take the inflatable. It'll do ten knots if we put the big Yamma on, could be with them in less than an hour.'

'No,' Dick was firm. 'One, we might not be able to find you again and secondly, under still conditions like this they would hear you coming. That would arouse even more suspicions.'

'Skipper,' the voice of Janice hailed from the cockpit with anxiety. 'There are red and green lights coming straight at us[35], looks like a bloody great ship.'

Dick sprang through the companion way and in an instant realised their position. The alteration of course had put them back inside the shipping lane and for some reason the vessel behind had probably not noticed them. He took the helm, turned to starboard and the tanker slid past.

'That gives me an idea,' Dick said as he returned the boat to her proper course and the helm to Janice. 'Sal! Rod! Up here pronto please.'

The other two scrambled into the cockpit. He turned to his daughter. 'Sal could you do a mast job for us out here? It won't be as easy as when we were at anchor as the boat is rolling quite a bit especially when it hits a wake.' He glanced upwards, 'I want that radar reflector off, then we can chance closing on that other boat. It's only secured by an aluminium strap, should be able to cut through it in a minute with a hacksaw.'

'Okay I'll have a go, let's get kitted up.'

'I'll go,' Rodney volunteered.

'I'm the lightest, so it's my job, don't be a male chauvinist. Get me the hardware out of the Bosuns locker.'

---

[35] *Every ship has to show a red navigation on its port side and a green one on its starboard and a white light facing aft. (A sailing yacht may, as an alternative, have one light on its mast head which is divided into three appropriately coloured sectors, this is known as a tricolour.) A motor vessel carries, in addition, a white forward facing light on its masts depending on its size. By interpreting navigation lights the nature, size and course of a neighbouring vessel can be estimated.*

'There's one other thing, we will have to wait until another big ship comes along and cut the reflector away when we are very close, then we can shorten the gap on that suspicious looking blob on our screen.'

'Why the wait?' Sally queried.

'Because if our friend is watching his screen, which he ought to be, he will think it odd if we suddenly disappear. However, if we wait until we're merged with the reflection from a bigger boat he'll probably overlook the fact that we should reappear sometime! Don't fret we won't have to wait long those two whites looming up astern will be with us in ten minutes.'

*

John Grimley did not sleep, he lay in his bunk worrying. He just could not convince himself that, no matter how organised the Dutch were with their emergency warning plans for flood alerts, they could evacuate all the people who would be in the danger zone from the explosion. He was a convinced socialist who hated the capitalist system. He believed in socialist Russia and had happily devoted his life to forwarding its cause. He had infiltrated Watersthorpe to help destroy the nuclear industries. His objective was to save life not kill innocent people. When Olive returned he would demand she changed the plan; after all, he reasoned he stole the plutonium in the first place, so he should say how it was used. The sound of someone climbing the ladder sent a flush of adrenaline through his system and he braced himself to face her. Footsteps came aboard, he hesitated.

'Mr. Brine?'

It was a male voice, not Olive's, he drew back from the cabin door.

'Yes,' he heard George reply.

'I'm Captain Petricoff, the weapon is bolted to your keel, there were no problems. We will have you back in the water in a few minutes, but now I must brief you on how it is triggered, first I have some bad news…'

'Olive?' Pete interrupted.

'Yes, I'm afraid her fall was worse than we thought, it looks as if her ankle is broken, she is in great pain and will not be able to complete the trip. I am to enquire if you can manage without her or whether you would like to have one of my men as a substitute?'

Grimley had heard enough. He knew he had to see Olive without delay. Quietly he opened the fo'c'sle hatch and climbed out. He found a mooring warp, tied it to the anchor winch and tossed the other end over the side then slid down and went in search of his leader. Petricoff continued as George Brine gave a negative shake of his head.

'The plan remains unaltered. You will be much slower with this encumbrance...'

'I am aware of that Captain,' Brine said with sarcasm.

'You must be into the Waddenzee before high water. Strong tides run through the Gats and you will have great problems if you are not through them before the ebb sets.' *Brimstone*'s skipper nodded in agreement.

'So I don't have time to waste,' he interrupted.

'I will not delay you longer than necessary.' He took a small black box from a shoulder bag. 'This is the trigger. There are three buttons, each has a cover. You can lift the cover from button one at any time, it primes the device. After one minute the cover over number two will be released and you can then activate the fire button. This delay is to prevent an unintentional operation. The weapon will detonate exactly two hours after button two has been pressed. Nothing can stop it and any attempt to dismantle the bomb at this stage will cause it to explode.'

'What about the third button?' Pete asked.

'We hope you don't have to use that, it is suicide. You can only access it after two has been operated; if number three is pressed then the device will explode immediately.'

'Thanks, I'll try not to press that one,' Brine said with a wry smile. 'Now let's get going.'

'In a minute, Olive tells me to say that the escape plans are the same, at the Den Oever sluice you will find four cycles locked to a lamp post. The combination is written on this paper. You will cycle north to the viewing lay-by on the dam where you will find a blue XR4i. The key is in the saddle bag on the green bike. After that it is up to you to make your way to the East German border where you are to ask for Comrade Colonel Ivan Zurkoff.'

'Everything seems to have been thought of, can we go now?'

'Yes, of course, good luck Captain.' Petricoff bade his opposite number on the smaller boat, 'I will have you lowered back into the sea. As soon as you are free, go ahead, we will put our engine astern until you are clear.'

'Shall I get Grimley out of his bunk?' Pete asked.

'No, let the little twerp sleep,' George Brine instructed.

John Grimley lost no time in discovering that Olive had been taken to the Captain's cabin. He made his way up the iron staircase that led to the bridge and the nearby door marked Captain. He paused and wondered if he should knock, decided on a surprise entry, pushed open the door and marched in. The room, set into a corner of the bridge, was lit by one porthole in the door and a window which faced aft. The walls were lined with knotty pine and the floor carpeted in grey. Along one windowless side was the Captain's bunk and against the other wall a desk at which Olive was seated, her back half turned to the door.

'Olive, I must speak urgently to you,' John opened the conversation even before she had twisted round to see who had entered.

'You! What are you doing here, has something gone wrong?' Her voice was raised and for the first time he thought she was rattled.

'Yes, I am not going to allow you to have the weapon exploded in Holland. I don't care what you say about a warning, people will get killed.' He looked his leader in the face and awaited her reply.

'You what?' she laughed.

'I won't agree to people getting killed. I stole the plut in the first place. Without me there would be no bomb so I reckon I have a right of veto and I intend to use it!'

'John,' her voice went ice cold, 'the matter is out of your hands. The weapon will be exploded as I have said and you have no means of stopping it. Did Brine send you up here?'

'No, he doesn't know I've come, he's still being briefed by the Captain.' He paused for a moment as he remembered Olive's injured ankle. It dawned on him that she did not appear to be in any distress or pain.

'Go back to the yacht and carry out the instructions.'

Grimley stood firm. 'Your ankle, it isn't bandaged, you've been moving it. I don't think it's hurt at all, why?' As he finished speaking he moved closer and started to bend down as if to inspect it.

'You're right,' as Olive spoke she brought her leg suddenly upwards, sending her toe into Grimley's groin.

'Y...,' his words were strangled by the searing pain that shot up from his injured genitals and filled the pit of his stomach. He bent forward and as he did so Olive stood up, hit him hard across the face with the back of her hand then kneed him again between his legs. As tears streamed down his cheeks he tried to speak, but the words would not come. He stood doubled in agony, Olive stepped to one side then with her right hand, slashed down at Grimley's neck. He fell to the floor poleaxed and lay on his side. Olive looked down on the crumpled, whimpering heap.

'I think you have just lost your veto,' she mocked. 'As you have found out, there is nothing wrong with my foot, I did not want to go on the remaining part of the trip. You see they are not coming back, there is no delay after the second button has been pressed.' She smiled again. 'Now what am I going to do with you?'

She stepped over the body on the floor and taking careful aim drove her foot into Grimley's kidneys. With a jerk his back straightened, then he folded again, almost into the foetal position. He clenched his lips determined not to let out any sound. Olive hesitated, then like a cat tired of its lifeless prey, turned away. She felt a sense of satisfaction having inflicted pain, but it could no longer be appreciated by her victim, so the stimulation it gave her faded rapidly.

'Now shall I finish you off or let you die with the others when we abandon the ship. I think I will have a word with Petricoff,' she muttered under her breath as she walked over to the door and went in search of the Captain.

Grimley had heard these words, and his brain was starting to function again. As he lay on the floor, body racked with pain, he realised that he would not be allowed back on *Brimstone*, moreover if they were doomed so, too, was he. They were no longer comrades, Olive was going to have him killed, it was only a matter of time. Perhaps if he could warn the others... It was a faint hope, but the only one. He took several deep breaths to try and regain some strength then forced himself to a standing position. He staggered to the self-closing door and, summoning all his remaining strength, pulled. It opened and he lurched out onto the steel balcony. Looking to his right, down the steps which a few minutes ago he had ascended, he saw Olive had already attracted a man's attention who, he assumed, to be Petricoff, they were walking towards the foot of the ladder.

Olive chanced to look up. 'Damn, he's recovered. I thought he was as good as dead,' she cried out. The Captain assessed the situation even before she had finished speaking.

'Ivan,' he shouted to one of the KGB agents on the port side of the boat, 'get that bastard. You take those steps I'll go this way.'

Grimley realised his access to the deck was barred, without any clear idea of what to do he turned to his left and ran across the bridge. The First Officer and the helmsman, unaware of what was happening, looked on bemused as he ran out of the port door. Grimley turned, then saw the KGB gorilla starting towards him. Numb with fear he edged backwards until he felt a hand rail press against his spine. He turned and saw climbing rungs leading down from the bridge platform to the after deck below. The KGB man was close behind and reached out to grab him. John turned, twisted and somehow broke the grip that was on his sailing smock. He stepped on to the rungs and scrambled down to the deck below. Now he found himself against the stern rail, the still sea slapping into the transom of the boat. He knew it was a desperate hope, the slenderest of straws to clutch but he was a good swimmer. He sidled over the rail and let himself fall into the water. If he managed a few strokes he could reach the yacht which was about to cast off.

The First Officer had not followed the Grimley saga and ignored the Captain's dash across the bridge, he was more concerned to get the yacht away. He saw the deck hand indicate that the small boat was clear so he rang the engine "slow astern". The big propeller started to turn and a surge of water was swept under the ship's keel, it caught John Grimley and carried him on to the blades. The metal cut into flesh and blood coloured the water. Petricoff and Olive looked over the rail.

'That seems to have solved our problem,' was all she remarked.

*

Harry England was in a quandary, he had moved three miles north east then held station to watch. The suspicious blob on his radar now lay east south east. As far as Rodney could tell it had not moved for about half an hour. It would not take that long, he reasoned to hand over a container of plutonium and possibly accept a cash package in return. Were they mistaken, could this be a fishing vessel?

'I don't understand why those two marks have not yet separated,' he muttered aloud.

'Perhaps they have,' Rodney suggested. 'It could be that the smaller boat, a yacht, passed close to the other one and then continued in the radar shadow of the larger vessel. It would not have had to have gone far before being out of our range.'

'Shit! I think you're right. All the time we've been here hove too waiting, the yacht has been on its way. Probably about fifteen miles ahead by now.'

'Or it could be that the small boat has been swallowed up by the larger one, might even have accidentally run it down. After all we don't know that it was the Yellow Peril, we might have been following some innocent fellow starting off on his holidays!'

'Don't think so, if the vessel had stopped following a rundown then she would surely have put out a 'May Day', 'Pan Pan' or 'Securite'. A pick up is possible, I have heard of stolen yachts being lifted out of the sea by South American bound freighters, but it would not have taken this long.' Dick England paused again, tugged at the lobe of his ear then continued. 'No, I think we've made a fool of ourselves, or at least I have, that must be a fishing boat on the Ridge. Now we've lost the other bastard.' As Dick plunged into thought the Scotsman returned to his screen.

'Dick,' Rodney called out from his radar watch, 'I think there's movement. It could be us drifting, but I don't think so.'

'Are you sure?' the skipper asked.

'No, not absolutely, but from the movement of the ships in the D.W. I don't think it's our drift. I'm sure that blob is moving north or north west, if it continues then it should clear us by only a few miles.'

Dick moved over to the set then looked at the chart. 'Sal engine full ahead, out with the genny and set the main, head east north east, we'll try and intercept. If we can get visual at least we'll know whether the plut has gone to Israel, Iran, Iraq or the USSR!'

Sally didn't hesitate, the Perkins Special burst into life as Janice let go the topping lift and then the jib furling line. The gentle breeze, which had been building in the last half hour, was enough to shape the sails but little else and *English Lady* managed just under six knots. Dick came on deck with binoculars, Rodney remained at the radar.

'How far are we apart?' the skipper asked.

'Closing, about eight miles bearing about one one ho.' Rodney read off the details from the screen.

'Still some mist about, will need to get to within a mile or so if we are going to be sure of a sighting, half a mile to read her name.' Dick was responding to a question from Janice.

'Won't they recognise us and try and sink us, nobody knows where we are?' This was fair comment Dick mused.

'Sal?' he called out. 'Remember that Dutch boat we towed off the Cork last year, what happened to the ensign they gave us?'

'Might be on board, but you were going to present it to the Club.'

'I know, but I don't think I did. Have a look behind the back of the saloon berth, starboard side.'

'What on earth for?'

'We'll borrow their nationality, after all it's only a few years off 1992, we are as good as one country. Our friends aren't expecting us, we are not coming on them from the angle they would anticipate and if we wear a Dutch ensign we won't even look British.'

'Want me to fly it if and when I find it?'

'No you clown, wipe your bum with it,' the tension and anxiety that Dick felt was starting to show, his daughter made no comment.

'Skipper,' it was Rodney calling from below. 'Come and take a look at this.'

'What is it, surely you can read a radar,' came the irritated reply.

'I can, that's why I've called you, there's another blip on the edge of the screen. Looks as if there have been two boats together.' Dick England hesitated no longer, gripping the top of the hatch he swung himself through the companionway and landed at Rodney's side.

'Christ, now what do we do? Two of the bastards to follow.'

'We're not going to get within a couple of miles of the bigger fellow, doubt if we'd learn much at that distance but if that other blip is a yacht, the one we were observing before, then we can follow her, might even catch up.'

Dick went over to the chart table, checked tides and laid out a theoretical course. He called up to Janice who had taken the helm while Sally was swapping flags.

'Change course, south south east, you'll need to trim in the main and genny.' He paused as he had second thoughts. The wind was south south west, perhaps he ought to get to weather of his quarry, 'Jan see how close you can get, make it south if she'll take it.' He returned to the radar before joining the females in the cockpit.

'What's happening?' Janice asked.

'Looks as if we've picked up the Yellow Peril on radar. We are also likely to miss the other boat I'd hoped we could intercept. I've decided to go after the yacht, we might just catch her.'

Daylight was now upon them, the sea looked very empty under the cold grey sky. A few dark clouds drifted under the high wispy cirrus. The glass had fallen a couple of millibars in the past six hours and the wind strengthened from the south west. Convinced that the high was giving way to an incoming depression he had freed a little and they were now making six knots in a south easterly direction.

'Not much to look at,' Janice remarked.

'Not up here, but we've still got that little blip on the edge of the radar and we're keeping pace.' Rodney reassured her from below.

'Good,' she replied and as a token gesture picked up the binoculars. 'Can't see anything.'

'You won't at this distance,' Sally, now at the helm, chipped in.

'I can see something,' Janice contradicted, 'but it's not a boat.'

'Sea gull?' Dick queried.

'No, looks like a bit of wreckage or a body floating in the water.'

'If it wasn't floating you wouldn't see it,' Dick declined to take her seriously. 'If it's wreckage give it a wide berth.'

'And if it's a body we still don't want to know. If you find a body at sea never pull it in.'

'Why?'

'Because then you have to take it ashore and may well get landed with the burial costs! We'll report the sighting as soon as we're within radio range of the Dutch coast.'

'But it might be alive,' Janice persisted.

'No chance,' Dick remarked. 'Survival time in the sea this time of year is only a matter of an hour or so. Unless it fell out of the sky it must have been there longer.'

Janice still clutched the glasses and stared intently ahead. 'It does look like a body,' she repeated, but this time there was a note of concern in her voice, all traces of flippancy gone.

Dick took her more seriously, 'Where?'

'About two o'clock, half a mile away. See it on the crest of the waves.'

'Okay we'll be suckers, helmsperson bring her up thirty five degrees.'

As he spoke he went over to the winch and wound in the genoa sheet. 'Jan bring the main in,' he called.

'Approach from loo'ard, then luff, we'll roll in the genny and loose off the main,' he instructed. 'Rod better leave your telly and come and give us a hand.'

Sally, still at the helm, executed the manoeuvre with precision.

'It bloody well is a body,' Rodney called from the bow. 'It looks recent, not bloated, what now? Christ I think it's still alive? It twitched.'

Dick didn't hesitate. 'Rod get a harness on. Jan get a line out of the starboard locker,' he shouted as he rushed forward and lowered the spinnaker pole, one end of which was permanently fixed to the mast. He attached a halyard to the outer end and also secured to it the length of warp that Janice had handed to him.

'Rod hook on, we'll swing you out and lower you down. Sal use the engine to hold her steady.'

As soon as he hit the water Rodney tied a bowline round the body.

'Secured,' he called.

It was a technique they practised as part of the man overboard drill. Dick had already run the tail of the halyard, which was deliberately longer than normally required, to the anchor winch and put four turns round the drum.

'Jan take this end while I crank,' he called and started the hard labour of winding in, for once he agreed with Rodney - it should have been power driven.

The winch made its usual noise and slowly Rodney and the body were hauled aboard. While Sally stayed at the helm Janice went forward to help. She looked at what they had pulled out of the water and had to turn away feeling sick. The body, which she presumed to be that of a man, was badly mutilated. The left leg was severed at the knee and there was no hand on the right arm. The lower clothing was torn to shreds revealing large gaps of raw scarlet flesh, the face was cut and blackened and one ear was hanging loose by its skin.

Rodney knew what had to be done. He gently laid the torso chest down on the deck, head turned to one side then with two hands he gave several firm pumps on the small of the back. Water gushed from the gaping mouth. Without wasting a moment of time in hesitation, he turned the body, pulled back its head and started mouth to mouth resuscitation. He paused to feel for a pulse then started again.

'He is alive,' he called out then continued blowing into the open mouth.

Dick stood by admiring the efficiency of his friend. After what seemed hours, but in all likelihood was no more than ten minutes, Rodney turned the unknown man onto his side and stood up.

'He is alive and breathing. Don't give much for his chances, must have lost a lot of blood and be in shock, if we could get medical assistance quickly he'd have a chance, but out here...'

'We'll do all we can,' Dick said as he turned and went below. He checked the VHF channel 16, picked up the mike and spoke.

'Pan Pan Medico, Pan Pan Medico, Pan Pan Medico. This is yacht *English Lady, English Lady*, position approximately fifty two degrees thirty eight minutes north, three degrees twenty minutes west. I am in urgent need of medical assistance, over.'

As he waited for a reply he realised that the yellow yacht would almost certainly have monitored the call and would now know they had been followed. He had decided that one immediate life was more important than a chase that would probably come to nothing anyway. The wait seemed long, surely some of the big ships in the area would have heard his call, maybe there were no doctors aboard. He tried again.

'Pan Pan Medico, Pan Pan Medico, this is *English Lady,* position Brown Ridge, I require medical assistance urgently. Can any vessel hearing this call please relay it to a coastal station. This is an emergency. Over.'

Again he waited an eternity, but there was no response. He pressed the transmit button on the mike and looked up at his set.

'Oh Jesus Christ, not now,' he cried in rage and despair. The performance monitor, which indicates transmitter power, was showing nothing. He ran his fingers over the microphone and aerial connections in the forlorn hope that one may have come loose. He thought back, when was the set last used? They had been receiving noise all the way over, and had maintained radio silence.

'Ye Gods,' he muttered, as a thought occurred to him. The marks on the boat when she had lain in the mud. Someone had been aboard, probably sabotaged the aerial...

'What's up Dad?' in the cockpit Sally had heard the oaths.

Before he could answer Rodney called from the foredeck 'Bring a blanket, we must try and get this Johnny down below, have you raised help Dick?'

Janice recovered her composure, Sally left the helm and Dick quit the radio. All four managed to carry the battered body below and laid it on the saloon berth. Sally returned to the helm, Rodney to the radar, Dick stood in the cockpit alongside his daughter wondering what to do next. Janice started to clean the injuries on the still unconscious man. After raiding the first aid box, which was hopelessly inadequate for this situation, she made up a week Dettol solution and started to wipe down the blackened face. Suddenly she stiffened and cried out.

'Oh no, Dick come quick, it's John Grimley.'

Rodney left the radar and Dick rushed down from the cockpit.

'Are you sure?' he asked.

'Of course I'm sure. I've worked with him long enough. Oh poor John, whatever happened? I didn't like him very much, but I wouldn't wish this on anyone. There must be something we can do.'

'I can't raise help on the radio, we're a good eight hours from land, there are no other ships around that would see a flare,' Dick shot a glance at Rodney who nodded in agreement, then he moved over to the chart table. 'We're a good eight miles from the Deep Water lane, we could turn round and head back in the hope of finding a large ship, we're forty miles from Ijmuiden and thirty from the Helm gas field, though the nearest wells are only twenty...'

'I think we should go back,' Janice interrupted. 'It is the shortest way to get help.'

'But may be not the quickest,' Dick countered. 'It would mean a beat or at least close hauled. Whether we sailed or motored I reckon it would take at least two hours, then we have to hope we find a ship that sees our flares. If we carry on north east we ought to make six knots with this wind helping, so in three hours we will be at the gas wells. Must be someone around there.'

'Let's do that,' Janice requested, as she turned to continue to tend for the injured. Dick quickly worked out the course and gave Sally instructions. Rodney returned to radar watch.

It was the best part of an hour later, that Janice noticed Grimley's eyes flicker.

'It's alright John you're safe now. We'll get you to hospital soon.' The eyes flickered again and a groan escaped from his lips. Rodney had left the casualty lying on his side in the recovery position, Janice bent down and whispered in his remaining ear. 'Everything will be alright now, we've found you, we'll get a doctor soon, try to relax.' She realised it was a stupid thing to say to a man who was probably more dead than alive, who had lost a hand and a leg and who was certainly racked with pain. The lips quivered again, Janice placed her ear as close as she could get.

'Where...?'

'You're with friends, on a boat,' she whispered, turning her head so her lips were close to Grimley's cheek. The return to consciousness was gathering momentum, the lips moved again. Janice wondered if she should call the others, but decided not to do so for fear of missing something. They knew little of what had happened, it was important they learnt as much as they could.

'Who...?'

'I'm Janice from work,' she responded, with tears starting to fill her eyes. Though she despised his treachery it pained her to see him suffer, she forced herself to continued. 'Tell us what happened John. Where's the plutonium?'

'I took it, fooled you all...' his voice weakened, his lips stopped moving.

'Yes we know that John, you were very clever,' Janice paused then continued to coax him, 'but where is the plutonium now?'

The Health Physicist from Watersthorpe waited, the lips moved again. She bent even closer in an attempt not to miss even the faintest of a whisper.

'Swapped...the Russians...a weapon...on the keel...now they're going to kill people...thousands...it wasn't in the plan...tried to stop...now it's over...they'll die...there's no delay...I tried to stop...' They were John Grimley's final words, the stress and emotion hastened his death. His lips froze, his eyes stared sightless and he lay very still. Janice screamed.

'He's dead, he just died. Oh God!' Rodney, deeply engaged in following *English Lady*'s approach to the nearest oil rig was startled by the cry and went straight to the body on the berth. He felt for a pulse and heartbeat, but there were neither nor was there any sign of breath. Without further hesitation he went into resuscitation procedure, first the pumps on the chest, then the mouth to mouth. It was of no avail, John Grimley was dead, but his legacy was very much alive.

As Rodney started to wrap the body in a blanket and Janice stared in horror, he muttered, 'Wonder what happened to the poor sod? Must have fallen overboard. Wonder how long he was in the water? Suppose the thermal jacket he was wearing kept him afloat and reduced hypothermia,' he turned to Janice.

'Cheer up, first time you've seen a dead person?'

'Yes, but it's not that, I knew him. All those terrible injuries, what on earth caused them?'

'Perhaps he was run down by a large vessel, maybe we should stooge around and look for wreckage. Did he say anything?'

'Muttered some words, hadn't we ought to tell the skipper?'

English Lady hove too, her helm lashed and jib pulled aback while the four had a quick conference in the saloon. John Grimley's body had been transferred to the fo'c'sle. Janice finished recalling his last words to her.

'What do we do Dad?' Sally asked. Dick pulled at the lobe of his ear.

'Well, let's try and think this through. We're now pretty sure that plutonium was taken from Watersthorpe by Grimley, seems you were right after all,' he said to Janice as an aside. 'All the evidence suggests that there was a meeting out here, and if Jan heard Grimley correctly, the plut was swapped for a bomb.'

'Agreed,' Sally and Rodney spoke simultaneously.

'Now where do we go from there? The bomb was probably fixed to the keel of the yacht, that would certainly slow it down and make it unwieldy, has it subsequently been run down?'

'Can't see how the stiff's injuries can be explained any other way,' Rodney remarked without regard to Janice's feelings.

'But there isn't any sign of other wreckage,' Sally reminded him. 'I've been on the helm and kept a good lookout. If a yacht had been run down there must be wreckage, cushions, life jackets, wash boards, all sorts of things float. Surely being run down would be like going through a mincer?'

'Sally's right about that Rod. Have you seen any other vessels on the screen which could have run down the Yellow Peril?'

'No, what's more we thought we had it under observation a little while ago.'

'Right,' Dick said continuing with the logic. 'First let us suppose it has been sunk and Grimley was the only survivor. The plut is safely on its way to Mother Russia and there's an atom bomb with Davey Jones. Our immediate problems are over, we might just as well turn for home. On the other hand suppose their yacht hasn't been run down, maybe this guy just fell overboard and wasn't noticed until it was too late. After all with an atom bomb under the keel a gang of terrorists aren't going to stop and search for a lost mate if they can manage without him. So if they haven't been run down where have they gone? I suppose they're out of radar now?'

Rodney nodded agreement.

'Holland?' Janice asked.

'Why?' Dick asked. 'These people do things for a reason, if we can work out their thought train then we can beat them.'

'You did say it was the nearest.'

'But why attack Holland? If Grimley is to be believed, they intend to let off the weapon in a place where it will kill lots of people. Holland hasn't any nuclear weapons and only a couple of power stations. I don't see the motive for abusing the Dutch.'

'I think they'll take it back to the U.K. and bomb London, or a power station, or Watersthorpe, or Windscale. Perhaps the IRA are involved,' Janice speculated.

'I think Janice is right,' Sally agreed.

'Me too,' Rodney added.

'She was right about the plut being stolen, maybe you're right this time,' Dick looked at Janice as he spoke. 'They have a nuclear bomb, what do we do? Even if we had the VHF working we couldn't call for help. One, who's going to believe us? Two, we would alert the enemy who would then say keep away or we all go bang. No, we must get ashore and alert the authorities. Janice can call Watersthorpe and I'll talk to Alf Carter. England's home and no lingo problems, Holland's nearer and international calls are on auto. So quo vadis.' Dick went over to the chart table and picked up the dividers, 'Seventy miles to Lowestoft, thirty five to Ijmuiden and forty to Den Helder.'

'Looks like Ijmuiden then,' Rodney suggested.

'Winds from the south west, it would be a close reach to Ijmuiden and there's also a lock to go through. On the other hand we could make Helder on a broad reach and that would be worth a quarter of a knot. I think we should make for there. One thing I'm not going back to the U.K. if we can help it.'

'Why?' Janice asked in innocence.

'Because we've a lot of explaining to do to the Customs who will undoubtedly be waiting for us. Not only did we not post them a form before we left, they'll want heaps of statements about our dead friend. By the time we've talked our way out of that lot it'll be too late. On the other hand last years entry papers are still valid for Holland. We wave them at our port of entry and the Douane aren't going to bother us any more.'

'So Helder it is?' Sally asked.

'Yes, let's go,' her father responded. 'I'll work out the course, should be able to carry the spi. Rod get the kite set[36], we'll need all the speed we can get. The more time they have back home to arrange a reception for our friends the better.'

'Aye Aye Skipper,' the others chorused.

---

[36]*Spi or kite is jargon for spinnaker. This is a large bulbous sail, set from the stem of a yacht and used when the wind is coming from astern.*

CHAPTER 17

George Brine sat in the cockpit and steered *Brimstone* with one hand lightly on the tiller. The wind was freshening and clouds had already covered the sun, reducing it to a hazy blob of brightness in the sky. The mustard coloured spinnaker steadied the boat as it ran down wind and surged along at five knots. The additional weight of the nuclear bomb under the keel had slowed *Brimstone*'s progress, but had reduced her roll. It was just coming up to 1100hrs, the Helm Field lay five miles to the north west, they were on course and on time. The skipper surveyed the sea. Two ships about three miles on port were on a parallel course probably also making for the Marsdiep. On all the other points the sea was empty. He felt tired and began to wish that the ship still had its compliment of four. He wondered why Grimley had deserted and what had happened. The night passage and disruption of loading the bomb had taken its toll on both of them. Brine did not like leaving the boat with only one person on watch. He knew it was common practice amongst some sailors, but he did not consider it safe. If the helmsman is concentrating on holding a course it is not easy to navigate and look out for other shipping. Even so he had managed alright for the past two hours, now Pete could relieve him. By the end of that watch they would be picking up the marks at the southern extremity of the Schulpengat. He would then take the boat into Marsdiep, through the Malzwin and into Den Oever. He did not want to stress the boat and wondered if he should leave the big sail pulling while he handed over to Pete.

'Cup of tea skipper?' an unusually cheery Pete's voice interrupted his thoughts and a tough muscular hand passed him a steaming mug. 'Go get your head down, I'll take her for a while.'

'Thanks,' he took the proffered drink and raised it to his lips. 'I've set the cursor to the course. Should bring us onto a red and white offing buoy. If you stray too far north then it'll be either a West or a South Cardinal. Anyhow if I'm not back on deck by then give me a shout as soon as you spot one of the marks.'

'Okay, anything else?'

'Yes, there'll probably be quite a bit of shipping about so don't hesitate to call me if anything comes too close. We don't want to be run down at this stage of the operation.'

'Don't worry skipper, I'll shout if there's any prospect of a problem. We're too damn close to success to risk a last minute disaster. Just think, in about six hours time our task will be over, the bomb will be primed and we will be on our way.'

'What's more we shall be giving back to Father Neptune what is rightfully his. The first real blow for restoring the environment. I always thought those Earth savers were a lot of charlatans, out for publicity, self glorification and achieving very little because they often get the wrong end of the stick. Our work will be anonymous, no hero worship, no appearance fees for media interviews, just one major counter attack for the true environment.'

*

Janice was at the helm, Dick below working out their position, Sally and Rodney catching up on missed sleep. *English Lady*'s big patriotic red white and blue spinnaker, with its thousand square feet of one and a half ounce non rip nylon was pulling them along at seven knots. They were a little to the north of their intended course, but Dick was not concerned, he could make out the gas structures on the Helm field to the north east, once a little closer they would give him a good fix. He glanced at the radar, there were two large ships six miles ahead and another one about eight almost due east. The latter he noted was moving only slowly and he concluded it was probably a small yacht. He went up on deck to take a look around.

'Lovely sailing breeze,' Janice remarked, she had let down her hair and the wind caught it and blew it over her face, she brushed it back with her free hand.

'Yes,' Dick agreed. 'Reckon it'll freshen before the day is through. Could get a seven or eight tomorrow.'

For a moment Janice looked alarmed. 'Don't worry,' he reassured her, 'we'll be snug in Den Helder long before then.'

Something nagged at the back of his mind, but he could not formulate what it was.

'Suppose the Yellow Peril will be in the Thames, how much further than us will they have to sail?' Janice did not realise it, but her innocent question would be the turning point of their venture.

'Oh about forty miles, taking Brown Ridge as the starting point,' *English Lady*'s skipper responded.

'That'll mean an extra six hours for them, hope it gives us enough time to get the authorities to take action. If young Graham has proved that plut is missing from the store then the Brigadier will move fast. I'll say this for him, when he decides to take action he...'

'It'll take them much longer than that, with the wind heading they won't make more than four knots under power and it'll be bloody uncomfortable at that, if they decided to sail then it would be a beat and...' Dick's voice trailed away.

'And what?' Janice prompted.

'I've been a crass idiot,' he responded, 'how stupid!'

'Why?'

'I don't believe the skipper of that other boat is a fool, he must have noticed the glass falling and heard the forecasts. Even if I didn't have an atom bomb under my keel I'd think twice about trying to make it back, more likely would have scuttled down to Ijmuiden, the Hook, or even Flushing and holed up for a couple of days until the blow was over.'

'You mean you don't think they're on their way back to Blighty after all?'

'I'm sure as hell they're not, there's something else as well. If they had headed back to England they would most likely have passed through our radar field, but we didn't see anything that could have been a yacht. Pound to a pinch of shit they've carried on for Holland. I suppose...'

'Suppose what?' Janice again prompted.

'I wonder if they intended to return to the U.K? May be they are going to bomb Holland...but if so where?'

'Be ironic if we warned the Brits and all the time the target was the Dutch,' Janice remarked.

'Ironic, it would be bloody tragic. Jan think hard, you were the only one who heard Grimley speak, are you sure he gave no indication of where the bomb was to be exploded?'

'No, it's just as I told you. He said, "it's all over now, there's no delay, lot's killed, wasn't in the plan" or words to that effect.'

The minutes of silence that followed were broken only by the sound of the sea on the hull and the wind in the rigging.

Dick reopened the conversation, 'Are you sure he said, "it's all over now," were those his exact words. Think carefully a lot may depend on your answer?'

'I...' Janice hesitated. 'I don't think he actually said "it's all over," more like, "it's over".'

'That's what I thought you reported originally.'

'Does it make much difference?'

'Could do, could do,' Dick repeated as he tugged at the lobe of his ear to indicate he was in thought. 'There's a place not a million miles from here called 'over', well Den Oever to be precise, but we can hardly expect a dying man to get the pronunciation correct.'

'Oh my God, where is it? Can we get there first? Can we stop them? Will we be too late?' Janice fired the questions at Dick.

'It's at the entrance to the Ijsselmeer, there's a large sea lock, approach channel fairly shallow and narrow, they'd probably want high water which will be...hold your course Jan. I want to go below and do some arithmetic.'

'But can we catch them?'

'I'll tell you when I've done my sums.'

It didn't take long before Dick had worked the answer out and returned to the cockpit.

'On the basis that the yellow yacht is making about four and a half knots, we are doing a good seven, then they should be about ten miles ahead, maybe as little as eight. In fact there is a blip on our radar which could be them, it's in about the right position.'

'Can we catch them?'

'In four to five hours.'

'Thank God for that.'

''fraid it's not that simple Jan. In four hours they will be at Den Helder.'

'So?'

'What do we do? Just sail up to them and say, "we've discovered your wicked plot, now be good chaps and give up." Or we could try making a citizens arrest even though we're in a foreign country,' Dick said with sarcasm in his voice. 'We know those people are armed, they could just shoot us. If they missed or had scruples over that they would simply say the equivalent of sod off or we'll explode the bomb and send us all to Kingdom Come!'

'There must be something we can do. Wake up Rod and Sal perhaps they could think of something. We've come so far we can't be beaten now!'

'Well I do have an idea, it's a long shot but might just come off. Somehow we have to take them by surprise and immobilise them before they can trigger the weapon. We could trail them until they moored up then try and find a way of enticing them off their boat, but I doubt it. If we come up on them from behind, the closing speed will only be two knots, we'd be under observation for a long time and almost certainly be recognised before we could do anything. No, as I see it, we have to get in front and approach them head on, we should then get an opportunity to ram or something like that.'

'Can we do that?'

'There is a chance, but it will be touch or go. There are two approaches into Marsdiep, either through the Schulpengat on the south side of Noorderhaaks...'

'Where's that?' Janice interrupted.

'It's a low lying island that is partly awash, well that's what the chart says, I've never been there. It divides the gap between Noord Holland and Texel.' Dick answered the question, then continued. 'Or the Molengat which is on the north side. Now from the angle of approach they will almost certainly use the Schulpengat, if we could come in through the Molengat we would meet them head on. What's more the island may provide some cover for us almost until the last moment.'

'Great, what're the snags?'

'The bad news is that we might lose them from our radar when we went behind the land, the resolution on our set is not the best. We would have to time our arrival by dead reckoning, also we would have to cut across some shallows, there is not time to go right up to the start of the Molengat. It'll be nearly high water and *Lady* has a shallow draft so the only problem would be the unpleasant rough water. I think it's time we briefed the others, let me take the helm while you give them a shout.'

'Aye Aye Sir,' Janice replied with enthusiasm.

*

'Skipper,' Pete called from *Brimstone*'s cockpit. 'There's a red and white buoy about a mile ahead.'

George Brine sat up in his bunk, rubbed his eyes and looked at his watch.

'Good, I'll be up,' he replied, as he threw aside the blanket which had covered him.

'There, on the nose,' Pete indicated.

'Got it. Are you alright or do you want to get a bit of shut eye, still about three hours to the lock?'

'I'm fine, I want to see this all the way in. I suppose nothing can stop us now?'

'Nothing. The wind is fair, the water is high and the channels are well marked.'

'What if the Dutch Customs stop us?'

'They won't, anyhow Olive fixed us up with an entry permit. So as far as they are concerned we crossed over two weeks ago, entered at Flushing and have been pottering around.'

'How'd she do that?'

'Easy, at Flushing the Douane have their office a short walk from the harbour, further from the marina, so they don't actually come and inspect your boat. Walk into the office, produce a set of ship's papers and say you've just arrived. They issue the permit and never doubt that you didn't bring your boat with you!'

'Olive thinks of everything,' Pete remarked.

'I hope she's thought about the bikes and our get-away car.'

'Don't worry she will,' Pete reassured his skipper. 'Are those some more marks ahead?' he asked as they slid past the offing buoy.

'Yes, red and greens about a mile apart, they show the channel, although there's plenty of water for us at this state of the tide even if we were to stray to one side. That low lying piece of land is Noorderhaaks.'

*

'I'm losing the target from radar,' Rodney called out to Dick, who was in the cockpit surveying the approaching shore through binoculars.

'What's the depth?'

'Three metres,' Sally replied after reading the helmsman's repeater.

'Well this is it, let's hope we get it right.'

'You will skipper, you will,' Janice reaffirmed her confidence in his ability. Dick ignored the compliment.

'In about a mile it should drop to about two, when that happens look out for a shoal patch, should see broken water. We'll skirt to its north then harden up and close reach down the Molengat.'

Sally held course, Janice alternated her eyes between the echo sounder and the sea in front, Dick kept the glasses occupied.

'There it is,' he called out. 'Go another fifteen degrees to port and we'll clear it.'

'What about the kite?' Sally asked.

'We'll need it in to get down the Gat. Rodney,' he called, 'come and give a hand on the spi, won't need your radar any more.'

In the fresh breeze *English Lady* surfed along at seven and a half knots as she reached down the last mile of the Molengat leaving the red can buoys to port and the green ones to starboard. Dick explained his plan.

'We should approach the yellow boat from ahead or abeam either close hauled or on a close reach. We'll run the engine and fly a black cone[37] so although we'll be on starboard the yellow boat will have right of way and won't alter course to avoid us. With a bit of luck they'll have a spinney up, it'll restrict their ability to manoeuvre. We're still flying our Dutch ensign so they should take us for a local boat passing to weather and across their stern. Rod, will you take the main and mizzen sheets? When I give the word, loose off the mizzen altogether and ease the main as we bear away to ram? Sal, you take the genny sheet and do likewise?'

'What about me?' Janice asked.

'Hold tight, the collision will give a hell of a jolt. Then once things are calm scuttle aft, haul down the Dutch ensign and put up the Red Duster.'

'Is that important? What will happen to the other boat?'

'Yes, Jan it is important because there will be a lot of questions to answer. We will probably cut the other boat in half, we want it to sink too fast for them to be able to trigger the weapon. The collision may well kill, but I hope not. If we've got the wrong boat then I could finish up facing a manslaughter charge. If we are seen flying the wrong flag they might add piracy as well!'

'Dick, I know getting the plut back is important, but no more killing please. Let's try something else first?'

'No choice,' Dick knew he had to be firm, after considering all the information available this was no time for change, at any moment the boat from Longsands would come into sight from the other side of Noorderhaaks. 'That lump of meat down below used to be a human

---

[37]*A yacht under power as well as sail should show a black cone, point uppermost, in her rigging. As such she becomes a power vessel for the purposes of the Collision Regulation and so loses her right of way as a sailing vessel.*

being, you should know that better than any of us, well I reckon he gave his life to try and stop those mad things in the other boat, that in my book is as good a reason as any to have to kill them. Look there they are, three o'clock, about half way between the East Cardinal and the red channel buoy. Trim your sheets in.' Dick swung the wheel to starboard and started the engine. 'Rod, black cone smartish.' He was too busy to notice Janice burst into tears and go below.

*

'Hey skip, what's that beacon thing on our starboard beam?' Pete asked.

'Kijkduin. Nearly two hundred feet high and, under good conditions, the light is visible for thirty miles. We'll hold this course to that East Cardinal then jibe her round and head in due east. About half a mile to go. May as well get the spinney down before the jibe as we'll come on a broad reach, we'll hang on to it for a few more minutes.'

'Sure, some other yachts about,' Pete remarked as he surveyed the surrounding water. 'Surprising really so early in the season.'

'No, the Dutch are born to float, there must be more yachts here per head of population than anywhere else in the world. If you ever enter Dutch waters and there's no one else sailing then it can mean only one thing.'

'What?'

'War has been declared,' George Brine retorted with a smile.

'See that one coming at us on our port side?' Pete ignored the joke. George Brine had not, the mast was obscuring his vision. He picked up the seven by fifties and focused on the fast approaching craft.

'Looks a bit like that big thing we left on the putty back in Walton,' he murmured aloud. 'No, can't be, she's wearing Dutch colours, I must be getting jumpy.'

'Do we have to give way?' Pete asked.

'Don't think so, she's got a black cone up, must be motor sailing. I'll say this for the Dutch they're sticklers for their regulations, hardly anyone in the U.K. bothers with such niceties. If we hold steady she'll probably pass close to weather, wonder where she's heading for. Good thirty miles between here and Ijmuiden and close hauled all the way. Think I'd rather wait or go through the canals with this falling glass.'

'Must be in a hurry, look at the waves breaking over her bow. What's she doing? Seven, eight knots do you think?'

'Looks every bit of eight, as you say she's in a hell of a hurry, coming a bit close but I still think we'll clear.'

Pete looked on fascinated, then pulled the helm to port.

'Steady,' George warned. 'You'll jibe us all standing and that could be trouble. Hold your course she'll pass a weather I can see her lee rail.'

*

Dick England bit his lip and gripped the wheel as the yachts converged. A hundred yards apart and as much up wind, it was now or never.

'Start the sheets,' he bellowed and swung the wheel to port.

Rodney let the mizzen off and then broke the main out of its jammer, but kept it tensioned as it ran through his hand. The sail had to pull all the time *English Lady* was turning. Sally was no less an expert on the genoa, easing the coils round the winch so the sails shape suited the ever changing course. Dick reached for the engine throttle and moved it to full ahead. The boat turned her stem towards the yellow Surfmaster, white angry water cascaded over her bows as she healed under the combined effect of wind and rudder. In a twinkling the hundred yards had disappeared, now they were only seconds to impact *English Lady* headed straight for a point abeam of its mast and well forward of the cockpit. Dick could see its crew react as they realised what was about to happen.

'Hold tight,' he commanded and added, 'Christ I hope we're right.'

George Brine had a look of satisfaction on his face. 'There, told you they'd clear us to weather by.... fucking idiots, what the.... quick give me the helm.'

Satisfaction changed to astonishment then alarm. He saw the big yacht start to bear down on him, sheets easing as she turned. In an instant he knew it was no accident. 'They're trying to ram us,' he shouted as he pushed Pete to one side and took charge of the tiller. 'Quick activate the weapon.'

Instinct told him impact was inevitable, he pulled the tiller as hard as he could to starboard to try and escape with a glancing blow.

Pete, alarmed, at first started for the saloon then ignored his skipper's instruction and reacted the way his years of training dictated. He reached inside his orange heavy duty nylon jacket, found the reassuring butt of the Magnum, pulled it from its waistband holster, steadied and, in the last second before collision, squeezed the trigger.

Dick saw it happen.

'Look out, the gun,' he called, but at the same instant a spurt of flame and an ear shattering explosion told the story. The bullet ricocheted off the mast then with a resounding crash the big powerful bows of *English Lady* smashed into and rode up over the cockpit of the smaller yellow yacht. Its chain plates pulled and the mast crashed down trailing sails in the water. Reinforced ferro cement struck the man with the gun full in the chest before he had a chance to fire again. Like his companion, crushed at the tiller, he died in an instant.

'Free the sheets,' Dick ordered as he recovered from the shock of the impact, at the same time he put the engine to full astern. Someone rushed past him, Janice had not forgotten her task of changing ensigns. *English Lady* pulled clear and, accompanied by the sound of gurgling water, the yellow boat sank under her.

Dick let out a cry of satisfaction as he looked round at the others. 'We've done...oh my God.' His eyes had turned towards his daughter who lay slumped in the cockpit, the genoa sheet still in her hand.

'Sally? Are you okay?' Rodney called, but he had not seen the red stain on her yellow jacket in the middle of her chest. Dick left the wheel and cradled Sally's head in his arms.

'Hold on love, hold on,' he urged. 'Help will soon be here.'

'Dad,' Sally's lips parted, blood ran from them down her chin and started to drip onto Dick's hand. 'We've saved the slender thread, haven't we?'

She died before her father could concur.

Epilogue

Within two hours of bidding farewell to *Brimstone* the *Gulf Queen* had been scuttled in the area of the North Sea designated for burning refuse material. Petricoff and Olga Kuznetsov had assembled the crew, then massacred them. All loose gear was removed from the decks and after the shadowing submarine had come alongside and taken them and their plutonium package aboard, charges blew out the bottom of the old coaster. She sank without trace in a matter of minutes.

It was not until the submarine had reached the Baltic did these two start to suspect something had gone wrong for the news broadcasts made no mention of any Dutch disaster. They persuaded the Captain to agree to a clandestine landing in East Germany. Petricoff was subsequently arrested and returned to the Soviet Union where, with a number of other conspirators, he was secretly executed. Olga evaded capture and eventually made her way to Libya where she was able to deploy her talents.

The story of the collision between the two English yachts was well contained thanks to close co-operation between MI6 and their Dutch counterparts. Only the local newspapers reported the accident, it seemed that the mishap had been caused by a steering failure on the larger boat. Four people, three men and a lady, had been killed. The sunken yacht was subsequently salvaged by a NATO recovery team as part of a training exercise. The public were completely unaware of the Russian advisers who helped defuse and recover the weapon which was then secretly returned to its country of origin.

At Watersthorpe the Brigadier had acted swiftly. The first results of the container survey, which had confirmed some plutonium to be missing, coincided with Janice's phone call and her extraordinary story. He made a call to the Secretary of State's office and the Head of Security. All documents that could be related to the affair were removed to his office for 'safe keeping'. Grimley's flat was searched and subsequently decontaminated in secret by a special squad from the Ministry of Defence. The same group spent some time on Site where their 'training' included an 'exercise' in decontaminating a locker in the Watersthorpe change room. It was, of course, a coincidence that the locker had last been used by John Grimley.

A similar squad, under the guise of Inland Revenue officers, went into Longsands House and removed all evidence of the past few weeks happenings. The case of the missing reporter, Clive Wordman, became one of those files the police never closed, but also never pursued. In due course, in the absence of a body, an inquest presumed his death from causes unknown. The Department of Trade, having first ensured there were no outstanding creditors, had Research Express put into liquidation.

Alf Carter had also acted swiftly once he heard from Dick. He had alerted his contacts and this provided valuable corroboration for the Brigadier. He was sent to Den Helder to assist the Dutch police in their investigations and was present when Dick, Janice and Rodney were debriefed. All three were warned that under no circumstances should they ever divulge the story of the Watersthorpe plutonium, they were read the relevant sections of the Official Acts and required to sign a document to that effect. It was also pointed out to them that the Russians wanted the matter hushed up and if there was the slightest suspicion of them telling their story then the KGB might well take action against them. Of course, the British Authorities would do their best to provide protection, but...

Janice Hardman returned to Watersthorpe after her 'holiday', but some months later was moved sideways to the Personnel Department in their London office. It was put about that this was part of her career development training, but she was told privately that her days with the nuclear industry were numbered. Going outside Watersthorpe without authority had raised doubts over her loyalty. By giving her experience in another discipline the industry expected that she would be able to find suitable employment elsewhere.

Both Dick and Rodney were heartbroken at Sally's death. Rodney threw himself into his work, but Dick sank into depression. *English Lady* was laid up almost as soon as she returned to the United Kingdom. Her owner, shunned by the industry he had worked so hard to support, became a recluse. That is until the New Year's Honours List was published. Two names associated with their adventure were included. Alfred George Carter was awarded the Order of the British Empire for services to sailing. Brigadier Claude Siegfried Whatley-Jones, for services to the nuclear industry, a Knighthood. It was then that Richard Harry England resolved to write a novel, he called it "By a Slender Thread".